MIDNIGHT

MIDNIGHT

KEVIN EGAN

FORGE®

A TOM DOHERTY ASSOCIATES BOOK
NEW YORK

MIDNIGHT

Copyright © 2013 by Kevin Egan

A portion of this book appeared in the January–February 2010 issue of *Alfred Hitchcock's Mystery Magazine*.

A Forge Book
Published by Tom Doherty Associates, LLC
175 Fifth Avenue
New York, NY 10010

www.tor-forge.com

Forge® is a registered trademark of Tom Doherty Associates, LLC.

Library of Congress Cataloging-in-Publication Data

Egan, Kevin
    Midnight / Kevin Egan.—1st ed.
      p. cm.
    "A Tom Doherty Associates Book."
    ISBN 978-0-7653-3526-5 (hardcover)
    ISBN 978-1-4668-2211-5 (e-book)
    I. Title.
    PS3605.G355M53 2013
    813'.6—dc23
                    2013003724

Forge books may be purchased for educational, business, or promotional use. For information on bulk purchases, please contact Macmillan Corporate and Premium Sales Department at 1-800-221-7945 extension 5442 or write specialmarkets@macmillan.com.

First Edition: July 2013

Printed in the United States of America

0 9 8 7 6 5 4 3 2 1

For MaryLou, Emily, and Greg, all at once

ACKNOWLEDGMENTS

I would like to acknowledge the efforts of:

Ben Bova, longtime friend and colleague, for bringing *Midnight* to life.

Paul Stevens, the best editor ever, for helping polish some fuzzy moments into high definition and for saving me from an embarrassing geographical blunder.

Vincent Graziano, the funniest undertaker in the world, for his technical advice.

Captain Michael Castellano and SCO Seymour Bobroff (Ret.) for answering my elementary security-related questions.

Emily and Greg, though both much older now, for continuing to connect me with the world of my younger characters.

And MaryLou, for once again contributing aspects of herself to the female lead.

PART ONE

New Year's Eve

CHAPTER 1

Halfway up the steps the judge stopped to grab the handrail. It was a silver metal handrail, stainless steel and so cold that if there had been any moisture on his skin it would have bound him immediately. But he had no moisture, not on his skin or even in his mouth. He felt dry, but not merely the midwinter dry from low humidity and blasting steam pipes. He felt desiccated, as if he could collapse into dust and blow away.

He took a deep breath, worked his free hand under his topcoat and between the two flaps of his scarf. His heart gave one more of those crazy thumps, then steadied. He slid his other hand up the rail, gripped tight, and pulled himself up and out of the subway station.

The sky over Foley Square was flat gray, brightening to yellow only where the sun hung in the notch between the two federal courthouses. The wind blew hard, tumbling flattened coffee cups and grimy newspaper pages across his path. Up ahead, a man stood with one foot raised on the edge of the fountain and his hands shoved into the pockets of his peacoat. He wore a floppy black cap, faded jeans tight to his stubby legs.

The judge thought he had seen the man before, but whether he was a litigant, a juror, or a punk he might have put away when he sat in criminal court long ago, he could not say.

The man suddenly turned as if sensing the force of the judge's stare. The judge realized then, in the millisecond before he lowered his eyes, that the man was a complete stranger to him.

The judge crossed Centre Street, passed the coffee cart at the bottom of the wide steps that were so popular in movie shoots and fashion ads, and began his climb directly up between the two brass rails in case the thumps returned and he needed to grab hold. At the top, a court officer stood between the two center columns, arms akimbo, breathing smoke in the frigid air. The officer said good morning as the judge reached the top. The judge, trying to conceal his heavy breathing, simply nodded.

In a few hours he'll hate me, the judge thought as he reached the revolving door.

"So what good is a frigging hour off in the middle of the day, huh?"

Jerry Elliott, his uniform already day's-end sloppy, sat at a small desk at the edge of the rotunda. Pale sunlight reflecting off the Federal Building across Foley Square filtered in through the windowpanes over the main entrance, silhouetting Foxx in a wintry glow. Foxx only half-listened to Elliott, which was all the attention Elliott's carping usually deserved, while a back-pack slid through the X-ray machine on a conveyor belt. The backpack belonged to a messenger who waited between the metal stanchions that ran the length of the sloping promenade from the lobby down to the rotunda.

"You're not even listening to me, are ya, Foxx?" said Elliott. He was a big guy who gave the impression of having been bigger, as if a sudden deflation left lines in his face and a sag behind his belt buckle.

"Sure I am," said Foxx, sweeping the messenger with a wand. "You're bitching about comp time."

Elliott sighed as the messenger grabbed his backpack and hustled to the elevators. He almost wished Foxx had not been listening, which would have given him something else to complain about.

"So tell me what the hell it's good for."

"Self-improvement," said Foxx.

"The only self-improvement I need is right here." Elliott slapped the wallet in his pants pocket.

"That's where you lack imagination," said Foxx. He was as trim and athletic as Elliott was big and dumpy, with a swayback posture and well-oiled joints that lent grace to every movement. "Think of what you can do. You can exercise, go to a library, take up yoga."

"I can't waste my time with that crap," said Elliott. "I got responsibilities."

"So do I."

"What are they? You got no wife, no kids."

"Responsibilities to myself, and to the greater good." Foxx smiled puckishly. "Besides, this was no surprise. OCA's been threatening to cut out overtime for years."

"Yeah, well this is the year those bastards at OCA actually did it."

"Because Werkman blew the contract negotiations."

"He'll get it back."

"With that lawsuit?" asked Foxx.

"The lawsuit isn't our only chance," said Elliott.

"What else is there?"

"I don't know, but Bobby will think of something."

"Bobby is it?" said Foxx. "Are you two buddies?"

"I worked with him in Westchester Supreme."

"And I worked with him in Bronx Supreme. He was thrown out of every courthouse he ever worked. He had no choice but to become union president."

"Maybe that was his plan. Work everywhere, get to know everyone so they'd vote for him."

"Then he better come up with another plan pretty damn fast," said Foxx. He snapped the band of his latex glove against his wrist. "Next election, he'll be out on his ass."

"Don't be too sure. Bobby's done a lot of good for a lot of people."

"I don't care what he's done. Overtime trumps everything."

Much as Elliott hated to admit it, Foxx was right. Overtime did trump everything, and the prospect of losing it was doing a number on his nerves. He checked his watch. It was seven fifteen, which left one hour and forty-five minutes in his last overtime shift of the year. Maybe forever, if his confidence in Bobby Werkman turned out to be misplaced. Overtime pay was precious to court officers. Other than moonlighting, it was the only way to supplement a civil service wage that did not go very far in a city like New York. But once the clock struck midnight tonight, all overtime pay would cease. Officers might still work an extra hour or two, but instead of double time pay Office of Court Administration regulations now decreed they would receive compensatory time. Or, as Elliott described it, a frigging hour off in the middle of the day.

"Hey, there he is," said Elliott. "The man who holds our fate in his hands."

Foxx followed Elliott's eyes to the front entrance, where Judge Alvin Canter had just pushed in through the revolving door. The judge was bean-pole thin, a long coat hanging on his longer body. He scraped the black schapska off his head, and even at a distance Foxx could see the strands of his comb-over flying apart with static electricity.

"Overtime equals fate?" said Foxx. "Isn't that overly dramatic, Jerry?"

"Not to me it ain't."

The judge unbuttoned his coat, shook the lapels loose, and headed past the coffee shop toward the judges elevator in the south wing of the lobby.

"Think today's the day?" said Elliott.

"For what?"

"The ruling on Bobby's case. What else?"

"How the hell would I know?" said Foxx.

"Didn't you have something going with Canter's secretary?" asked Elliott.

"Who told you that?"

"I don't know. No one. I thought . . ."

"Keep thinking, Jerry. Think all you want. Just keep your thoughts to yourself." Foxx peeled the latex gloves off his hands. "Excuse me."

He squeezed between two stanchions and glided smoothly up the promenade to an alcove where two banks of phone booths once had stood. He opened his cell phone and pressed in all ten digits of the number. Unlike most people, he did not rely on stored contact information. He refused to upgrade to a

smart phone. To him, people who outsourced their brain func-
tions to devices were in for an unpleasant surprise someday.

"What's up?" asked Bev.

"What's up? No hello? No Happy New Year?"

She sighed. "Hello, Foxx. Happy New Year, Foxx. Now what's
up?"

"Canter just walked in."

"This early? You think today's the day?"

Did she need to use Elliott's exact words? thought Foxx.

"New Year's Eve," he said. "Most of the judges will be no-
shows. The ones who are here have something important they
need to get done. Yeah, I think today's the day."

"Keep an eye. I don't trust either side."

"Don't you work for the administration?"

"Aren't you a member of the union?"

"Touché," said Foxx, and cut the call.

Viewed schematically from above, the New York County Courthouse resembled a hardware bolt: a hexagon of courtrooms
and back offices surrounding a central rotunda. The first four
floors were designed with mezzanine levels constructed around
two-story courtrooms whose original magnificence had dete-
riorated over time into a stately decay. The judges' chambers
were located on the fifth and sixth floors. Depending on the
interior architecture and the position along the hexagonal outer
face, chambers consisted of either a two- or three-room suite.
But regardless of size or shape, all chambers shared a common
attribute: They were completely private, utterly self-contained
worlds.

The judge reached his door, unwedged the two copies of the
New York Law Journal from the mail slot, and slipped the key

into the lock. His chambers were one of the three-room varieties, with a large outer office that Tom and Carol shared, a narrow middle room filled with file cabinets and thick with potted plants, and a sizable inner office that was his private sanctum, his true chambers. He flipped the switch, and the triple bank of fluorescent lights in the outer office came on one, two, three. The third bank, the one over the conference table, flickered before strengthening. A buzz, loud enough to annoy but soft enough that he could not remember having heard it when he departed chambers last evening, vibrated in the air. He made a mental note to have Carol call the custodian.

The judge lit the full spectrum lamp in the middle room and reached behind a lush schefflera to switch on the humidifier, then moved into the studied order of his inner office. Two black velvet couches faced each other across an Oriental area rug laid atop the bland industrial wall-to-wall carpet that covered the entire suite. Laying an area rug atop an existing carpet seemed counterintuitive to him, but Carol had suggested it and he had to admit that it pulled the office together. Beyond the rug, his teak desk stretched almost the entire width of the office, its orange cast accentuated by the light from two Tiffany chandeliers.

The judge crossed between the two couches, successfully negotiating the curled edge of the rug that tripped him when he did not pay attention. Behind the desk, the green and red bindings of the New York case reporters filled a broad set of floor-to-ceiling bookshelves. On one side of the shelves was the closet where he hung his coat. On the other was the door to the lavatory where he washed his hands. Finished, he dragged the pile of decisions Tom had left for him last night from the corner of his desk to his blotter.

Motion practice was a staple of all civil litigation, and no-where more so than in Manhattan. Judge Canter decided approximately five hundred motions each year, the decisions ranging from two-sentence knockoffs to carefully reasoned and precisely worded opuses. In his twenty years on the bench, the judge had employed three law clerks, and Tom definitely was the best of them. He had a literary, almost poetic facility with language, and his legal reasoning, except in those few areas of law he admitted he never could understand, was usually flawless. As a result, the judge basically read Tom's work for typos.

He dismantled the pile quickly, skimming and signing. The last decision, and he was sure Tom had positioned it this way, was *Werkman v. Office of Court Administration*. Rather than skim, he lingered over this one, weighing each word and following the flow of Tom's reasoning. At the end, he lifted his pen to stroke his characteristic *AC* and then hesitated. Ruling against the court officers union was distasteful, but neither he nor Tom could devise any other legally acceptable result. He slipped the pen into his shirt pocket, took his checkbook from his desk drawer, and went through the middle room to Carol's desk. He would come back to that decision later and give it one more read.

Carol was neat and organized, pencils and pens each in separate cups, two sizes of paper clips in magnetized dispensers, coffee cup wiped clean with a paper towel still crumpled inside, running shoes tucked under her desk. He sat on her chair, feeling a tingle at the thought that this was exactly where she parked her ass. The tingle faded, and he waited for that heart thump to return. Nothing happened, though, and he wondered whether the thoughts that kept him up last night had been simply nighttime thoughts.

He wrote the two checks, sealed them in an envelope, printed Carol's name, and lay the envelope in her top drawer.

Relieved, he went back to his own desk. He reread that decision one last time and muttered, "Sorry, guys," before etching his initials on the signature line and *31* between December and the year.

He was watering the plants in the middle room when Carol breezed in at eight thirty. They called hello to each other, the judge maneuvering himself into position to watch her arch her back and shed her coat. Her coat was long and red, with a sateen lining that slid easily over her wool turtleneck sweater. The sweater, combined with her plaid skirt and black boots, showed off her figure nicely.

He retreated to his desk and listened to the familiar sounds of Carol logging onto her computer, checking the chambers' voice mail, firing up the coffeemaker. She did not, as far as he could hear, open her desk drawer.

Eventually, as was chambers custom, she appeared in the avenue of doors that linked the three rooms, the judge's own coffee cup in her hand and a steno pad tucked under her arm. She set the coffee on his blotter and sat at the edge of the closest chair, her arms folded across her stomach and her knees primly pressed together. He took his first tentative sip of coffee, and she settled back and crossed her legs.

"What plans do you have for the big night?" he asked. Despite his skinny torso, he sat rigid and straight.

"Making popcorn and hoping my one glass of wine doesn't knock me out before the ball drops."

"I expected something more exotic."

"Well, you know me."

"I do," said the judge. "Hence my expectations."

Carol had been with him for nine years, four years longer than Tom. He knew that she dated, could see a certain look cross her face whenever she answered her cell phone and quickly took the call to the corridor outside. The specifics of her relationships were a complete mystery, but he could detect the fitful rhythms as infatuations flowered and faded. Lately, though, he sensed a difference in Carol. She was not exactly flirtatious; she was too reserved for that. But she seemed to have developed a connection with Tom that he doubted Tom even noticed. She seemed to be declaring her availability, something he recognized well.

"What about Tom?" he asked. "Does he have any plans?"

"Not that I know. Why?"

"Just wondering." The judge swiveled his chair sideways to hide his relief.

Carol rubbed her thumb across the inlays on the judge's desk. The judge liked to say that the desk had been carved from a single block of wood and that the inlays were African ivory. Carol had accepted these claims without question until Tom told her no block of wood was that big and the inlays were elaborate decals.

"Are you all right, Judge?" she asked. In profile his lips looked thicker, his chin weaker, his comb-over scragglier.

"Fine. Just didn't have a great night's sleep." He could have mentioned how those thumps in his chest kept him up all night, how he had trouble walking up the stairs from the subway station. But he wanted her concern, not her pity. And since he could not control which he would elicit, he turned back to face her and patted the pile of folders. "I signed all these, so you should get them filed today."

Carol nodded.

"I left you something in your desk drawer. Don't forget it when you leave today. And close my door on your way out. I think I'll lie down for a while."

Carol carried the folders to the table in the middle room, closed the judge's door, then went to her desk. "Goddammit," she muttered when she saw the checks.

She marched right back and opened the door, but the judge was already asleep on one of the couches.

CHAPTER 2

Tom spotted Dominic from a block away, standing beside the fountain with a phone stuck to the same ear that, up close, had the Mr. Clean hoop punched through its lobe. At the sight of Dominic, Tom instinctively shoved his hand into his left front pocket and fingered the thick wad of bills.

Tom's idea, really no more than an idle notion, rose from a sudden confluence of circumstances. He was half an hour earlier than usual, which gave him the element of surprise. He was wearing jeans and a jacket instead of a suit and topcoat, which allowed him to blend in with a different element of people. And he was unencumbered, no briefcase, no brown bag, not even a newspaper. As he reached the edge of Foley Square, not actually a square but a triangle wedged among courthouses and government office buildings, the light at the intersection turned red, and the quickly bunching traffic screened him from the fountain. He stopped behind a coffee cart. He was certain Dominic had not spotted him and, as he peeked around the side of the cart, he fingered the smaller wad in his right pocket. Seventy-five bucks, all he had till payday.

The notion was an idea now, and a plan of action formed in Tom's mind. He peeked out from behind the cart again. The traffic still formed a solid wall with Dominic somewhere on the other side. Tom tested his idea in the Socratic method of a law professor. *What do you hope to gain, Mr. Carroway? Resistance, sir. But you know, do you not, that resistance is futile? I know, sir. Then why resist? To make a point, sir, and it's only for a little while.*

The light changed, and traffic flowed again. Dominic, off the phone now, had drifted from the fountain and faced completely in the opposite direction. Tom crossed the bottom of Foley Square and lost himself in the crowd until he reached the wide, imposing steps of the New York County Courthouse. He climbed quickly and then peeked down from the colonnade. Dominic stood at the fountain, flipping a coin like a football referee.

Only for a little while, thought Tom.

Even when she was at the courthouse, a part of Carol remained home with her son and mother. The image persisting in her mind right now was typical. Nine-year-old Nick, half-dressed for a day of snowboarding with a friend, sat at the kitchen table and played a handheld video game, his hearing aids at his elbow, his cereal soggy in its milk. Rose lay sideways on the hospital bed that now dominated the small dining room, her glasses steeply slanted as she watched a cooking show on a TV that sat on a spindly snack table. Carol spun around them like a whirlwind, fixing lunch for Rose, tucking a few extra bucks into Nick's snow pants, assembling her own things into her shoulder bag. Still, she would be on the phone with one or both of them ten or fifteen times before day's end, and she was on the phone with Nick when Tom walked into chambers.

"I want to invite a friend, too," said Nick. "You said last year I could invite a friend this year."

"You're right, I did. Sorry. I forgot. Are you thinking of Jeremy, because his family could have their own New Year's plans."

Nick stayed silent.

"Well, when Jeremy picks you up, ask his mother to call me."

"Okay."

"You have fun today."

"Okay."

"And wear your helmet."

"Okay."

By the time Carol hung up, Tom already was seated at his computer at the conference table.

"Why is the door closed?" he asked.

"He's taking a nap," said Carol. "He was here before me this morning."

"That early? Did he say why?"

Carol thought of the checks. "No, but he did sign a bunch of decisions."

"Maybe he just wants us all to go home early," said Tom.

He scrolled through his partial draft of the *Berne* decision, which involved a young girl who lost her leg after a bicycle accident. The decision could potentially throw the girl out of court, and Tom, to divert himself from the responsibility, occasionally peeked out from behind his monitor to look at Carol. Early in the spring, she had started a regimen of long midday jogs—down to the Battery, up Broadway to Houston and then back down Bowery to Chinatown—that had sculpted her cutely round figure into something more lithe and athletic. Her waist tucked nicely between the swell of her breasts and the spread of her hips. Her thighs, hemline permitting, showed a pleasing hint of muscle. Even aside from their parting kiss on Christmas Eve, which included a quick dart of her tongue, he had sensed a subtle shift, as if their orbits had aligned and they were now within each other's gravitational pull. He deliberately had not reacted to the kiss, passing it off as one of those let-your-guard-down holiday moments that rarely survived into January. But he did find her floating through his mind at odd times and he had awakened more than once this week with the distinct impression of having dreamt about her.

"Tom," Carol said now. "Do you have plans for tomorrow?"

"No," he said. "Why?"

"I'm cooking New Year's dinner. Nothing fancy, just a few people. My mother. My son. My son usually invites a friend. Some neighbors might drop by for a drink. Would you like to come?"

"Sure," said Tom. "I'd love to."

For the next hour, Carol and Tom worked in silence. Carol plowed through the pile of signed decisions to enter information in her complicated set of records. Tom continued fiddling with the *Berne* decision, though the thought of Dominic still waiting out by the fountain poked holes in his concentration. What exactly was he trying to prove?

The division of labor between the judge and Tom had evolved into two separate tracks, with the judge exclusively handling some areas of law and Tom exclusively handling the rest. High-profile cases, like the union's overtime dispute, were collaborative efforts, with the judge stating the decision he wanted to reach and Tom constructing the legal reasoning to get it there on paper. But a case like the *Berne* case, something critical to the litigants but unimportant to the wider legal world, was totally Tom's call. He had heard rumors about dishonest lawyers who would pay for favorable decisions, and he supposed with his free rein under Judge Canter he could make a buck or two. It would be nice to come up with a chunk of cash to hand over to Dominic and free himself from these demeaning monthly installments. But he just wasn't that desperate. Squeezed and unhappy, but not desperate.

Tom let his mind drift away from Dominic but not back to the little Berne girl. For years, Carol simply had been "the woman at work" who always was on the phone with her mother and son, who always batted out of chambers at five o'clock sharp and left an eddy of dust in her wake. He had started to notice her—she had entered his ken, as he liked to phrase it—at precisely the time he had capitulated to Monty's advice to get his life together. In fact, Carol was one of the people Monty had urged Tom to reconcile with, even though Tom was certain he never had done anything to her. But Monty had opened his eyes to Carol. And if the Christmas kiss was not a sign they were headed somewhere, the dinner invitation surely was.

The phone rang. Carol answered, listened briefly, then hit the hold button.

"The lawyers on the union case," she said. "They want to talk to you."

"Which side?"

"It's a conference call."

Tom went to his desk and picked up his phone.

"We'd like permission to submit a reply," said the union's lawyer. "Nothing lengthy. Just an affidavit from the union president and a short memorandum of law to address some points in the OCA's opposition papers."

"If you wanted a right to reply, you should have asked for it earlier," said Tom.

"We know, but the court has discretion."

"What does the other side say?" asked Tom.

"We don't oppose," replied the other lawyer. "We expect this will go up on appeal no matter who wins, and a full record can only help."

"We can have it to you first thing on January second," said the union's lawyer.

Normally, Tom had the discretion to grant this request, especially since both sides agreed. But with the decision already written, he needed to run the request past the judge.

"I'll be right back," said Tom. He put the call on hold. "Did he sign the decision in the union case?"

"I don't know," said Carol. "I'm only through half of what he signed. The rest are on the table in the middle room."

Tom went into the middle room, pawed through the pile of motion folders, and saw that the judge had signed the decision. Then he opened the door to the judge's office. He could not remember the last time the judge napped in the middle of the day. But there was the judge, contorted on a couch that was too small, his head awkwardly bent against one armrest, his ankles propped on the other, his eyeglasses askew.

"Judge?" Tom said softly.

The judge did not stir. Tom took two steps closer.

"Judge," he said, sharper now and with a little more volume as he reached the couch.

"Judge," he said, louder again.

The judge did not react, did not even flutter an eyelid. Tom pressed his knuckles against the judge's shoulder, feeling the sharp bone beneath the soft flesh and flaccid muscles. He pressed two fingers against the judge's neck where he guessed the jugular to be. His mind was already in overdrive.

"Carol," he called. "Tell the lawyers I'll get back to them."

"Sure," said Carol.

Tom heard her pick up the phone, speak to the lawyers, then drop the phone back on its cradle.

"Come in here," said Tom.

A moment later, Carol peeked her head in.

"Close the door behind you," said Tom.

"What's wrong?" she asked.

"Touch right here, like this." He held two fingers together and pointed to the judge's neck.

Carol gingerly did as she was told.

"What do you feel?" said Tom.

"Nothing," said Carol.

"Me, too," said Tom. "He's dead."

CHAPTER 3

At about the time that Tom found Judge Canter dead on the couch, Foxx relieved the officer posted at the information desk in the main lobby. The officer's sole job was to direct the general public to the magentometers and to check the IDs of attorneys and court employees who did not need to clear security.

Foxx had settled at the desk for only about five minutes when a squat, burly man pushed in through the revolving door. The man stood at the point where the metal stanchions formed two distinct entry lines and sniffed the air. He had a pig face, a shaved head beneath a black cap, and a hoop earring in one earlobe. Liking what he smelled, he turned toward the coffee shop.

"Hey, you," called Foxx.

Pig Face did not stop, so Foxx got up from the desk and intercepted him at the coffee shop door.

"You need to go through the mags," he said.

"Hey, alls I want is a cuppa coffee," said Pig Face. "Those A-rab carts outside are all in the wind."

"You need to go through the mags," said Foxx.

"For coffee?"

"This is a courthouse, not a coffee house."

Pig Face stepped back and looked Foxx up and down, as if taking in the blue uniform that gave Foxx the balls to confront him. Foxx, amused by the moronically certain expression, stifled the urge to bait Pig Face into a fight. He did not need that kind of hassle on New Year's Eve.

With a theatrical sigh, Pig Face headed around the stanchions and down to the first set of mags. Foxx sat at the desk. Pig Face glanced over his shoulder as he dumped his wallet, watch, and pocket change into a tray. He glanced back again after passing soundlessly through the mags and again as an officer swept him with a wand. Foxx studiously did not react. But he kept an eye out as Pig Face ceremoniously strapped on his watch, rounded the stanchions at the bottom of the promenade, and headed slowly up toward the coffee shop.

Pig Face stopped at the desk.

"Betcha thought I was carrying," he said.

Foxx shrugged. He already had decided that Pig Face might not be as dumb as he looked.

"I'm not carrying because I don't need to carry. Catch my drift?"

Foxx shrugged again.

"I'd buy you a cuppa coffee, 'cept you being a civil servant it might be a bribe."

"Thanks for the thought," said Foxx.

In Judge Canter's chambers, Carol broke away from Tom and lifted the phone on the judge's desk.

"What are you doing?" asked Tom.

"Calling the captain's office for help."

She stabbed numbers, but Tom reached across to hit the hook switch.

"Why'd you do that? He needs help right away."

She pushed his hand off the phone and started pressing numbers. Again, Tom killed the line.

"Carol, listen. He's dead."

"But people can be revived."

"Forget it, Carol. Whatever hit him hit him very hard. I know dead, and he's dead. We need to think this through."

"Think what through? We call the captain. Don't court officers have CPR training?"

"He's probably been dead for an hour. What's the difference if we call now or five minutes from now?"

"We should, that's all."

"I know we should," said Tom. "But there are things we need to think about first."

"Like what?"

"Like what this means for you and me. Five minutes. Just give me five minutes."

Carol slowly set the phone back onto its cradle, then followed Tom to the other couch. They sat with some distance between them, then Tom slid close and placed his hand lightly on Carol's shoulder. They stared at the judge's lanky frame, his head pressed against one armrest and his feet spilling over the other. He looked more asleep than dead, and, if Carol used her imagination she almost could see a slight rising and falling of his chest. But she knew it was only her imagination. The judge was dead.

"Do you know what happens to a judge's staff if the judge dies?" asked Tom. He spoke softly, barely above a whisper.

"I never thought about it," Carol replied.

"The staff keep their jobs until the end of that year," said Tom. "So for us, right now, that means we're out of our jobs at close of business today."

"But we'll keep our jobs, won't we? They'll let us keep our jobs."

"Carol, the court system is in terrible financial shape. Haven't you been paying attention?"

Carol had heard about the unemployment rate, the falling property values, the unbalanced state budgets on the news. But that was just stuff happening out there, beyond the personal concerns that buzzed around her like so many gnats. She was in a permanent state of financial crisis, a permanent state of stress as she attended to everyone and every thing in her life. So no, she had not been paying attention to the court system's budget. And she never thought about what would happen if the judge died because, why pay attention to something she could not control.

"There are four judges retiring today," said Tom. "Their staffs are all out of their jobs, too. Four law clerks and four secretaries."

"But at least they knew retirement was coming," said Carol. "We've been, like, totally surprised."

"The result is the same," said Tom.

"But that's so unfair."

"Which is exactly my point. We need to think about ourselves."

"What's there to think about? The judge is dead, and we're screwed."

"Well, yeah," said Tom, "if we call the captain's office and report that the judge is dead. It's December thirty-first, and we would be screwed."

"What are you saying, Tom?"

"I'm saying that the judge is dead. We can't change that. And there's only a few hours left in the year. We can't change that, either. But what if we take the two things we can't change and put them together?"

"I'm not following," said Carol.

"The judge is a bachelor, right? No family to speak of except for his brother in Florida and those cousins somewhere out West. Nobody who's going to miss him till . . . probably till he doesn't turn up here the day after tomorrow."

"Tom, what are you saying?"

"I'm saying that for us it would be better if he died tomorrow."

"But he died today."

"Only if we report it. What if we don't?"

"Isn't that illegal?"

"I'm not sure. I'd need to check."

Suddenly Carol started to cry. Her sobs erupted and her tears flowed. She buried her face in Tom's chest and blubbered violently. Tom smoothed her hair. He looked at the judge and imagined a slight rising and falling of his chest. But he couldn't have seen that. Dead was dead. And he had no plan to hide the body—no present plan, anyway. He was just cataloging the facts and thinking how someone desperate enough and clever enough could—this one time only because the conditions were near perfect—make it look like the judge died after midnight tonight.

Carol said something into his chest.

"What?" asked Tom.

She spoke again, but her words were no more intelligible. Tom pushed her off his chest. Her face was red, wet with tears, stained with running eyeliner. She sniffled. He took out a tissue and dabbed at the corners of her eyes, ran his fingers back all the way through her hair.

"He gave me thirty-three hundred dollars today," she said.

"He gave you thirty-three hundred dollars? What did you do, sell him a car?"

Carol laughed.

"He gave me three hundred for next semester's tuition. He's been helping me get my degree because he thinks I should be more than just his secretary. Of course, at the rate I'm taking classes, he'd have been retired before I got my degree."

"I didn't know that," said Tom.

"He's been doing that since before you started. He didn't want anyone to know."

"What about the three thousand?"

"He kind of forced that on me," said Carol. "I mentioned that Nick's hearing aids were falling apart, but that insurance wouldn't pay for new ones till June, and he decided Nick shouldn't wait. I kept refusing, but today he wrote the check and left it in my desk. I never got a chance to talk to him about it."

She leaned back into the corner of the couch and folded her arms across her chest. Her eyes softened as she drifted into thought.

"Those checks are worthless now," said Tom.

"Why?" asked Carol.

"The law of principal and agent. When the judge wrote those checks, he was acting as the principal telling his agent, the bank, to give you that money. When a principal dies, the agent has no authority to complete any transaction."

Carol pushed herself forward, leaning with her elbows on her knees and her head in her hands. The complicated pattern of the Oriental rug blurred as the focus of her eyes went to infinity. Okay, the three thousand was over the top; she could use it, of course, but since it was something she never expected, it was something she could live without. Ironically, the three hundred at the start of each semester was something she had come to rely on.

"But," said Tom. "If I hadn't come in here to see the judge and you had gone out to the bank at lunchtime to deposit those checks, they still would be good."

"Even though the judge actually was dead?"

"The line is fuzzy," said Tom. "There's no time stamp on any of this."

Carol stared at the floor. Tom rubbed her back.

"Come on," he said. He stood up and extended his hand. She took it, and they went into the middle room, closing the door behind them.

"What would you have done," he asked, "assuming I didn't need to wake up the judge?"

"I'd have gone to the bank at lunchtime and deposited the checks," she said.

"And what about him?"

Carol routinely did the judge's banking. He had taught her how to forge his name, both the full signature he used at the bank and the distinctive *AC* initials he used at court. Sometimes, in his absence, she even signed court orders. She withdrew four hundred dollars cash for him each week, usually on Friday, though with tomorrow being a holiday she would have withdrawn that same amount today.

"His usual," she said.

"Okay," said Tom. "Let's just do this. Right now, and for the next half hour or so, we are going to act like we never went into his office. You'll go to the bank, I'll stay here and work. When you get back, we'll decide on our next move."

"But won't we . . ."

"Sure. We'll probably just call the captain's office." Tom saw doubt cloud Carol's eyes. "Carol, the judge wrote you those checks. Don't you think he'd want you to have the money?"

Tom waited exactly one minute after he watched Carol take the angle at the end of the corridor. Then he locked chambers and headed in the opposite direction. Unlike Carol, he had thought about what would happen if the judge died. It would enter his mind each year as Christmas approached and hover like a specter on the periphery of his consciousness until January first came and he could put those fears away for another year. But, looking back on those other years, the judge's death would not have been so dire a situation. The court system had money then, and a massive institution like the New York County Supreme Court had enough folds in its financial flab to hide a couple of employees whose judge died out from under them. There was no money now, and though Tom occasionally stretched the truth for effect, he had been totally truthful when he told Carol that the court could not afford to retain the staffs of the four judges scheduled to retire that same day.

Hard enough as it was to stay with the court system today, it was harder to find a decent job in the private sector. And for someone who had been in the court system as long as he had been, leaving was near impossible, even in a good economy. Lawyers in the private sector looked askance at most longtime government employees. Anyone who stayed in the court system for more than a couple of years, went the conventional wisdom, was either lazy or incompetent or both. Tom considered himself neither and perhaps he was right. But try convincing the hiring partner of some midtown Manhattan law firm otherwise. Tom already had tried and failed.

Plus, few people had sympathy for lawyers. Tom had a law degree, he was a member of the bar. If he lost his job, he always could open his own office. Couldn't he? Well, he could, he supposed—if he had enough money in the bank to survive for the time it took to cultivate a cash flow. But he didn't. Even before his recent troubles, he literally found himself counting pennies at the end of every month. He was entitled to two more paychecks if he lost his job, from which he could make one more payment to Dominic. After that . . . a parade of horribles danced in his head. Broken bones, eviction, a life on the run, the constant fear of turning a corner and walking into Dominic. And so, despite his assurances to Carol, that rhetorical question still floated in his head: How could he take the two facts, that the judge is dead and it's New Year's Eve, and put them together?

The two small elevators in each wing of the front lobby were still called the judges' elevators. These elevators originally were operated by real human beings and the passengers restricted only to judges, but over time the operators retired, the elevators were reconditioned to be self-service, and chambers staff as well as senior back-office clerks earned the right to a key. Tom took the south elevator, which landed a few steps from the courthouse coffee shop. Outside the shop, Dominic slouched against a trash bin.

"Well, Mr. Carroway," he said. "Fancy meeting you here."

"I was just on my way out to see you," said Tom.

"Really?" Dominic twisted the sleeve of his peacoat to expose his wristwatch. "This piece o' shit must be broke. It says ten o'clock instead of eight."

"Sorry," said Tom.

"Sorry don't cut it." Dominic locked onto Tom's elbow and pushed him through the revolving door, then grabbed the back of his neck and dragged him down the steps at a sharp angle. At bottom, just beyond the abutment, was a small park. The trees were bare, the ground frozen, the benches empty. It was the middle of the morning and few people were on the streets.

Dominic stopped in front of a bench.

"You duckin' me?" he asked. He squeezed Tom's neck.

"No goddammit. I wouldn't. You know that."

Dominic let go and dusted his hands.

"I don't know that," he said. "Alls I know is that I was waiting at the fountain and freezing my ass off."

"I got in early. Lots of stuff needs to get done today. I started working, then the judge came in, then the next thing I knew it was almost ten."

"So you're not duckin' me?"

"I have your money." Tom patted his left pocket. "What's the point of avoiding you?"

"Ain't no point," said Dominic. "Let's see it."

Tom scraped out the thick wad and handed it over. Dominic held the bills tight to his chest, counting quickly, his mouth moving.

"Good," he said. The inside of his jacket had many pockets, and he shoved the five hundred dollars into a particular one. "Thanks."

The punch came out of nowhere. It caught Tom beneath the sternum, lifted him into the air, and dropped him onto the bench.

Dominic leaned close.

"Don't you ever fuckin' make a fool of me again, you hear?"

Tom barely nodded. His stomach felt like a cannonball tore through it.

Dominic dug a hand into Tom's other pocket and pulled out the thin wad. He peeled off a ten, stuffed it into Tom's collar, and pocketed the rest.

"Finder's fee," he said. "Because I had to come find you. Asshole."

Tom rolled sideways, trying to catch his breath. The pain in his chest was so intense that he did not notice the cold slats of the bench or the presence of someone settling next to him. Then a hand slapped his cheeks.

"You okay, Tom?"

"Foxx?" Tom's eyes swam. He rolled back until he was sitting straight, then felt his stomach heave as if he would vomit. He leaned forward with his knees spread and swallowed hard until the feeling passed.

"That guy do this to you?"

"What guy?" asked Tom.

"Short stocky guy with a pig face."

"I don't know any guy."

"You just walked out with him."

"I don't know any guy, Foxx. Okay?"

"You're telling me you just came outside by yourself and collapsed on the bench?"

"That's what I'm telling you."

Foxx had a stare people told him could peel the paint off wood, and he aimed that stare at Tom.

"Thanks, but my problems are none of your goddam business."

Foxx pressed something into Tom's hand and stood up.

"It was sticking out of your collar," he said.

Foxx climbed the steps and stood on the abutment above the park. Foley Square was empty except for a handful of pedestrians bent against the wind. Pig Face was not among them.

Foxx lit his first cigarette of the day, took a long drag, and replayed what he had seen in his mind: Pig Face dragging Tom out the door and then steering him down the steps. He hadn't seen Pig Face punch Tom, but he could infer what happened just as surely as if he had seen Pig Face holding a smoking gun while Tom bled from his chest.

Down on the bench, Tom slowly assembled himself. Foxx had planned to wait for him, but someone heading down the steps in the opposite direction caught his eye. He stubbed out his cigarette and followed.

CHAPTER 4

Carol did not head directly out of the courthouse, but stopped into the ladies' room just beyond the first angle in the corridor. Most judges and employees took off the entire week between Christmas and New Year's, and all the chambers she had passed were locked up tight with several issues of the *Law Journal* spilling out of their mail slots. Carol slipped off her coat and closed herself into a stall and hunkered down to pee. She was glad the courthouse was so empty, because if she ran into another secretary or law clerk she might confess that the judge was dead or, more likely, start to sob. The deserted courthouse lent a dreamlike quality to an unreal circumstance, and in those odd moments between her thoughts turning away from and then back to the judge, she almost could believe that he was still alive.

She left the ladies' room and walked past an officer idly paging through a newspaper at the security desk to the public elevator bank on the inner circular corridor. She rode alone down to an empty rotunda and walked up the promenade past a skeleton crew of officers manning the quiet mags.

Outside, the sky seemed much grayer than when she had arrived, the air colder and the wind more biting. The Emigrant Savings Bank that both she and the judge used was three short blocks south and one long block west across Broadway. Normally, in bitter weather, she would have taken the shortest route. But on a troubling day like today, she needed time to consider what she was about to do. She headed south along the square, with the tall federal courthouse and the massive municipal building looming beside her. Traffic swept off the Brooklyn Bridge, and when the signals changed in her favor she crossed the street.

A neatly laid granite path curved between City Hall and the Tweed Courthouse. Protected by the two ancient buildings, the path enjoyed a microclimate where seasons arrived early and lingered late. Daffodils sprouted in January and bloomed by Presidents' Day. Trees stayed green well into October and held onto their peak autumn colors till Thanksgiving.

Sheltered from the wind, Carol walked slowly. She was hyperaware of the two checks in her pocketbook, and their monetary value, as if transformed into physical mass, weighed on her shoulder. Tom's reasoning made perfect sense. The judge wanted her to have the money. The tuition check was such a ritual that it had become routine. And the check for the hearing aids, well, they had been up and down that topic for weeks, the judge suggesting, then cajoling, then insisting, and she refusing, then resisting, then outright shutting down all conversation. So he had found a way around her, left the check in the drawer for her and then conveniently died. Of course, that last part of the plan wasn't quite true. He couldn't have known he was going to die. But he had, and now she had the checks, so she would deposit them, and because this whole trip to the bank was predicated upon the plausibility that the judge was still napping, she would withdraw his usual four hundred dollars.

Not reporting the judge's death was something else entirely. She would have preferred that the judge not die at all. And if he had to die, if today had been the day, it would have been better to have occurred at his apartment after he had crawled into bed. But that's not what happened, and so in a few short hours she would be out of a job.

Inside the bank, three tellers worked the windows while four customers stood in line. Carol, wanting as much cover as possible, found a spot where a glass counter joined a thick pillar. Holiday music played in a ceiling speaker directly over her head. A Christmas tree decorated with origami ornaments stood in a corner with dummy presents piled on a cottony white mat. Decorations and music fit Carol's mood only until Christmas Eve. After that, she would just as soon see them gone.

Carol tried to endorse the first check, but her hand shook so much she dropped the pen. She couldn't sign her name, and if she couldn't sign her name how could she sign the judge's? But then she heard Tom's calm, soothing words in her head. She picked up the pen and, taking a deep breath, endorsed both checks and signed the judge's name on a withdrawal slip.

A teller called her to the window. Carol slipped everything through at once: the checks and the deposit slip and the four-hundred-dollar withdrawal. The teller separated the two transactions. Carol took another deep breath. She wanted to be done with this banking and hurry back to chambers and to Tom. She thought about how it felt to lean against him on the couch. He was solid, not hard; gentle, not weak.

"How do you want the cash?" the teller asked.

"Ten twenties and four fifties," said Carol. It was the mix of bills the judge preferred.

Her cell phone buzzed in her pocketbook.

"Hi, Nick. Is everything all right?"

"Great," said Nick. "This is fun. We're at the top of the mountain and it's snowing. Thanks for letting me go."

"Of course, dear. You're welcome."

"This is really great and . . ." His voice faded.

"Sorry, Nick. I missed that."

"About tomorrow . . ."

"Did Jeremy say he could come?"

"I . . . asked . . ."

The connection broke. Snow, a remote mountain. It was lucky Nick reached her at all. He sounded so excited, and so thankful, too. It was nice to hear him shake out of his video-game torpor and gush the way a nine-year-old boy should gush when happy.

Carol dropped the phone back into her pocketbook and thanked the teller. Rather than walk through the park, she headed back to the courthouse by the most direct route up Broadway. In the middle of the next block, a thought stopped her.

She was about to lose her job.

Just minutes ago, it seemed, that same thought had been theoretical. But now, after the phone call from Nick, the realistic implications of losing her job exploded before her: mortgage payments, her virtually empty savings account, her mother's small pension, her mother's poor health, the cost of maintaining medical coverage for herself and Nick, the terrible job market. She had scraped through some pretty bad times, but these times felt much worse. Forget about the likelihood that she might never hear that excitement in Nick's voice again anytime soon. Her family's survival was at stake.

When her thoughts faded, she found herself leaning against a bus shelter. A man pushing a shopping cart full of deposit bottles stared at her.

"You okay, lady?"

Carol pushed herself off the shelter and tightened the pocketbook on her shoulder.

"Yeah, I'm okay," she said.

She walked off quickly. She needed to get back to chambers before Tom did anything stupid.

Tom waited for the judges' elevator to close before collapsing against the wall. He felt like there was a big bubble of air riding up against his heart. He pounded his chest and tried to force a burp, but the bubble remained.

The elevator dinged, and the door opened at the fifth floor. Tom shuffled across the corridor and into the men's room. In the mirror, his hair was mussed and his face was as red as a fresh sunburn. He took off his glasses, folded them onto the sink, and ran the water hard. Up close, his eyes were bloodshot and bugged as if the punch had popped them out of their sockets. He splashed cold water on his face, then raked his wet fingers through his hair.

What the hell had he been thinking, he wondered. Sure he resented the monthly ritual of meeting Dominic at the fountain, not only because it had been going on for so long but also because it stretched so long into the future. But resistance, as the professor in his head told him, was futile. And what did his resistance cost him? His stomach, maybe. A couple of cracked ribs, probably. All but his last ten bucks till next payday, definitely. A finder's fee, that dumb bastard had called it.

He dried himself with paper towels, then took one more look at himself in the mirror, inhaling carefully to calibrate exactly how deeply he could breathe before a cough erupted. Carol would be back from the bank soon, and he hoped she would not notice.

He unlocked chambers, looked in at the judge quickly, and then sat at his computer. He found that if he angled his body just slightly to the right that bubble in his chest did not seem so big. That same question returned to his mind: How could he take the two facts that the judge is dead and it's New Year's Eve and put them together? The question no longer was rhetorical. And after a few keystrokes, he found the answer.

On her way back from the bank, Carol needed to restrain herself from breaking into a run. She just wanted to get back to chambers and talk to Tom about their next move. As she hurried past the fountain, someone came up from behind her, slipped a hand under her arm, and tugged at her pocketbook. Her heart seized, and she thought, of all days to be mugged.

Then she saw who grabbed her.

"Foxx, dammit, I thought you were a mugger."

"Hey, kiddo," he said. "Who says I'm not. Who says what any of us are in the deepest recesses of our hearts?"

Carol groaned. Foxx could wear you out with his dime-store philosophical questions. Carol knew *that* firsthand.

"I've been meaning to stop by chambers," said Foxx. "Wish you and the judge and Mr. Carroway the tidings of the season."

"They're busy," said Carol.

"Busy with the *Werkman* case?"

"Among other things. The judge likes his docket as clean as possible at the end of the year." At least she could say that without lying.

"Any preview of his ruling?"

"I don't know, and I couldn't say anything if I did. And why do you want to know? It's not like overtime is anything you care about."

"Let's say I have a sporting interest."

Carol removed Foxx's hand from her pocketbook.

"Everything okay in chambers?" he asked.

"It is. Why wouldn't it be?"

"Even with your law clerk?"

"Tom?"

"That's his name, isn't it?"

"He's fine. Just the usual year-end hysteria."

"I should come up and say hello to the judge."

"I'll say hello for you. Trust me."

"I do. And by the way, do you want red or white?"

"Red or white what?"

"Wine. For tomorrow."

"What's tomorrow?"

"New Year's Day," said Foxx. "Dinner at your house. Nick invited me. Don't you two ever talk?"

Carol's mind went completely blank as Foxx guided her across Centre Street. It was only when they reached the steps that her mind reengaged and her anxiety level began to climb. Did he plan to follow her all the way back to chambers? Would he insist on saying hello to the judge himself? With Foxx, all things were possible. But as they reached the top step, he was no longer beside her. Carol felt disoriented at first. Foxx had this ability to slip into and out of physical spaces in the same way he could slip into and out of a person's consciousness. When he was gone, he was gone, leaving behind more of a void than simply an absence. And when he was present, boy, was he present. It was as if people, objects, even empty space organized themselves around him. Carol blamed his eyes. They were an amazing blue—Caribbean blue, she called them—but they were also intense and challenging, even in tender moments. She took a deep breath and pushed in through the revolving door. God, she was glad those days were over.

In chambers, Carol took off her coat and tossed it onto her chair. Tom sat at the conference table and stared intently at his computer monitor.

"I did it," she said.

Tom clicked the mouse and unglued his eyes from the monitor.

"Are you all right, Tom?"

"I'm fine. Why?" He coughed.

"You look all red in the face."

"Like someone punched me in the stomach?"

"More like you ran a mile."

"I did, sort of," said Tom. "I went down to the coffee shop, then took the stairs back up. I need to get into better shape, like you."

Carol smiled weakly. She dug into her purse for the four hundred cash and slapped the bills onto the table.

"The judge's usual withdrawal in the usual denominations. Ran into Foxx, too. He came up behind me near the fountain. Startled me, actually. He said wanted to wish you and the judge

Happy New Year. I thought he was going to walk me all the way back to chambers."

"Where is he now?"

"I don't know," said Carol. "We got to the top of the steps and he just disappeared."

Tom came out from behind the conference table.

"You done good, kiddo," he said. He put a knuckle under her chin and lifted her head just slightly. She thought he was going to kiss her, but instead he just winked. "Gotta show you something."

Tom led her into the middle room and opened the judge's door.

The judge still lay on the couch, only now he was on his left side, facing the back cushions with his knees drawn up so that he fit between the two armrests.

"What the . . ." said Carol, and for a moment she believed the judge hadn't died, that he really had been asleep, and that he had moved to make himself more comfortable. And in the moment after that she thought about how silly and pointless all her heartache and stressing had been.

"I moved him," said Tom.

"You did? Why?"

"When a person dies, bodily fluids stop circulating. Gravity pulls them to the lower parts of the body, and, because most of the fluid is blood, the person's skin turns reddish purple. That's why it's called lividity, and it's a way to estimate how long a person has been dead. But if you turn the body every two hours, the fluids circulate artificially. The circulation minimizes lividity, and it becomes harder to establish the time of death."

"So we're going to call the captain's office?" asked Carol.

"Who said that?"

"You did."

"That may be what I said, but it's not what I meant," said Tom. "I told you to deposit the checks because the judge would want you to have that money. And because making the judge's usual withdrawal gets us a couple more hours into the day. And because I needed time to do some research."

"On what?" asked Carol.

"Getting to midnight."

"You mean not telling anyone about the judge?"

Tom nodded.

"Tom, I don't want to lose my job any more than you do. But we're not playing a game here."

He put his arm around her shoulder, but she spun out from beneath him and sat on the other couch. He sat beside her, careful to give her some space.

"Carol, I have a plan. I think it will work, but I need to know you're with me on it. If it works, we win. If it doesn't, we lose big time. But it definitely won't work if we're not together on it."

"We have twelve hours till midnight," she said. "And we can't keep turning him on the couch till then."

Tom took her hands in his. They were nice hands, a little chafed in the palms but soft and smooth on top.

"It's not really twelve hours," he said. "It's a lot less because the building will clear out fast after lunch. And we're not going to keep him in chambers. We'll leave as soon as we can."

"We?" asked Carol.

"Yep. All three of us," said Tom.

CHAPTER 5

Tom stood over the couch, staring at the judge's body and carefully sniffing the air. The judge had been dead for close to three hours now, and according to Tom's research, internal gases would build and the odor of death eventually would leak out of the body. He detected nothing yet.

The office had two windows facing east, though the federal courthouse blocked most of the sunshine. Tom lifted each window, and frigid air immediately swirled in. The room would cool quickly and slow down the process of decomposition.

Tom opened the closet and patted the pockets of the judge's suit jacket until he found the keys. He recognized one for the apartment house lobby, two for the apartment itself, and the silver one with its embossed Buick symbol worn like an old coin. He went back to the judge. He pulled the four hundred dollars from his pocket, peeled off a fifty, and gingerly worked the rest into the judge's pocket. His finger touched a folded handkerchief, and he immediately pulled back and quickly left the room.

"Stick to the story," he told Carol. "Anybody asks for the judge, you say he closed himself in for a nap ten minutes ago."

"What if an order to show cause comes in?" asked Carol.

"Call me and we'll talk it through."

"What if . . ."

"Carol, we can't foresee every little thing. If anything comes up, call me. I'll be back in an hour."

The walk to Canal Street did Tom good. The bubble in his chest dissipated. The pain in his ribs waned to a dull, not entirely unpleasant ache, enough to remind him that he was alive, which was not a fact he took for granted today. Dominic's punch was still sharp in his mind, but its import had begun to fade now that Tom had a plan. Not that Tom could not hold two serious thoughts in his mind at the same time; after all, law clerks were masters at maintaining a mental balance through the shifting focus of the day as cases, issues, and legal emergencies boiled like clouds over a mountain range. Tom's relationship with the judge had been multifaceted: the older man had been a boss, a friend, the dominant personality in Tom's professional life. His death was a tragedy, and he, like Carol, would need time to deal with the emotional fallout. But right now it presented a problem to be solved and a disaster to be averted. They could get to midnight; they needed to get to midnight. And the odds of getting to midnight—a wrinkled boundary where probable met doubtful—were a heady mix.

Canal Street was thronged as usual, and after feeling naked walking up a virtually deserted Centre Street, Tom gladly lost himself in the crowd. The first store sold mostly laptop cases and pocketbooks and no luggage bigger than airline carry-ons. The second store carried huge wheeled contraptions with thick straps and deep pockets and telescoping handles. He dragged the biggest one he could find to the register and paid with the judge's fifty. He got almost fifteen dollars change.

At the Canal Street subway station, he bought a single ride fare card and lifted the suitcase over the turnstile. A train arrived in less than a minute. This excursion was going well so far.

Twenty minutes after Tom left chambers, Carol looked at her watch for the twentieth time. He probably was at Canal Street already, she thought, maybe even in a luggage store.

Tom's plan was irresistibly simple. But no matter how many times she ran it through her head, no matter how many times she told herself the judge would want this for her, she could not ignore its basic dishonesty. Keep the judge's death a secret, turn the body to prevent lividity, bank on the judge being an old bachelor with only distant family relations.

"What about friends?" she had asked.

"He's a judge," Tom had answered. "He has no friends, just acquaintances, allies, and enemies. We're his friends. No one else."

She had been excited in that brief span between Tom accepting her invitation to dinner and the words Tom had spoken as they stood over the judge's body, "He's dead." She finally had done something to break her seemingly endless parade of guys who were going nowhere. The judge's death left her no good choice. If they reported it, chambers would be dismantled and they would go their separate ways. Tom's plan, if it worked, would keep them together for the following year. But would their secret be the original sin they could not erase from their souls, one that would eventually tear them apart?

Carol shook the thought from her head. What basis did she have for accreting an entire shared life around a speck of sand that was a dinner invitation? She was acting crazy. She needed to divorce her attraction to Tom from the immediate situation. They needed to keep their jobs.

She called home. Her mother answered on the second ring.

"Didn't you just call?" her mother asked. A cooking show played loud in the background.

"Two hours ago, more," Carol replied.

"What?" said her mother.

"Can you lower the TV, please?" Carol asked.

The sound faded.

"That's better, Mom. I'm going to be late tonight."

"That's okay."

"It's not, really, but I can't help it. Sorry."

"We'll be all right, me and Nicky."

Yeah right, thought Carol.

"There's a cup in the back of the cabinet over the dishwasher," she said. "It has, like, thirty dollars cash in it. You can order a pizza."

"Okay. Are you going to a party?"

"No, I have to work late," said Carol. "The judge has a big decision he needs to get out. And then he wants to take us to dinner as a reward for working late. I'd rather not stay, but he's insisting on taking us."

"Who else?"

"Tom, the law clerk. You'll meet him tomorrow. I invited him to dinner."

"Is he nice?"

"I think so. You'll see for yourself tomorrow, Mom. Bye for now. I'll call again later."

Tom did not expect to see anyone he knew on a midday, up-town local train. But when the door opened, there was Moxley gripping the center pole not six feet away. Moxley cut his usual dapper figure, not a blond hair out of place, camel hair coat padded in the shoulders and tapered to the waist, a sleek designer briefcase wedged between his patent leather shoes. At another time and in another circumstance, Tom would have backed away and let other people shuffle aboard. But there was no one else on the platform and hardly anyone on the train. Tom calculated quickly. He had little time to spare, and these midday locals were running on a leisurely holiday schedule. The next one could be twenty minutes away. Plus, Moxley had spotted him, so Tom swung the suitcase across the gap between the train and the platform and stepped on. The door banged closed behind him.

Moxley shifted, inviting Tom to grab the same pole.

"Mr. Carroway," he said.

"Mr. Moxley," said Tom.

The train lurched into motion. Moxley played his eyes over the suitcase.

"Going somewhere?" he asked.

"Not until spring," said Tom. "I needed a new one, so I bought this today."

"Big."

"I travel heavy," said Tom.

"Where are you going?" asked Moxley.

"Huh?" said Tom.

"Your trip."

"Ireland," Tom answered. "Maybe Italy. I still need to decide."

"I see." Moxley's smile carried a hint of doubt.

Moxley was a partner in Harrington & Stone, a high-profile, plaintiff's negligence firm that specialized in complex medical malpractice actions. Though his name was not on the firm's masthead, Moxley was its most recognizable face at the courthouse where it raked in most of its fees. He charmed judges, schmoozed with clerks, and caused heart palpitations in the courthouse women whether they were court officers, court clerks, or court reporters.

A few years earlier, during his brief infatuation with the idea of working for a law firm, Tom landed an interview with Harrington & Stone. Moxley himself squired Tom around the firm that day. But the interview went nowhere; Tom never got a call back, in fact, never heard from anyone at the firm again. The experience left a bad taste, and years later, that taste still rose up from his gut whenever he saw Moxley.

The halting subway ride mimicked their tortured trade of banalities. Spring Street, Bleecker Street, then Astor Place. Tom hoped that Moxley would exit at Fourteenth Street. But Moxley stayed on and actually moved closer as several people boarded.

The train reached Twenty-third Street.

"My stop," said Tom. "See you."

"Happy New Year," said Moxley. "And give my best to the judge."

Tom shouldered his way off the train and looked back through the window. Moxley held his eye until the train rolled away. People always mentioned the judge to him: "How is the judge?" "Say hi to the judge." "Tell the judge I was asking for him." Tom never once conveyed these ass-kissing sentiments, and if he ever had, the judge would not have been impressed. The judge understood his place in the world; if he hadn't been a judge, he would have been just another old white guy people overlooked.

But a second, more troubling thought hit Tom as he climbed to street level. Did Moxley know that Twenty-third Street was the closest subway station to the judge's apartment?

CHAPTER 6

Tom knew that the judge parked his car on the street and paid
the apartment super to move it on alternate days in keeping
with the parking regulations. The trick was to find the car,
which was, as Tom thought emblematic of the judge, a stodgy
Buick sedan.

He found it on East Twenty-second Street, half a block east
of the entrance to the apartment building. It was hemmed in
between two hot-looking sports cars, the type temperamental
enough to ignite their alarms if someone even brushed too
close. Tom could not get to the Buick's trunk, so he opened the
back door and shoved the suitcase inside. The super must have
been short, because Tom needed to roll the front seat backwards to fit behind the wheel. He turned the ignition. The
engine sputtered.

"Don't you die on me, too," Tom groaned.

But the engine caught and began to hum. Tom worked the
car off the curb, making several back and forth moves before
he cleared the car in front. He checked the dashboard clock. He
was doing well timewise, and now he needed to make a choice:

go west and fight the lights heading south on Bowery or head east and zip down the FDR Drive. He chose east and drove smack into a traffic jam.

The fifth floor was quieter than quiet. Quiet implied only a lack of sound: no slamming doors, no squeaky wheel on the cleaning lady's cart, no conversations passing in the corridor. This was the quiet of desertion, what remained when people shut down their computers, turned off their lights, and slipped out of the building.

At one thirty, Carol ate her hummus sandwich on seven grain bread and her six carrots and drank her bottled water. She was not hungry, but she decided to force the food down. She did not know what the rest of the day held, so better to eat now when she had the chance than to wait for later and regret she hadn't. She wished she could have run today. Running helped her sort out her problems, and if she could not sort out her problems at least the endorphins kicked in and lifted her mood. But no number of miles, no time devoted to thinking, no amount of endorphins could have helped today. She wished she had not become involved in this plot, but the truth was that she had no real choice. Jobs were scarce, and with the judge gone she needed this job more than ever.

Her cell phone buzzed, and she saw Tom's number on the screen. The phone buzzed twice more as she swallowed down the last of her sandwich and slugged a mouthful of water.

"Where were you?" Tom said.

His voice sounded tense; she hoped nothing had gone wrong.

"Eating lunch," she said.

"In chambers?"

"Yes, in chambers, Tom. Do you think I'm an idiot?"

"No. Sorry. It's just that I'm in the mother of all traffic jams on the FDR Drive. I can't even get off."

Carol heard a thump, Tom slamming the steering wheel with the heel of his hand.

"No way I'm making it back before two o'clock," he said. "That means you need to do something for me."

Two o'clock came, and Carol decided to wait another minute in case Tom miraculously walked through the door. Then she gave it another minute and a minute after that. Finally, at 2:05, she knew she could not wait any longer. These two-hour cycles were probably general guidelines. But what if they weren't? What if at precisely two hours the blood printed a red wine stain on the judge's cheek? She got up from her desk, checked to make sure the entry door was locked, and went into the judge's office.

The room was cold, a steady breeze lifting the gauzy curtains. The judge's face was pressed against the back cushion, and his arms had uncrossed themselves and flopped down in front of his chest. Carol held her breath and examined the underside of his face. There was no hint of a wine stain, and she wondered if she could give Tom more time to get back and relieve her of the distasteful task of touching the judge. But no, she thought. She had better not take the risk.

She straightened up and studied the body, trying to decide the best way to turn him. He already touched the back cushions with his face and his knees, so she would need to pull him out and then rotate him.

"Here goes," she muttered.

She shoved her right hand, palm up, just below the judge's waist. She could feel the slackness of his flesh, the point of his hip. She turned her head, forced out a breath, and pulled in another. Then she shoved her other hand under his ribs. They felt like chicken bones, and the thought sickened her. She pulled out and paced across the office, panting, flapping her hands as if to shake off the feel of the judge's flesh and bones.

"I can't," she muttered. "I can't."

But she knew that she needed to. She was in this deeper than she wanted to be. She had touched the judge's body, and though she didn't know Tom's plan down to its most minute specifics, she knew its general shape. They were conspirators.

She went back to the couch. A shiver coursed through her, part cold and part fear. There was no way she was touching the judge again. No way. She knelt at the side of the couch and grabbed each of the cushions firmly. She yanked the cushions toward her. An inch, two inches. The judge came with them, the bend in his knees supporting the body enough to balance it. When she had pulled the judge far enough from the backrest, she worked her hands under the cushions and pushed up. The judge tumbled face down into the gap between the seat cushions and the backrest. She thought she heard his bones rattle.

Tom's cell phone rang at two fifteen. He answered it without taking his eyes off the crawling traffic. Crawling was a big improvement over a dead stop.

"Carol," he said.

"Tom?" The voice was male.

"Yeah, who the hell's this?"

"Monty."

"Monty. Damn. Sorry. I was expecting someone else."

"You all right, Tom?"

"I was till I got stuck on the FDR."

"Traffic jams are only temporary."

"Easy for you to say. What's up?"

"Just calling to see how you are."

"I'm fine," said Tom.

"I mean with tonight being New Year's Eve."

"Which reminds me. Who do you like? Auburn or Michigan? The spread's seven," said Tom.

"That's not funny, Tom."

"Sure it is. Joking about a thing means you have control over it. You said that yourself."

"I'm not in a joking mood," said Monty. "What are your plans for tonight?"

"Spending it with a lady who has no interest in sports."

"Sounds like a good idea."

"Hey, I'm your prize pupil."

"Keep it that way. Call if you get stuck on something."

"Will do," said Tom. "Taking no chances. Not tonight."

"Damn," Tom said. He unzipped his jacket and tossed it onto the conference table. "I never thought it would take that long. Sorry."

"I'm glad you're back," said Carol.

"Me, too. I'm freezing. The heater in his car doesn't work very well." He had the sense that he should hug her, but she sat at her desk, and if he went to her and she did not respond he would feel like a fool. Instead, he pulled a chair away from the table and sat down. He stamped his feet to get the circulation going.

"Did you turn him?" he asked.

"Oh yeah." Carol bit her lower lip, an expression Tom saw whenever she thought she had done something wrong.

"What does that mean?" he asked.

"It was . . . well, I didn't enjoy doing it."

They went into the judge's office.

"Oh," said Tom, seeing the judge face-planted into the gap between the seat cushions and the backrest.

"Sorry," said Carol.

"Nothing to be sorry about. You did fine. You turned him a quarter turn and that's the important thing. We just need to make an adjustment."

"Tom, I really don't want to touch him again."

"You won't need to," he replied.

He explained what he wanted Carol to do, and then they did it. Tom lifted the judge by the shoulders, and Carol shoved the first seat cushion back into place. Then Tom lifted the judge by his hips and knees, and Carol shoved the second cushion back into place. Then Tom angled the body in an exact facedown position with the judge's arms at his sides and his feet hanging over the cushion.

"There," he said. "Perfect."

They closed the door and went into the outer office.

"I'm nervous, Tom," said Carol.

"About what?"

"What we're doing. You mean you're not?"

"I feel the kind of nervous that keeps you sharp."

"Not me. I feel the kind of nervous where I can say or do the wrong thing."

"That's not going to happen," he said.

"How can you be so confident?"

"Because we're lucky this happened today and not yesterday."

"But not lucky enough for it to happen tomorrow."

"No, that's true," Tom allowed. "But we have a plan that's just simple enough to work."

"You really think that?"

"I'm feeling more confident by the minute."

"And I'm feeling less."

"Come here," said Tom. He lifted his arm as if inviting her to tuck herself under it. But instead of embracing her, he guided her around the conference table to the window. He opened the blinds.

"I know there isn't a whole lot of good going on," he said. "It's dark and depressing, and the judge is dead. I feel like crap, too. Sitting in his car in that traffic jam on the FDR, I felt like crying. But we can't do that, Carol. We can't give up when a few hours of effort can buy us another year."

"You really felt like crying?" asked Carol.

"Yeah," he said. "Only for about a minute, but it was real. And when traffic began to move I felt stronger than ever that he'd want us to do this."

"Do you think he would, Tom, because I'm having a hard time with that."

He put his thumb under her chin and, for the second time, lifted as if to kiss her.

"Yes," he replied. "I really believe it."

The winter dusk had fallen by the time Tom went out to the judge's car. He had parked half a block north of the courthouse, curbside next to Columbus Park, which separated the Criminal Courts Building from Chinatown. The park was empty except for a trio of Chinese men performing the slow, sweeping moves of tai chi. Beyond the park, holiday lights twinkled in the windows of the restaurants lining Mulberry Street.

Tom pulled the suitcase out of the car and rolled it along the sidewalk. The wheels made a deep scuffing sound that, amplified by the empty suitcase, rumbled like a bass drum. He crossed Worth Street, then lifted the suitcase by the handle and carried it to the back door of the courthouse.

A single officer sat at the mags. He nodded as Tom flashed his ID card and made no comment about the suitcase. Tom descended a long ramp to the basement level, then rode one of the public elevators to the fourth floor. From there, he climbed a back stairway to the fifth floor, reaching the hexagonal corridor just a few doors from chambers. He met no one along the way.

Inside chambers, Tom swung the suitcase onto the conference table and opened it up. The suitcase, cluttered with plastic bagging and pieces of corrugated cardboard, suddenly did not look big enough. But when Tom pulled out all the crap he saw that, yes, the suitcase would work.

He sensed reluctance from Carol, the way she followed him at a distance, the way she slowly closed the door to the inner office, the way she stood off to the side as he staged the open suitcase below the couch and studied the judge with his hand stroking his chin. Soon, though, he was lost in thought, visualizing lines and angles and superimposing them on the dimensions of the suitcase.

"A tight fetal position should work," he said. "What do you think?"

Carol grunted, then, feeling she should be more supportive, added, "I suppose so."

Tom now did the reverse of what they had done to fix the judge earlier. He grabbed the judge under each armpit, lifted him away from the backrest, and rolled him onto his right side.

"I need you to hold him here," he said.

Tom waited for Carol to place her hand on the judge's left shoulder before removing his own. Almost instantly, the judge toppled backwards.

"You need to hold him, really hold him," said Tom.

"Sorry," said Carol. She dragged the end table away from the armrest and positioned herself where she would have better leverage.

Tom bent one knee and then the other. The joints felt surprisingly stiff, and where Tom had visualized bending the judge's knees enough so that his heels touched his ass, he barely got them to ninety degrees.

"What's that smell?" asked Carol.

Tom caught a whiff of rancid meat.

"We pushed his breath out of him," he said.

He nudged the judge's chin downward and then bent the torso forward. Again, he had visualized sharp angles, but what he got instead was the judge in a perfect sitting position, his hips and knees both at right angles.

"He won't fit like that," said Carol.

"I know. But maybe . . ." Tom stroked his chin again. "Okay I'll lift him and swing him out, you move the suitcase directly underneath him."

"But he's not going to fit."

"Not now. But if we get him most ways into it, we can make him fit. I don't know how long I can hold him, so do it fast."

Carol knelt beside the suitcase and gripped it with both hands. Tom worked one arm behind the judge's back and the other in the crook of his knees until his hands met underneath. He locked his fingers, tested his grip, and then lifted. The judge, though barely more than skin and bones, literally felt like dead weight. Tom raised him just six inches off the couch before the muscles in his arms and back began to burn.

"Damn," he breathed.

He swung the judge out from the couch. One of the judge's arms dislodged and dropped free, dangling.

"Put it back," said Tom. He meant the arm. "Fast."

Carol caught the arm, bent it, and wedged the hand between the judge's knees and chest. It felt like a handful of long, thin twigs.

"Hurry . . ." Tom said through a grimace.

Carol ducked beneath the judge, aligning the suitcase at the best angle to receive the body. Tom lowered the judge as his back gave way and his grip broke. The judge hit the suitcase with a thud. His head lolled over one side, his legs splayed over the other.

Tom straightened up, wincing. His back hurt like hell.

"Are you all right?" asked Carol.

"No. Damn. I think I pulled something." He walked in a slow circle, his spine arched, his hand pressing the small of his back. First the punch to his sternum and now a muscle pulled in his back. What a goddam day this was.

"He doesn't fit," said Carol.

"He will," said Tom. He took one more deep breath as the pain ebbed, then knelt opposite Carol. "Take his head and tuck it inside."

Carol gingerly lifted the judge's head, bent it forward, and lowered it into the suitcase. It felt like a grapefruit in a sock.

Tom pushed against the back of the judge's thighs, trying to press his knees to his chest. The judge's waist gave a little, then the entire suitcase began to move.

"Hold it," he said.

Carol crawled around the suitcase and wedged her knees against the other side. Tom pushed again, closing the angle of the hips, then worked on the knees. Then he stopped.

"I can't push him any more."

"So what do we do now?"

Tom stood up. He could not jam the judge into the suitcase without breaking bones and bruising flesh, and from what he read on the Web any mortician with half a brain would see that the body had been moved after death. The suitcase idea would not work; it was as simple as that. He began to pace.

"Tom . . ." said Carol.

"I'm thinking," said Tom. But he was not really thinking; he was panicking. He had no goddam idea how to get the judge out of here until his toe caught the edge of the Oriental rug.

"Let's take him out of the suitcase," he said.

He grabbed the judge under the arms and pulled while Carol held the suitcase. Conveniently, the judge unfolded as his heels dragged on the rug. Tom centered him parallel to one edge, gently laid him down, and crossed his hands on his waist.

"The rug?" asked Carol.

"Exactly," said Tom.

They knelt side by side. Then together they lifted the edge of the rug, curled it over the judge, and began rolling until they reached the other end. The rug looked lumpy, but not terribly so, at least not for a New Year's Eve when no one would likely see them.

"We need to tie it," said Tom. "Hold him steady."

He got up and rifled through the judge's desk. He found

nothing. Then he went into the judge's lavatory and, in the utility closet, found a roll of duct tape. Coming out of the lavatory, he grabbed the *Law Journal* off the judge's desk.

"What's that for?" said Carol.

"First we stuff the ends, then we tape it closed."

Carol tried to lift one end.

"How are we going to carry it?"

"We're not. We'll use the cart."

"But someone will see."

"No one will see," said Tom. "Hell, no one's here."

He was right. He walked around the entire fifth floor and saw not a single light burning in any transom. He climbed the stairs to the sixth floor and walked that entire corridor as well. Again, not a light to be seen. He and Carol and the Oriental rug containing judge's body were the last occupants in any chambers.

He walked back down to five and passed the security desk. He wished the court officer a Happy New Year, and the officer responded in kind. Tom took the public elevator down to the rotunda and walked up the promenade to the lobby. One court officer stood at the mags, another sat at the information desk. Each exchanged a Happy New Year with Tom.

Outside, the streetlights had taken hold, bathing Foley Square in a golden glow. Tom angled across the steps, passed the bench where he had been punched, and swung around the north side of the courthouse. Traffic was light, pedestrians sparse. He got into the judge's car, started it up, and tacked about from one street to the next, eventually backing into a driveway that ended near a heavy bronze door known as the Worth Street entrance.

Tom opened the door with a swipe of his ID card. A security

camera hung from a short post about twenty feet from the door. But the car was obscured, and a law clerk entering through the Worth Street entrance was not out of the ordinary. He rode the judges' elevator to the fifth floor and passed the security desk, which was now empty, on his way to chambers.

Carol waited at her desk with the judge's coat across her lap.

"All clear," said Tom.

CHAPTER 7

The rug was heavy by itself, and even heavier with the dead weight of the judge bound up inside. They needed to park the cart right beside the rug, squat like weightlifters to snake their hands and forearms underneath, and then use all their strength to lift.

The cart was made of thin metal painted gray. It had a flat top and was used primarily to truck motion folders and case files into and out of chambers. The rug sagged where it hung over the front and back. Tom inspected both ends, making sure the balled-up pages of the *Law Journal* were stuffed tight.

They bumped the cart into the outer office. Tom pulled the judge's coat over his jacket. Carol opened the door and peeked out in both directions. The corridor was empty and quiet.

The cart rolled smoothly, the combined mass of the rug and the judge dampening the squeaky wheels into silence. The door to the judges' elevator opened immediately at Tom's touch, further proof that the building was empty. The rug was too long to fit inside, even on an angle. But Tom lifted its head end with his shoulder while Carol maneuvered the cart. With the rug set diagonally from one top corner to the opposite lower corner, the door could close. At street level, Tom jockeyed the rug back onto the cart, and they rolled through the big brass door.

The streets were even quieter than when Tom moved the car. Traffic was thin. A single pedestrian walked along Worth Street with his head down and hands in his coat pockets. Tom waited for him to pass out of sight before opening the back door of the Buick and collapsing the front passenger seat. Together, he and Carol fed the rug through the door, balancing one end on the center console and the other on top of the backseat.

"One of us needs to bring the cart back," said Tom.

"You do it," Carol replied. "I'll wait in the car.

She watched Tom go back inside the brass door, then slumped down in the seat. The car was cold. She had been in it once before, many years ago, on a frigid night like this, and she remembered how the stiff ribbing of the vinyl upholstery felt through the fabric of this very same coat. She did not want to think about that now. She wanted to think about what they were doing and how, as Tom told her, the judge would have wanted them to do it.

She sniffed the air, but smelled nothing of the judge, not death, not a whiff of breath loosened from the depths of his lungs, not even the particular old man odor that she could detect even across the breadth of chambers. Tom had packed those *Law Journal* pages well.

She closed her eyes, let her chin drop. She almost dozed, and maybe she had, but then the trunk slammed and Tom slid behind the wheel.

"Did you put something in the trunk?" said Carol.

"The suitcase," said Tom.

Carol sat up and forced a smile, her face pale in a patch of streetlight. Tom reached over the rug and massaged the back of her neck. She flinched just enough for him to withdraw his hand.

"Hey, it's not like we killed him," he said. "We're only floating him for a while."

"I suppose so," said Carol. "Maybe tomorrow we'll look back and say it wasn't so bad."

Traffic was light all the way to Twenty-second Street, and miraculously, a car left a curbside space right in front of the apartment house door just as they arrived.

"Anybody asks," said Tom as he wiggled the rug out of the car, "we're delivering a rug."

"That's kind of obvious, isn't it?"

"Right, but we won't say for who."

They carried the rug on their shoulders. It was heavy, but not terribly so. And they were just as lucky entering the judge's apartment building as they had been leaving the courthouse. They encountered no one, not in the lobby, not in the elevator, not in the corridor on the way to the judge's apartment. Tom, still wearing the judge's coat over his jacket, braced the rug on his shoulder as he fished for the keys. The floor was quiet except for music playing in the next apartment.

Tom unlocked the door, and they went in. They set the rug on the living room floor. As they stripped off their coats and turned on the lights and lowered the shades, Tom felt his old confident edge again. *This is going to work,* he thought. *This is going to work.*

They set about executing the plan they had hashed out during the afternoon and then rehashed during the drive. Carol pulled the bedcovers down while Tom unrolled the rug and dragged the judge into the bedroom. Together, they lifted the body onto the bed. Tom removed the judge's clothing, handing each piece to

Carol. She dropped his socks in a hamper and hung his suit in the closet. She counted five suits in all and saw, from the way they hung, the precise order in which he wore them.

"We should dress him in what he usually wears," said Tom. "Sweats. Pajamas."

"I doubt he ever wore sweats." Carol lifted the edge of a pillow. A set of powder-blue pajamas, wrinkled but neatly folded, lay underneath.

"How did you know that?" asked Tom.

"Lucky guess," said Carol.

They dressed the judge in his pajamas and plumped the pillows. Tom checked his watch. It was just past six o'clock. The timing was perfect. He could start the judge on his back and roll him quarter turns at eight, ten, and midnight. Carol took the shoes out of the suitcase and set them carefully on the floor of the closet. Tom zipped the suitcase closed and stood it outside the bedroom doorway. Carol went back into the closet and emptied the judge's pants pockets. She dropped the handkerchief into the hamper, then folded the judge's glasses over the cash on the nightstand.

"Nice touch," said Tom.

They did not pull up the covers. They would do that only after they turned the judge for the last time. Tom took one more look around the bedroom, then shut the light.

"I'll be right there," he said.

After Carol left the bedroom, Tom cracked the two windows. He tested the cold drafts with his hand and raised each window sash first one inch and then two. Satisfied with the air flow, he peeked out the doorway. He could see Carol seated on the couch, leaning forward to look through the open drawer of the coffee table. This will be a long six hours, he thought as he lifted the judge's glasses and slipped a fifty dollar bill into his pocket.

On one level, Tom thought that they needed a break from the judge. All of their hard work was behind them, and though they had six hours and three turns ahead of them—turns that he could think of as the turns in the Belmont Stakes—they were on the homestretch. They also needed to get out on another, more practical level. The judge's apartment was stocked worse than any bachelor pad imaginable. The cupboards were bare: three punched-in boxes of cereal, a jar of unsalted almonds, peanut brittle, saltine crackers, and several boxes of Jell-O in assorted flavors. The refrigerator pickings were even slimmer: a head of lettuce turning brown, three celery hearts as limp as cooked spaghetti, a ketchup bottle and mustard jar with hard red and yellow collars oozing out from the caps, a pint of fat-free milk dated DECEMBER 26, and half a pastrami sandwich wrapped in wax paper.

Tom peered out the fish-eye and then eased the door open a crack. The neighbor had turned up the volume, and Tom recognized the song as "You Meet the Nicest People in Your Dreams." He knew the song from *The Big Broadcast,* a weekly program featuring music from the 1920s and 1930s aired on Fordham University's radio station. When he was certain the corridor was empty, he opened the door wide and beckoned Carol to follow. They padded down the stairs and out the door and said not one word aloud until they were well away from the apartment house. They walked close, not touching but with a psychic connection that was palpable to each of them.

The atmosphere on Second Avenue was more festive than the quiet of Twenty-second Street. The lights were brighter, the sidewalk alive but not crowded. A scratchy rendition of "Auld Lang Syne" played from speakers attached to the awning of a greengrocer.

Carol stumbled. Tom caught her under the arm.

"Clumsy," she said. "I should have changed into sneaks."

She kept two pairs of sneakers under her desk, one for her lunchtime runs and the other, when she remembered, for commuting.

"I'm glad you kept the boots," said Tom, still holding her arm. "I like them."

"You do?" she said. She snuggled against him, and he patted the top of her hand.

A block later, they came upon a deli with the same name as on the label of the half-eaten pastrami sandwich wrapper in the judge's refrigerator. It was small and crowded, so Carol stayed on the street while Tom went in to order. Seeing that Tom would be awhile, she pulled out her cell phone and called home.

"How's it going, Ma?" she said.

"Oh fine. Fine. Nicky got home from snowboarding. I haven't ordered the pizza because he's dozing."

"Did he have a good time?"

"I think so. You want to ask him?"

"No," said Carol. "Let him sleep."

"You'll be home soon, right?"

"Mom, I told you. I'm working late." Carol was extremely patient, but sometimes she could not help the incredulity from creeping into her voice whenever her mother forgot the obvious.

"That's right. Sounds like you're outside."

"Tom and I went out for food."

"Tom is the fella you work with?"

Carol smiled to herself. "That's right."

"I thought the judge was taking you to dinner?"

Now *that* she remembers, thought Carol.

"We had a change in plans," she said. "Too much work to go out to dinner."

"Well, don't work too hard," said her mother. "Keeping you late on New Year's Eve. Wait till I see him. This Tom, he's the one coming tomorrow?"

"Tomorrow," said Carol. And she smiled to herself again because suddenly tomorrow did not seem so far away. "Tell Nick I love him."

Tom came out of the deli with a bag stuffed surprisingly thick.

"All that for just the two of us?" said Carol.

"It's mostly air," said Tom.

A few doors down, Tom stopped in front of a liquor store.

"Wait here," he said, and handed Carol the bag.

Inside, he turned directly to the wine cooler. The sandwiches, chips, and salad had eaten a good portion of the judge's fifty, but there was still enough left to cover a moderate bottle of champagne. He picked a brut from the rack and calculated the price plus tax in his head. As he walked to the register, the front door opened, and for the second time today, Tom found himself face to face with Dominic.

"Well, lookee who's here," said Dominic.

"Jesus Christ," muttered Tom.

"Whatcha got there?" Dominic's hand darted from his peacoat and deftly twisted the bottle in Tom's hand. "Nice taste. I didn't think ten bucks went that far."

"It doesn't."

"Really? Were you holding back on me this morning?"

"I gave you what you're due and then some," said Tom. "And anyway this isn't my money."

"No? Whose is it?"

Tom looked through the door glass, and Dominic followed Tom's eyes to Carol leaning against a light pole.

"I don't know how some of you fuckin' guys keep getting chicks to bankroll you," said Dominic.

"It's not . . ."

"Hey, Carroway, save it. I ain't working right now. In the spirit of the season, have a happy."

Dominic stuck out his gnarly hand. Tom took it, and they shook.

"Who was that?" Carol asked as Tom joined her on the street.

"Some guy I knew a long time ago," said Tom.

The judge's apartment had a dining area with a small round table. The table was covered with neat piles of newspapers and mail, including the mail Carol had taken from the judge's mailbox on the way in. After Tom rolled up the Oriental rug and lugged it to the compacting room at the end of the corridor, they sat on the couch and ate on the coffee table. The TV played without sound, showing a retrospective of the year's events intercut with scenes of New Year's celebrations from around the world.

Neither Tom nor Carol felt they had much of an appetite, but once they opened their sandwiches hunger overtook them and they ate ravenously.

"Music's awful loud from next door," said Carol.

"We could turn up the volume of the TV," said Tom.

"No, I kind of like it." Carol dabbed at her mouth with a

napkin, then tossed it onto the table. "What do you think happened to him?"

"Stroke, heart attack. Probably heart attack. Didn't his father just drop dead?"

"He did," said Carol. "But the judge always said he had his mother's genes."

She laughed, and her skirt rode up to expose a good bit of leg. Tom could not help stealing a glance. He especially liked the strength of her thighs, and he wondered how he had overlooked her for so long.

"He looked like a nerd," he said. "But he was strong in his own way. The lawyers knew they couldn't push him around." He slapped the coffee table. "Shit, I forgot to call those lawyers back."

"The union case lawyers?" asked Carol.

"Right." Tom slipped a single chip into his mouth and chewed it slowly. "Oh well, nothing I can do about that now."

"Who is going to find him?" said Carol. Tom had avoided this question during all their planning.

"We'll wait until midmorning, then leave a message on his answering machine. You know, something like, 'Judge, it's ten thirty and you're not here and we haven't heard from you. Hope everything is all right.' We'll wait awhile longer, then call the administrative judge's office and ask if the judge called in. When they tell us no, we'll call the super. He'll find the judge."

Carol nodded; that plan made sense. She balled up her sandwich wrapper and tossed it into the white plastic bag from the deli. She sank back into the couch and sighed, staring at a scene of people partying in London, where it already was well past midnight. Tom leaned back as well, but rather than stare at the TV he reached a hand to her and flipped a lock of hair back over her ear.

"How about we crack that champagne?" he said.

"Sounds good," she replied.

"First, I need to turn him. You clean up out here. Throw one wrapper and the chips bag into the trash. Tie the rest of it up in the plastic bag. If anyone notices, it'll look like he ate dinner alone."

Carol turned her head, brushing her lips across his knuckles.

"You're smart," she said.

"No, just accustomed to dealing with evidence."

He went into the bedroom and closed the door behind him. The inside air was as cold as a walk-in freezer. He opened the blinds and worked with the ambient light. Turning the judge on the bed was much easier than on the chambers couch. Tom quickly rolled the judge on his left side, bent up his knees for balance, and extended both arms for additional support.

Back outside, Carol stood at the kitchen counter and separated the garbage. Tom opened the refrigerator, but paused before taking out the champagne. The lettuce head, messy condiments, the expired carton of milk all spoke of a bleak, lonely life, and Tom, who sometimes saw himself as following the judge's path to the bench, often worried that he might share the same fate. Now he thought he should be so lucky.

Tom placed the champagne bottle on the counter, but rather than uncork it pressed himself against Carol from behind. She went rigid, but only for a brief moment until he snaked his arms under hers and cupped her breasts. She turned. They kissed hard. Tom lifted her onto the counter, pushed her skirt up to her waist, and rubbed her glorious thighs as he insinuated himself between her knees.

CHAPTER 8

They lolled naked on the couch with a scratchy woolen throw as their only cover and the shimmering blue glow from the quiet TV as their only light. Cold air flowed from beneath the bedroom door and lapped against them like the waves of a silent lake. At ten o'clock, Tom untangled himself from Carol and went in to turn the judge for the second time. He worked quickly, his breath cloudy in the half light, breaking down the judge like a pup tent and letting him fall facedown onto his stomach. Tom's own nakedness felt creepy.

Back in the living room, he huddled under the throw and poured the last of the tepid champagne into their thin paper cups.

"I had a funny thought while you were in there," said Carol. "It was like you were checking on a baby."

Tom grunted, his thoughts, unlike the traveler in the Robert Frost poem, simultaneously following separate implications down diverging roads.

"I'm joking," said Carol.

"It's a good point," Tom replied. "He was like our child. We attended to his every need, professional and personal. Well, maybe not his every need, right?"

Carol knocked back the last of her champagne.

"Anyway, he's awfully big for a child," said Tom.

"Yeah, and my ex never once checked on Nicky like that. He hardly ever was around."

Tom thumbed one of her nipples.

"Mmmm," said Carol. "Don't start something you can't finish."

"I never do," said Tom.

This time it was slow and sweet, not quick and tart like in the kitchen.

"Much as I want midnight to come," said Carol, "I almost wish it never does."

"Ironic," said Tom, nestling against her.

But midnight came. The ball drop occurred electronically on the TV screen as it occurred physically some twenty blocks up and crosstown. They kissed, and Tom tweaked a nipple while Carol stroked the inside of his thigh. But unlike earlier, the kissing and touching did not start something they could not resist finishing. They unwound themselves from under the throw and, urged by the knee-high layer of frigid air, dressed quickly. The magic they had created on this strangest and most exciting of nights dissipated quickly in the new year.

Tom went into the bedroom, rolled the judge from his stomach onto his right side, and pulled the covers up to his shoulder. The cold had worked. Only a hint of odor floated in the air. He started to close the windows, then thought better. Midnight had come, and no one else knew the judge was dead. But they could not be too careful. Another few hours of cold air would tip the odds even further in their favor. He calculated the risk of returning tomorrow against the benefit of further scrambling the time of death and decided to leave the windows open.

The corridor was quiet except for muffled music from the next apartment. Tom carefully slipped a key into each of the two locks and turned slowly. He worried about the impossibility of sliding the security chain. But he told himself it was a detail that could not be helped and, likely, would not be noticed.

Outside, they headed west toward the subway. Tom waited until they were halfway between Second and Third Avenues before cramming the deli bag and champagne bottle into a trash basket. He waited until they crossed Third before parking the suitcase in the shadow of a brownstone stoop. They didn't speak, as if the need for quiet had pursued them from the judge's apartment down onto the street. But half a block on, Tom's unburdened hand caught Carol on the elbow, then slid down her arm and entwined her fingers in his.

PART TWO

New Year's Day

CHAPTER 9

Tom had not made a New Year's resolution in many years. He thought the concept was stupid. You were essentially the same person on January first as you had been on December thirty-first. Why should a new year cause you to change? People did change, of course, but usually because of a traumatic or miraculous event or an epiphany of major proportions, not the unfolding of a new pictorial calendar.

For Tom, all three things happened at once: the traumatic (finding the judge dead), the miraculous (getting to midnight), and the epiphany (Carol). Even the punch from Dominic, a completely separate trauma, had receded into the soft focus of nostalgia since it was all of a piece with the rest of the day's events. The fact that these events coincided with New Year's Day had Tom thinking in terms of resolutions.

He bounced out of bed at eight o'clock. He had slept on his back, with his arms crossed over the exact spot where Dominic's fist had landed. The pain was largely gone, he noticed, as he took several deep breaths and probed his sternum with his fingers. Another miracle, perhaps, but more likely the restorative powers of sex, rest, and his own body heat.

He got into the shower. The water was hot, and the spray from the showerhead felt good. Marvelously good. In fact, he never had noticed what a great old showerhead he had. The pressure was strong, the stream thick; it felt like expert fingers massaging his shoulders and back.

And so, with his bright mood and physical locale, Tom made five resolutions. First, he was going to stay clean. He had been clean for over a year, ever since he had replaced bookies with loan sharks, one subdivision of what people still called the mob with another. But he rarely spoke to Monty anymore, and so he resolved, second, to call him more often. Not today; he had dinner at Carol's house. Not tomorrow; they, along with the rest of the courthouse, would hear that Judge Canter had died. Soon, though, he would begin a regular schedule of calling Monty. Third, he would pay Dominic on time, with no foolish gambits like yesterday. Fourth, he would continue his frugal lifestyle, but at least he still would have a job. And if he kept number four, he eventually would be done with Dominic and his boss. He would be spending the year with Carol, too, because they had made it to midnight. That was number five, cultivating a relationship with Carol.

Tom dried off and dressed in jeans, a polo shirt, and a pullover sweater. His hair was thick, flecked with just enough gray to lend character. His belly was slightly rounder than flat, but the sweater covered that nicely and accentuated the width of his shoulders.

He checked his wallet. The ten-dollar bill Dominic had left him was still there, folded into fourths, along with seventy-odd bucks he had taken off the judge's nightstand before closing the apartment last night.

"Early this morning," he muttered, correcting his own thoughts. The distinction was critical.

He would use the cash to buy wine and, possibly, flowers. Right now, though, he would get a newspaper, eat breakfast at a diner, and enjoy the anticipation of seeing Carol. That's what he would do.

New Year's Day always gave Carol a sense of renewal. It never lasted very long, having all the permanence of a coffee rush, but she could think back on the many New Year's Days of her life and pinpoint exactly what she, in her optimism, believed would come to pass that year. Nothing ever did, at least nothing good.

Today, as she quickly dumped bone-hard shards of pizza crust into the trash and swirled little pillows of popcorn into a pile on the counter, the feeling was purely and simply bitter-sweet. Yesterday, Tom's plan had carried her over the shock of the judge's death. Now, with the morning sunlight at its particular January angle exposing smudges on the kitchen window, reality took over. The judge had been more than just a boss or even a friend. He had been a lifeline. She could not have survived the rough years of her separation and divorce without him, and now she would need to survive the rest of her life.

She had teared up briefly yesterday, then put her emotions away. Now the tears came freely, the sobs pulsing in blubbering waves. In the dining room, the hospital bed creaked as her mother rolled over. Carol turned on the faucet. She stood there and cried, her hands stuck to the silver metal bowl dotted with corn kernels as it filled and then overflowed.

She cried herself out, then turned off the tap.

"Carol?" called her mother.

"Yeah, Ma?"

"You all right? I thought I heard you crying."

How could she have heard, thought Carol. But that stroke had done strange things, not only disconnecting her mother from her considerable ability to invent worries but also sharpening some of her senses into superhero proportions.

"Not me, Ma," she said, rubbing her eyes with the back of her wrist.

Carol started dinner, loading the heavy roast into the slow-cooker, then cutting the carrots, chopping the onions, and peeling the potatoes. Half an hour later, the kitchen looked like a tornado had ripped through. Half an hour after that, it was clean. The roast bubbled in the slow-cooker, the scalloped potatoes browned in the oven, and a ginger snap gravy simmered on the stove. The kitchen smelled great.

Carol climbed up to Nick's bedroom. Nick sat in bed, headphones clamped to his ears and attached to the video game player pressed against his knees.

"Happy New Year," she said, and kissed the top of his head.

"You already said that," Nick replied.

In fact, she had said it dozens of times, as she carried him up to bed when she arrived home, just after two in the morning.

"Sorry, I'm saying it again."

"What time's dinner?" he said.

"Three-ish," said Carol. "Which reminds me, mister, why didn't you tell me you invited Foxx?"

"You said a friend. Foxx is my friend. He's bringing me a surprise."

Carol sighed in a way she knew her son could not possibly understand just yet.

"Foxx sure is a man of surprises," she said.

She changed into running clothes, tied back her hair, and went for a run. The air was cold and calm, the neighborhood quiet. Carol's mind was quiet, too, simply taking in what she saw. Wreaths hung on doors. Christmas decorations that inflated and illuminated at night lay like broken balloons on the iron-hard front lawns. A few people already had dragged dried-out trees to the curb. During the second mile, her thoughts began to bubble.

Her ex-husband had been her first boyfriend. They met the first day of tenth grade and married the day after he graduated from law school. In between, they dreamed. He—even in her thoughts she referred to him only by pronoun—opened a personal injury practice in the Williamsbridge section of the Bronx, not far from where they both grew up. Bronx juries were the most generous in the state, he told her. He would make a killing. After a year, he moved her to a house in White Plains. It was not the greatest house; from the way he bragged about his verdicts she expected a mansion. But the neighborhood was a great place to raise a family. Plus, even though he was doing well now, they needed to live within their means. "It's a long time between drinks," was how he described personal injury work. Young lawyers got into trouble overextending themselves.

Looking back, she realized he had been stating his true intentions all along, not in words but in actions: the late-night phone calls with his secretary, the files he suddenly decided he needed to retrieve from his office, the house in White Plains, even her pregnancy with Nick. It was all part of a grand design to keep her occupied and removed while he pursued his secret life. One day, during the eighth month of her pregnancy, he simply vanished. He left behind an empty office, empty bank accounts, scores of angry clients, leases on two BMWs he had tricked her into cosigning, and several criminal investigations.

The next three years were a blur. Her mother moved in, newly retired from her job as secretary in Bronx Supreme Court. Rose took over the house, attended to young Nicky while Carol tried to heal her wounded soul. It was Rose who suggested that Carol go to work, Rose who found out that a secretary in New York County Supreme was planning to retire, Rose who connected the name of that secretary's judge with a young lawyer she remembered from her days in the Bronx. Carol took the job, and after two years, with Nick starting kindergarten, decided she wanted to return to school as well.

For two years, Judge Canter had been a remote boss. It now seemed so odd to recall that she actually had been scared to ask permission to leave work early one day each week to attend a class at Westchester Community College. The judge not only assented, but waxed eloquent on the value of a classical education. He had been a nerd in high school, he explained. He went to college and then, without any forethought, to law school. He regretted leaving academia, saw himself less as a judge than as a college professor in exile.

When time came for her to register for her second semester, the judge asked to see the course catalog and suggested which courses to take. When the third semester rolled around, he gave her not only his suggestions but a check to cover the tuition. That, she only realized much later, was a turning point.

* * *

Carol finished the run with a quarter mile sprint, then walked back and forth in front of the house for several minutes. "Warming down," the running magazines called it, though Carol could not understand the distinction between "warming down" and "cooling off." Her mind warmed down as well, returning slowly to the present. She was grateful now that Tom had convinced her of his plan. Those extra few hours meant nothing to the judge, but a lot to her and her mother and her son. And maybe something else—Tom—would come out of this as well.

She refused to dwell on that possibility just yet. After all, there was still tomorrow to get through. And before that there was today's problem—having both her old boyfriend and her (quite possibly) new one at the same table.

The thing you don't do, Monty told him long ago, is buy the *News* or the *Post*. The sports coverage was too good; the sports gambling coverage was too good, too. So, nine hours into the new year, Tom followed Monty's advice and opened *The New York Times* as he waited for his bacon, eggs, and pancakes to arrive. It was odd being more interested in food than in checking the scores to see how he might have done betting last night. But he was hungry, hungry not just in the empty stomach sense but on a cellular level as well. He hadn't had a night of sex like that in a good long while and he needed to replenish his energy. Who knew what today held, though given what he knew about Carol's home life he doubted that they would have any chance to be alone together.

The diner was quiet. A large, flat-screen TV mounted high over the counter played soundlessly. The hosts of a morning news magazine sat on a couch amid a sea of poinsettias. A crawl along the bottom highlighted the major news stories of the day. Next would come the weather. And after that would come the sports, a mix of yesterday's scores and today's schedule. Tom looked down, not only feeling noble but candidly telling himself it was easy to feel noble when events broke your way. He folded back *The Times* to the puzzle and, not having a pencil, began to work it out in his head. The food arrived. He cracked the strips of bacon with his fork. He sawed into the pancakes with his knife. Long-forgotten facts from college biology returned to his consciousness as the food slid down his throat. He could feel his cells absorbing nutrients.

Something rapped on the window glass right next to his ear. Tom turned, and Dominic crooked a finger.

"Come out here," he mouthed.

Tom speared a perfect wedge of pancake, then pointed his fork at the empty bench seat opposite. Dominic shook his head. Tom repeated the gesture, mouthing "Come in." Dominic lifted his middle finger. The spirit of the season had left him.

Tom slid out of the booth, taking his jacket but leaving his newspaper and gloves behind and signaling the waitress he would be right back. Dominic met him at the door and immediately grabbed him by the collar. Though Dominic was much shorter, his leverage and strength lifted Tom's heels off the ground.

"Hey, what the . . . ?"

"Shaddup," said Dominic.

"I just saw you yesterday."

"Yeah, what's that supposed to mean?"

"I didn't expect to see you today."

"Yeah, well, you're seeing me."

Dominic pushed Tom around the corner, where a big white

SUV with darkly tinted windows idled. He opened the door, shoved Tom inside, then climbed in after him.

"The boss's wheels," said Dominic. "He loaned it to me because I gotta deliver a message to you and select other sorry bastards."

Tom righted himself on the seat. The leather was slick with coconut oil, which greased the side of his face.

"The boss is calling you in," said Dominic. "Payment. In full. Everything."

"He can't do that," said Tom.

"Oh no? Who's gonna stop him? You?"

"We had an agreement."

"So? Whaddaya gonna do, Mr. Lawyer? Sue him?"

"Why is he calling me in?"

"'Cause other guys are calling in what he owes them. Shit flows downhill, Carroway, and you're at the bottom of the goddam mountain."

"How much?" said Tom. He had no idea how much he owed, minus the generous vig Dominic's boss charged for being so accommodating. The regular bimonthly payments had been going on for so long they left him financially numb and yet in a constant state of anxiety. He had adjusted. Life was a constant set of adjustments, of adapting to new normals. Unfortunately, Tom's current adjustment had set him on the edge of a precipice. This new one would push him over.

Dominic closed his eyes, his eyeballs darting beneath the lids like REM sleep. He may have sounded like a dumb, punch-drunk pug, but he never needed to write anything down.

"Eight," he said.

"I don't have that kind of money."

"Get it," said Dominic.

"Where?"

"Hey, that's your problem. I'm in collections, not financing."

"Can't I talk to him and work out a different plan?"

"You don't want to," said Dominic. "Believe me."

Tom felt that bubble in his chest start to inflate. He opened his mouth and thumped his chest with his fist. Nothing came out.

"Hey, Carroway," said Dominic. "You aren't going to gork on me, are ya?"

"No, I'm fine," Tom said, panting to catch his breath. "Just fuckin' great."

"Good, because I gotta move on to my next sorry bastard."

Dominic opened the door and backed out of the SUV. Tom slid over, following. He never saw it coming, just like he never saw the punch the day before. Dominic pitched him onto the sidewalk.

"Tomorrow," he said. "No money, I get unpleasant."

CHAPTER 10

Tom held it together long enough to return to the diner, pay for his breakfast, and lock himself in his apartment. Then pure panic set in. He paced in front of his living room window, his breath catching anytime something remotely resembling a white SUV passed on the street below. His knee ached from landing hard on the edge of the curb. That bubble in his chest was still there, too.

How the hell could he come up with eight thousand dollars by tomorrow? He had no savings to draw from, no investments to liquidate, no ready-credit he could access, and no friends with the wherewithal, never mind the inclination, to bail him out of a jam. His family was largely gone, and he barely spoke to those who remained. Carol had that three thousand from the judge, but he couldn't ask her for that, at least not without admitting things he would rather not admit.

The phone rang, freezing him in the center of the room. He let the answering machine pick up and then resumed pacing. He had a few antiques in storage, along with some World War II artifacts his father had inherited from an uncle. The stuff could bring significant money "in the right market," but a forced sale wasn't the right market, and Tom did not have the time to get them to a dealer before Dominic got unpleasant.

He settled on the edge of a chair, gingerly bending his knee as he listened to the recorded message. The caller had been Carol, who, in hasty words whispered against a backdrop of noise, told him she couldn't wait to see him this afternoon. Tom listened to the message a second time, his eyes closed and his head in his hands.

The revolving door was locked, so Tom pounded on the glass of the swinging door beside it. He could see into the darkened lobby. An officer sat at the information desk, his head resting on his hand. Tom pounded again, then waved both arms. Finally, the officer got up. He squinted at Tom through the glass, then pointed at his lapel. Tom, taking his meaning, slipped his picture ID from his wallet and held it up.

"Some things I need to do in chambers," Tom said when the officer cracked the door.

"Whose chambers?"

"Canter's," said Tom.

"I see." The officer pulled the door back just enough for Tom to shuffle through sideways. "How long do you expect to be?"

"Couple of hours, maybe." It was just about eleven, and Tom was due at Carol's house in White Plains by three.

Tom rode the public elevator up from the rotunda to the fifth floor, then walked the perfectly quiet hexagon to chambers. It had been less than a day since he and Carol carted the judge out of the courthouse. So much had happened since, a lifetime in mere hours, some good, some bad. Right now, mostly bad.

He let himself into chambers and stood in the outer office,

his mind completely blank. He had no set plan in coming down to the courthouse, other than it was a place where he felt safe and, perhaps, could think logically and productively. His last brilliant thought, just before he banged the door, was to come clean to Carol and ask to borrow the three thousand dollars. This he could use as a down payment against Dominic's unpleasantness and buy more time to come up with the rest of the money. Sell the antiques, see what he could borrow against his pension. He could slap it together if he had time, but he needed to convince Dominic to give him the time, and that's where the three thousand came in.

The plan sounded plausible out on the street, the imaginary conversation with Carol zipping like dialogue in a witty off-Broadway play. But inside chambers, in sight of Carol's sneakers tucked under her desk and her coffee cup stuffed with a paper towel on the credenza, he could not imagine himself uttering any of his lines. He drifted through the middle room. Except for the missing rug, the judge's office looked as if nothing had happened.

Tom drummed his fingers on the judge's desk. Since this latest encounter with Dominic, the judge's death had faded into irrelevance. But that was not quite true. There was relevance to the judge's death. Much as Tom might have liked to deny it, the judge had been an anchor in his life. Maybe, given what Tom now knew about the judge's generosity with Carol, he might have loaned Tom the money.

He went back into the outer office and sat at the conference table. This was a waste of time, coming down here. No amount of thinking could save him because there was nothing to think about. He needed eight thousand dollars and he needed it fast, and because there was no possibility of getting it fast, he was screwed. He should just run. Clean out what was left in his bank account, hock the few possessions he could, hop a train and just keep going. But he couldn't do that; he couldn't leave Carol to deal with the aftermath of the judge alone.

His thinking had been so clear yesterday: seeing the possibilities, designing the plan, and then executing it step by step. He had taken two facts, rubbed them together like two dry sticks, and created the spark of an idea. The judge is dead and today is New Year's Eve, and therefore . . . What about today, Tom wondered. The judge is dead and no one will find out till tomorrow and therefore . . .

The idea exploded before him.

Two years into his tenure with Judge Canter, Tom decided to parlay his law clerk's experience into a job with a private firm. Two years, he had been told, was the perfect time to jump. It was long enough for him to have learned the inner workings of the court system but not so long to require him to disprove the assumption that working for the court system had turned him into a lazy hack. The *Law Journal* ran pages of classified ads every day. Most of the ads described candidates who Tom definitely was not, like the "aggressive self-starter" or the attorney with "a loyal client base." He concentrated on ads that wanted someone with "an intimate knowledge of New York practice" or simply "two years relevant experience." He figured that someone somewhere would consider two years of working for Judge Canter to be relevant.

The ads listed anonymous post office boxes rather than firm names. Tom sent out fifty résumés before he got his first response. The firm was Harrington & Stone, and the person who called to set up the interview was Derek Moxley. Tom knew

about Harrington & Stone. The firm advertised on the sub-
ways with slick posters trumpeting huge recoveries in medical
malpractice and construction accident cases. Tom had encountered Moxley only twice in two years, both times at pretrial
conferences. These encounters were not enough for Tom to
form any opinion about Moxley. But he could tell from the way
the judge handled the conferences that he approved of neither
Moxley nor his firm.

Tom did not tell the judge about the interview with Harrington & Stone. He asked for the afternoon off for personal
reasons, and the judge, never one to pry, simply nodded. The
firm was located in midtown, and Moxley himself—who Tom
could see from his position on the letterhead was ranked just
below Messrs. Harrington and Stone—squired him around the
offices. He met the Messrs. Harrington and Stone, who shook
his hand and professed close personal ties with the judge. He
saw, at a distance, regiments of associates working away in tiny
cubicles.

Weirdly, there was little talk. Moxley asked Tom virtually
nothing about himself and seemed, from the few questions
he did ask, not to have glanced at Tom's résumé. Tom's
attempts to ask about the job opening evoked only silence.
The interview literally trailed off when Moxley left Tom at the
reception desk to take a phone call and simply did not come
back.

About a month later, the judge issued a decision dismissing
a construction accident case. The decision was noteworthy
enough for a front page story in the *Law Journal,* and, in reading the story, Tom learned that the plaintiff had been represented by Harrington & Stone. Suddenly, that weird interview
did not seem so weird.

About a month after that, Tom found himself alone with Moxley in a courthouse elevator.

"You didn't bring me in for an interview," he said. "You wanted to influence the judge's decision on that motion. Well, guess what? I didn't work on it."

"What do you think, Tom?" said Moxley. "You think you're brilliant? You think you can offer us something we can't find in a top graduate from a top law school? You're a law clerk. There are forty of you in this building alone. But stick around. You and I may be able to do business some time."

The incident had so devastated Tom's sense of himself that he never sent out another résumé. Time passed. His interactions with Moxley were cool but cordial, though not cordial enough for Tom to ask what Moxley meant by doing business some time. But there were rumors, and right now Tom wondered if those rumors could be true.

At any given time, Harrington & Stone had five or six lawsuits in Judge Canter's inventory of cases. The young girl in the *Berne* case, the motion Tom had been working on when Judge Canter died, was represented by Harrington & Stone. Tom booted up his computer and skimmed his partially drafted decision. After the bicycle accident, the young girl was treated at a municipal hospital, where, through a series of blunders, gangrene set in and required the amputation of her leg. The case was worth several million dollars, but there was a big problem. A lawsuit against a city hospital required that a written notice of claim be served on the hospital within three months after the incident. The girl's parents had not served this notice of claim when they retained Harrington & Stone six months later. The firm immediately filed a petition for permission to serve a late notice of claim.

Tom wrote twenty of these decisions each year; it was one of the areas of law that Canter had ceded to him. These were high-stakes petitions because, if unsuccessful, the injured party was barred from suing forever. Rarely had Tom seen a case so troubling. The hospital's negligence was obvious, but so was the family's failure to serve the notice of claim. And, according to the controlling case law Tom was obliged to follow, the extent of the injuries was to play no role in the decision.

Tom thought about meeting Moxley on the subway and if it was a sign or, if not a sign, at least a harbinger of his current problem. Feeling suddenly decisive, he picked up the phone. Though it was New Year's morning, he remembered the image of those associates slaving away in their cubicles. But with each buzzing ring, Tom felt his stomach tighten, his decisiveness fade.

"Harrington and Stone, may I help you?"

"Is Derek Moxley in?"

"I'm sorry, not today. What's this in reference to?"

"It's a personal call," Tom replied.

"Hold on."

The line went silent. Tom's heart thumped, and then that bubble returned to his chest. Maybe, he mused, Dominic had permanently rearranged his anatomy and that bubble would inflate whenever he felt the slightest tug of nerves. The silence lengthened. The bubble expanded enough to constrict Tom's throat. He could not have talked, even if he wanted to, and right now the thought of talking to Moxley was even more intimidating than facing Dominic. He hung up the phone. He dropped into a chair, panting, praying for the bubble to shrink. Finally, he cleared his throat, tested his voice, stood up and paced along the conference table. He was out of ideas. And then suddenly, looking at the pile of decisions on the table in the middle room, he wasn't.

If Bobby Werkman raised his head, he could look out his window and east along Worth Street to the edge of Chinatown. In between, foreshortened in Renaissance perspective, he could see the huge gray metal of the Federal Building, two of the columns that supported the pediment of New York County Courthouse, and the gold flourishes of the federal courthouse. But Bobby had no intention of raising his head or taking the view from the executive offices of the New York State Court Officers Union that had been his private domain for the last nine years. He was poring over a draft affidavit that had arrived by fax from his lawyers' office and was taking a blue pen to it the way a butcher took a knife to a side of beef. The affidavit was a four-page piece of crap. Worse, the lawyers didn't even know if the judge would accept it. They had phoned chambers yesterday morning and spoke to the law clerk, but never received a return phone call.

The office door opened, and Anton Vuksanaj poked his head in.

"Got a call for you," he said.

"What? Another eejit arrested for drunk and disorderly last night?" said Bobby. The office already had gotten three of those calls since Bobby blew in at eight this morning. Bobby fielded each call, patiently listened, then made his own call to dispatch one of the union lawyers to help.

"No," said Vuksanaj. "The landlord."

"Shit," said Bobby. "Tell him I'm not here."

"Too late," said Vuksanaj. He had spiked platinum hair and

a scar across his chin that sharpened when he did not shave. "He saw you come in."

"All right," Bobby sighed. He waited for Vuksanaj to close the door, then lifted the phone and spoke heartily. "Gogo, how goes it?"

"It goes," said Gogolak, who strictly speaking was not the landlord but the executive vice president of the agency that managed the landlord's properties.

"I know we are two months behind. I told you this is a bad cash flow time of year."

"I'm not calling about that. A guy named Dawson came to my office yesterday. Said he was running against you for union president."

"What did he want?" said Bobby.

"Information about the lease."

"What did you tell him?"

"I gave him the term, the base rent, how the additional rent is calculated. All the numbers."

"What about the arrears?"

"I lied. But I don't think he believed me. He said he'd come back, and when he did he'd bring his lawyer."

"Did he say when?"

"No, but soon."

It would be, thought Bobby, if he planned to make a campaign issue out of a union president who couldn't pay the rent.

"You need to square up," said Gogolak.

"I know. I know. Thanks for the warning."

Bobby hung up and looked out the window at the exact moment that a cloud crossed in front of the sun. There was a time he might have considered this happenstance to be an omen.

That time was gone. His luck had been so consistently bad that he wouldn't have noticed an omen if one bit him in the ass.

His nine years as union president had been a personal and professional success. But the economic downturn came at the exact worst time. He might have survived the loss of overtime early in his term, but not in an election year. Truth be told, even he believed there needed to be changes to the overtime rules. A number of officers had been piggish about padding their pension numbers with huge amounts of overtime during their last three years on the job. They were his pigs, though, and he had defended them. But he also believed that the total loss of overtime punished the vast majority of officers who did not abuse the privilege, who understood how an extra twenty or thirty bucks in a paycheck could translate into a night at the movies with the spouse or a take-out Chinese dinner for the family.

Bobby's empathy for his brethren, however real, also was a convenient front for a more personal concern. Early in his tenure as president, Bobby had used union funds and union labor to buy into and expand his uncle's chain of funeral homes. The union had been flush then, and Bobby, foreseeing a long stretch of successful reelection campaigns, deferred paying that money back. Now the books were in disarray, and he needed another three-year term to square them. Otherwise, he would go to jail for embezzlement.

Bobby picked up the phone, started to punch in his lawyers' number, then slammed the phone down. He twirled around in his chair, rubbed his eyes. The new year was not even half a day old and it felt like the same old shit. He had three weeks to reverse his bad streak.

The phone rang again, and Vuksanaj picked up on the second ring. *Tell 'em I'm not here,* Bobby thought. And when Vuksanaj poked his head in, Bobby put those thoughts into words.

"No, I think you'll want to speak to this guy," said Vuksanaj. "He's Judge Canter's law clerk."

"Our Judge Canter?"

Vuksanaj nodded.

"You can't be fuckin' serious," said Bobby. "What does he want?"

"To talk to you."

Bobby got up from his desk and went to the window, where he now took in the crowded perspective of buildings between Broadway and Chinatown. Canter's law clerk calling him on New Year's morning? It couldn't be about accepting the stupid affidavit. He would call the lawyers for that. Something else was up.

Bobby sat back at his desk, picked up the phone, and spun his chair to face the window.

"This is Bobby Werkman. Who's this?"

"Tom Carroway. I'm Judge Canter's law clerk. We need to talk about your case."

"In what connection?"

"Let's just say you'll want to talk about the case."

"Elaborate."

"Not over the phone," said Tom.

CHAPTER 11

The restaurant Bobby Werkman named was below ground on a narrow, crooked lane deep in Chinatown. Tom left the courthouse immediately, planning to arrive first, but found Bobby and Vuksanaj already seated in the back corner of the cramped but empty dining area. Bobby looked older and heavier than the file photo the *Law Journal* ran whenever it covered a union story. Lines etched his face, the deepest descending from the corners of his mouth to his jaw and rising from the bridge of his nose to his hairline as if he were a marionette with his brow permanently knit from worry. His shoulders were thick, and his shirt, open at the collar, stretched over an expansive gut. One button threatened to pop.

"Carroway," he said, and kicked a chair out from the table.

Tom caught the chair before it tipped over. He sat, pulled his arms in through his sleeves, and let his jacket fold itself over the back of the chair. A Redweld folder stood on his lap, a rubber band holding the flap shut. Vuksanaj, seated diagonally across the table from Bobby and directly to Tom's right, drummed his fingers on the table and tapped his feet on the floor.

"What's so important we need to meet today?" asked Bobby.

"Judge Canter is dead," said Tom.

Bobby leaned forward. His chin dropped between his two frown lines.

"Say again," he said.

"Judge Canter died yesterday in chambers."

Bobby swung a sharp glance at Vuksanaj.

"Something like this happens, and I don't know about it?" said Bobby. "How can I not know about this?"

Vuksanaj lifted his hands helplessly, but Tom cut in.

"Because no one does," he said.

In quick strokes, Tom explained smuggling the judge's body out of the courthouse and planting it in the apartment.

"Why all that?"

"To save our jobs. You know the rules."

Again, Bobby glanced at Vuksanaj.

"So why are you telling me?" he asked.

"Because you and I can help each other," said Tom.

"Really?" Bobby leaned back and smirked. The wooden chair made cracking sounds as it strained against his weight. "How?"

"The judge signed the decision in your case. It rules in OCA's favor."

The smirk left Bobby's face as he leaned forward toward Tom.

"Prove it," he said.

Tom opened the Redweld and angled it so Bobby could see the papers stuffed inside. Then he pinched out a few pages and laid them gently on the table in front of Bobby. A silence descended as Bobby traced his finger over the typescript. Tom watched closely for any reaction, but Bobby's expression did not change from one of total concentration. Vuksanaj sat motionless, hardly breathing. Finally, Bobby turned over the last page, then pushed the draft back to Tom.

"What time did he sign it?"

"Early. Before I got to chambers."

"So why, when my lawyers called, did you let them think the judge would take their reply papers if he already signed the decision?"

"Because the judge didn't want to dismiss your case. But looking at the arguments, he felt he couldn't rule in your favor. We even discussed asking for supplementary papers, but I told him that was a dangerous thing to do in a high-profile case like this. So he signed it, and when your lawyers called I couldn't say the decision was signed because it wasn't filed and technically didn't exist. But I thought the judge would accept your reply papers and possibly find something that would allow him to change his mind. I went into his office to talk to him. That's when I found him dead."

"Let me get this straight," said Bobby. "You keep the judge's death a secret to save your jobs. I have a decision in my case that no one knows exists. What are you going to do? Destroy the original and hit me up for hush money?"

"No. There is a more interesting possibility."

"Which is?" said Bobby.

"I rewrite the decision and file it first thing tomorrow before anyone learns he's dead."

"Really?" said Bobby. "And how do you suddenly write a decision in my favor when you and the judge together couldn't figure out a way to do that?"

"The judge was always concerned about being reversed by the Appellate Division," said Tom. "He wanted to be careful with this case because a reversal would have been an embarrassment. Now there's no embarrassment factor."

"How do you get him to sign a new decision?"

"I don't need to." Tom held up the first page of the decision. "What do you see?"

"The caption," said Bobby. "Some introductory language. A description of the parties."

"Now look at this." Tom held up the last page.

"The signature line and the date. One other sentence," said Bobby.

"Read me the sentence."

Bobby squinted. "'This constitutes the decision and judgment of the court.'"

"Which could end any decision," said Tom. "I can keep the first page and the last page and rewrite the seven in the middle."

Bobby tipped back his chair. His eyes glazed for a long moment, then focused on Vuksanaj long enough to see him shrug.

"That simple, huh?" he said.

"Simple to a degree. I still need to write it to make sense and fit it within those page breaks."

Bobby brought his chair forward and stretched his arms along both sides of the table as if to engulf Tom.

"Say we do this," he said. "I get my decision. What do you get?"

"Me?" said Tom. "Now that's simple."

Bobby asked Tom to leave because he needed a few minutes to think. Tom put on his jacket, tucked the Redweld under his arm, and climbed the stairs to the street. Bobby waited until he saw Tom's feet disappear and felt the subtle changes in air pressure as Tom opened and closed the door.

"Things happen for a reason," he said.

"Are you considering this?" asked Vuksanaj.

"I need to win this case," said Bobby. "Even if the Appellate Division reverses it later, the election will long be over."

"So you are considering this," said Vuksanaj.

"This is what I'm considering. Carroway's no dope. That was a photocopy of the decision, which means he hid the original somewhere."

"I can find it," said Vuksanaj. "And destroy it."

"That doesn't help. If the decision is destroyed, the case will just get reassigned to another judge once news of Canter's death gets out. There's no guarantee the new judge will decide the case before the election. Which means Dawson wins and I'm screwed."

"But can you trust Carroway?" said Vuksanaj. "He's already saved his job. Why does he need to stack a scam like this on top?"

"Money," said Bobby.

"Money you don't have."

"And what did I say to him?"

"Nothing," said Vuksanaj.

"Right. Because I want to find out why he needs it."

Tom shifted the Redweld from one arm to the other and stamped his feet. This had to be the coldest spot in all of Chinatown, maybe even the entire city. With the angle of the street and the height of the surrounding buildings, the sun probably didn't strike pavement here until May. Tom cupped his hand to the glass door and peered down the stairs. He hadn't seen anything before and didn't see anything now. Just the carpet and the tables closest to the landing. All empty.

He had been out here for almost fifteen minutes, slowly and now not so slowly beginning to freeze. He wondered what they could be talking about. Did they think he had made the story up? He didn't like that Vuksanaj. There was something unpredictable about him. Bobby actually seemed like a reasonable sort, someone Tom could deal with. He hadn't blinked when Tom named his price. Then again, he hadn't said anything, either.

Another five minutes passed. Tom stamped his feet harder. He wondered if he had made the plan sound too complicated. Rewrite the middle seven pages to break just right and preserve the judge's signature. The easier play would have been to write a completely new decision and have Carol forge the judge's signature *AC* as she had done countless times. But he wanted to keep her out of this. For many reasons.

The door opened. Vuksanaj came out first, then Bobby, huffing with exertion, behind.

"Come with me," said Vuksanaj.

Tom followed him around the crooked corner. Beyond the post office, a large black SUV straddled the curb. As they drew even with the darkened post office, Vuksanaj suddenly grabbed Tom by the wrist, twisted his arm up behind his back, and pinned him against the post office door.

"You sat in there and lied to Bobby, but you're not going to lie to me. What are you trying to pull here?"

"I told you, I need money."

"Why do you need money?"

"I'm in trouble. I owe money to some guys. I don't pay up, they'll come after me."

"How much?"

"Eight."

"You asked Bobby for ten."

"My bargaining position."

Vuksanaj laughed. "Is the judge even dead?"

"Yes. I'm not making that up."

Vuksanaj let go. Tom unbent his arm and rubbed his shoulder. Vuksanaj pressed a button on his key chain. The SUV's lights blinked and the doors unlocked.

"Get in the back," he said.

Tom climbed up and half sprawled on the enormous backseat. Bobby settled in the passenger seat as Vuksanaj started the engine.

"Where are we going?" said Tom.

"To see the judge," said Vuksanaj.

CHAPTER 12

"Feels like somebody left a window open," said Bobby.

"I wanted to keep the body preserved as long as possible," said Tom. He turned the dead bolt on the apartment door. They had seen no one in the lobby, the elevator, or the corridor. The building seemed wrapped in a holiday slumber, except for the music still seeping from the next apartment.

He led them into the bedroom, where the air was frigid enough that a glass of water on the nightstand would have frozen solid. But there was no glass of water on the nightstand. Everything was just as Tom and Carol had left it at one o'clock that morning. The judge lay on his back, the covers pulled up to his chest, one arm in, the other out and bent across his stomach. His glasses still lay atop the money left from Carol's withdrawal. Tom would not have minded slipping a couple more twenties into his pocket right now.

Bobby lifted one slat of the blinds and peered out through the slit. The window faced another apartment building across a back alley. All the windows in the other building were closed, their blinds down or curtains tight. He let the slat fall and glanced at Vuksanaj before turning his attention to the judge. Vuksanaj silently left the bedroom and closed the door behind him. Bobby crouched, lowering his face mere inches from the judge's. He shut one eye, sniffed, then shut the other eye. He walked around the bed and repeated the inspection. Then he straightened up.

"Pretty well preserved, I'd say," he said. "Of course, that's just an eyeball assessment. I can't tell what's gone on inside. But on the outside he doesn't look like he died yesterday."

"Then we have a deal?" asked Tom.

"I have some concerns before we start talking about a deal. Your secretary knows, and you know the old saying about keeping a secret."

"And you have him," said Tom.

"I trust him," said Bobby.

"Just like I trust Carol," said Tom.

"But I need to be able to trust her, too."

"She helped me hide the judge, so she's not going to expose anything. Besides, I don't want her to know about our deal, either."

Bobby seemed to consider this for a moment.

"Okay," he said. "Talk."

"I said I'd do it for ten, but I'll take eight."

"I don't have eight. Eight's out of the question."

"Seven," said Tom.

"Four," said Bobby.

"I can't do it for four," said Tom. "I do it for four, I might as well do it for nothing."

"Five," said Bobby.

"You win the case, you win the election. That's got to be worth more than five to you."

"Maybe it's worth a million, but that doesn't change the fact that five is all I have. You don't like it, I'll report the judge's death and you'll be out of a deal, out of a job, and face jail time, too. How would you like that?"

Tom felt that bubble rise, but he folded his arms tightly across his chest and squeezed it back down. Five was a big comedown from ten, but it got him close enough to eight to convince Dominic's boss to give him time to come up with the rest. Maybe if he could come up with the exact right words at the exact right time he could convince Carol to loan him the three the judge had given her.

"Okay, five," said Tom. "But can you advance me one now?"

"Carroway," said Bobby. "You've got some pair of balls."

After they locked up the apartment, they drove back to union headquarters. Tom waited in the idling SUV while Bobby and Vuksanaj went into the building. He had heard some words pass between Bobby and Vuksanaj on the way, Bobby saying something about the bail fund, Vuksanaj questioning his wisdom, and Bobby responding that New Year's was over. They wouldn't need to bail anyone else out for a while.

Tom hugged the Redweld to his chest and settled into the warmth of the SUV's backseat. This is going to work, he told himself. And he remembered repeating that same mantra yesterday when *this* meant something entirely different.

Bobby lifted the portrait of his predecessor off the wall and set it on the floor. Vuksanaj sat on Bobby's desk, the angle of the light on his face etching his scar deeper into his chin. His scowl, however, was not an optical illusion.

"You think this can get messy," said Bobby.

"It already is."

"I thought that's why I have a director of security."

Bobby opened the wall safe, removed a metal strongbox, and set it on the desk. Vuksanaj waited until Bobby lifted the lid before sliding off the desk and leaving the room.

The strongbox held a mix of personal and union business, symbolic of how Bobby ran the union for the last nine years. He walked his fingers across the tightly stuffed brown envelopes, finally extricating the one with BAIL FUND printed on the top edge. Inside were five one-hundred-dollar bills, less than half of the running total he had kept in his head, but then again it had been a busy holiday season. He lay the bills on the desk, stuffed the envelope back into place, and walked his fingers in search of an envelope labeled PETTY CASH.

Vuksanaj, meanwhile, had unlocked a file cabinet in the outer office and was pawing through a Redweld. The file was a personal project, something Bobby did not even know about. It was a compendium of personal and professional information about judges and their staffs. Most of the information was public record—newspaper articles, published opinions, official OCA press releases. But a small portion was private information that Vuksanaj unearthed in chambers after hours.

The public information on Judge Canter portrayed him as a good and decent judge who ought to have been sympathetic to the union. But no one ever could predict how a judge would rule in any particular case, and so despite all the positive indicators, here was Bobby, in trouble and being squeezed. Vuksanaj had something that could help.

Vuksanaj stuck the file back in the drawer and locked the cabinet just as Bobby came out of his office.

"Needed to pull from petty cash," he said.

"That bad, huh?" said Vuksanaj.

"Don't let my sunny disposition fool you."

"I came across something interesting on that issue of trust," said Vuksanaj.

He spread his find on the top of the file cabinet. Bobby squinted, then capitulated to his reading glasses.

"Where did you get these?" he asked.

"Web cam. You'd be surprised what goes on after hours."

"Why didn't we use this earlier?"

"It wouldn't have worked," said Vuksanaj. "But now the context is different."

Bobby looked closely again.

"Not bad," he said. He folded his glasses into his pocket.

"*This*," said Vuksanaj, "is why you have a director of security."

Back down on the sidewalk, Bobby motioned for Tom to come out of the SUV.

"Walk around the block with me," he said.

The two headed west, away from Broadway. The streets were almost empty, the shadows deep. They rounded a corner, and Bobby handed Tom the envelope.

"Don't make a spectacle by counting it," Bobby said. "It's all there. Trust me."

They walked on for another block.

"This is what's going to happen," said Bobby. "Tomorrow at ten sharp someone's going to come to chambers. He'll verify that the decision rules in our favor and then he'll make sure you file it. Understand?"

"What about the rest of the money?" asked Tom.

"He'll attend to that, too," said Bobby.

"And you'll be able to prevent any kind of inquest into the judge's death?"

"One isn't a union president for nine years without developing significant political contacts. So I believe we're square."

"Square enough," said Tom.

"Good. You go that way. I'll head back this way. Happy New Year. And don't spend that grand all in one place."

Dinner was all done except for the magic of the slow-cooker, and Carol, having just finished cleaning the kitchen, drew herself a glass of water from the tap and plopped onto a chair. She was still dressed in her running gear: tights and top, sports bra, training shoes, gym shorts worn less because they served any useful purpose than because she still was unaccustomed to her new, chiseled figure. Her sweat had long since dried, leaving salty tracks on her forehead, cheeks, and neck.

From outside, she heard the rhythmic thunk of Nick throwing a ball against the wooden basement door. The ball was a Spaldeen, something Foxx had given him long ago. Carol supposed Nick had resurrected the ball in anticipation of today's visit. He was excited, and, though she did not share his excitement, she refused to dampen it. Her mistake was not warning Tom. Yesterday, with everything that had happened, it slipped her mind. Last night, well, the thought had come to her but she did not want to spoil the mood. This morning, she had tried. But Tom's answering machine had picked up, and this wasn't the sort of news one left in a message. Tom probably had been sleeping. Men were like that after sex, sleeping and satisfied, while women, or at least those she could speak for, were so alive with the implications of having had sex that they couldn't sleep at all. So she did what she did best; she ran and she tried to sort out the day's singular problem. We're all adults, she had concluded. We'll get through it.

Carol gulped the last of the water and trudged upstairs. The Spaldeen still thunked against the basement door. Oh well, if nothing else the prospect of Foxx got Nick outside in the fresh air and away from those video games. Maybe Tom would prove to be an inspiration as well. She caught herself immediately. She couldn't start running with this one just yet.

She ran the water in the bathtub and after it heated switched the diverter to the showerhead and stripped off her running clothes. Steam rolled across the ceiling. She pressed her breasts with her palms and turned side to side, assessing herself. She looked okay, more than okay. She hoped, no, she believed that Tom had been pleased.

She got into the shower. The water felt great, and even though the tub had been draining slow lately, she didn't care how high it rose on her legs. She was going to stay in here, in the sound and steam and water, and savor the start of a very new year.

CHAPTER 13

Tom pressed the doorbell, heard a two-tone chime ring inside, and stepped back to wait. Traces of mildew stained the white siding near the base of the door, and Tom, orienting himself with the pale disk of the lowering sun, saw that the house faced north. He adjusted his grip on the bouquet of red and white carnations he had bought at the train station. Water seeped through the wax-paper cone, running over his fingers and dripping onto the stone of the front stoop. He heard a rustling behind the door, and then the door opened and there was Carol. She wore a black pleated skirt and red tights that matched a thin red top. Her hair was brushed back and knotted.

"Tom!" she said, as if he might have been someone else.

She pulled him in and kissed him hard on the mouth, then reared back and focused on the flowers.

"They're beautiful," she said. "Come in. Don't worry about the floor. I'll grab a vase."

She disappeared into a closet and emerged with a smoked glass vase before Tom finished wiping his feet on the rug.

"Ma," she called. "Tom's here."

The foyer was a modest square with an ornate radiator cover under a window and, on a sliver of wall, an antique mirror hanging over a small table. To the left, it opened into a living room with two old couches, an oval coffee table, and a large Christmas tree. Straight back it narrowed into a hallway that led to the kitchen. He heard a clicking sound, and then a woman leaning on a cane filled the kitchen doorway. She was short and bosomy, wearing a large white sweater, embossed with shiny red and green Christmas ornaments, and black stretch pants.

"Mom, this is Tom," said Carol. "Tom, this is my mother."

"Hello, Mrs. Scilingo," said Tom.

"Call me Rose." She reached out a hand, which Tom gently shook. "So you work for Big Al Canter, too? I knew him when he was just a kid lawyer."

"Mom worked in Bronx Supreme Court," said Carol.

"I didn't like many lawyers," said Rose. "Too pushy, too arrogant. And this one goes and marries one, but that's another story."

"Right, Mom. Another story we're not going to tell right now."

"But that Al Canter," said Rose. "He was a nice guy, the kind of guy Carol should have married. He was a good lawyer, too. Those two things don't usually go hand in hand. You're either one or the other."

Tom caught Carol rolling her eyes.

"Which one am I?" he asked playfully.

Rose Scilingo looked him up and down.

"I need some time to figure that out," she said.

"Mom, I need to get in here," Carol said, trying to squeeze past.

"Okay, okay. I'm going. Nice to meet you, Tom."

"Same here," said Tom.

Rose worked her way down the hallway, her cane clicking.

"Company dislocates her," said Carol. "Usually she'd be in bed watching TV."

"Sorry," said Tom.

"Not your fault. It's New Year's. It's good for her to see other people." Carol turned on the faucet and threw her arms around Tom's neck. "I'm so happy you're here. I missed you."

"Me, too," said Tom.

"I called you this morning," said Carol. "Early. Like around nine. I got your answering machine."

"I went out for coffee and a paper. I didn't look at the machine."

Carol walked her fingers across his chest, stopping to tweak each nipple through the thin wool of his sweater. Tom felt two jolts.

"I was going to call your cell," she said. "But then I thought that was too forward. Funny how I was able to do that yesterday, but not today."

"I went to the judge's apartment," whispered Tom.

Carol's arms dropped to her sides. "Why?"

"I left the bedroom windows open last night to keep him cold another few hours. Don't worry, no one saw me."

"What was it like?" said Carol. "Inside."

"Creepy. I just closed the windows and left. I took only a quick look at him. He looked pretty good."

"Let's not talk about this right now," said Carol.

The water, running hot, had steamed the window, which looked out over the tiny backyard. Tom wiped at the steam, revealing a boy and a man fiddling with a milk crate and a stick.

"Is that who I think it is?" he said.

"Yes," said Carol. "It's Foxx."

"What's he doing here?"

"Remember when I said Nick invited a friend?"

"Foxx is the friend?"

Carol nodded. "Foxx and I dated for a while a couple of years ago. It lasted only a few months."

"I never had a clue," said Tom.

"No one at the courthouse did. That's the way we both wanted it." Carol sighed. "Look, I'll be honest with you. There was a time Nick was meeting a string of supposed boyfriends. He felt comfortable with Foxx because Foxx was the only one who paid any attention to him."

"Interesting," said Tom.

"Nick didn't mean anything by inviting Foxx, if that's what you think. He doesn't know you, other than as a name. I'm sorry I didn't tell you. I was going to and then, well, it wasn't uppermost in my mind. And then I didn't want to ruin last night."

Tom smiled. "What are they doing out there?"

"I don't know," said Carol. "But they've been at it a long time."

"Does Foxx know I'm coming?"

"No."

"Then we're even."

The backyard was a triangular patch of frozen dirt and dead grass that had grown long before the first frost killed it. A stockade fence, gray with age, ran along one side, and a line of hemlocks ran along the other, meeting behind a rubberized tool shed with a missing door.

Nick and Foxx crouched behind a barbecue grill. Foxx

called it their bunker, but Nick, either not hearing or not under-standing, had not said anything, so Foxx let it go. In the mid-dle of the yard, a stick shaped in the perfect Y of a slingshot held a bright blue milk crate like a yawning mouth over a pile of broken crackers. Twine tied to the stick ran back to the bunker, the end curled around Nick's fingers. Two squirrels hopped along the top of the fence, occasionally dropping into the adjoining yard where, Foxx had noticed earlier, a treasure trove of birdseed lay beneath an upended bird feeder.

"Why isn't it working?" said Nick.

"We need to attract them," said Foxx. "You know how if you really like a girl you wear a nice shirt or comb your hair really cool?"

Nick looked at Foxx silently.

"Bad example," said Foxx. "Let's say you're at a barbecue and there are grilled vegetables on one table and hot dogs and potato chips on the other. Which table do you go to?"

"The one with the hot dogs."

"Right. They have the hot dogs in the next yard."

"Real hot dogs?"

"No. There's birdseed on the ground, which is like hot dogs to squirrels. So we need something better."

"Like what?" said Nick.

Foxx didn't know much about kids, but he knew Nick well enough to allow him complete control over whatever they did together. Sometimes these activities were a success, but mostly they failed and it was only after Nick had given up, which by the tone of his voice he was close to doing now, that Foxx would take over.

"This," said Foxx. He lifted the grill lid, where he had stashed peanut butter, a knife, and a pine cone.

"Peanut butter?" said Nick.

"Squirrels love it," said Foxx.

He watched Nick slather the peanut butter onto the pine cone, then run out from behind the bunker to set the bait under the milk crate.

"How long?" Nick said after he scampered back.

"Not long once they smell it," said Foxx.

On the fence, one of the squirrels raised up and sniffed the air. It hopped along the top of the fence, then descended on a twisted vine into the yard.

"Look," said Nick.

"Shh." Foxx pressed a finger to his lips.

The squirrel slinked along the ground, stopping every few feet to raise up and sniff.

"Get ready," whispered Foxx.

Nick tightened his grip on the twine as the squirrel crawled toward the open mouth of the crate. Foxx whispered to wait until the squirrel started licking the peanut butter before he yanked the twine.

"He needs to forget about the danger," he said.

Nick nodded.

The squirrel was just about to crawl under the crate when the back door opened. The sound chased the squirrel away.

"Ma!" whined Nick.

But her mother wasn't on the back stoop; it was a man Nick never had seen before.

"Hi, guys," said Tom.

"Carroway," said Foxx.

"You scared him," said Nick. "Damn."

"Nick," said Foxx. "Language."

"Sorry," said Tom. "What did I chase?"

"A squirrel," said Foxx. "We've been trying to trap one all afternoon. Now either go back inside or come down here."

Tom chose to stay and crouched behind the bunker.

"This is Carol's son, Nick," said Foxx. "I don't suppose you've met."

"We haven't," said Tom. He introduced himself and shook Nick's hand. "So what do we do?"

"We wait," said Foxx. "Quietly."

Tom could do that, especially the quiet part, which was better than talking to Foxx. But Foxx did not follow his own advice. He whispered constantly to Nick, who worried that the squirrel never would come back.

"He will. He knows the peanut butter's there and he wants it. He's going to try again and again."

The squirrel came down from the fence and crept along the ground toward the trap. Tom, crouched slightly behind, divided his attention between Foxx and Nick. Carol was right; they did seem comfortable together. Then Nick flicked his hair over the back of his ear to expose a dirty hearing aid held together with tiny strips of duct tape. Tom closed his eyes, feeling Foxx and Nick and the entire backyard fall away from him. How the hell could he ask Carol to borrow money?

"I got him!" Nick screamed.

Tom opened his eyes to see Nick and Foxx running across the yard. The crate was down flat on the ground, the squirrel bouncing and whirling inside.

"What do we do now?" said Nick.

"We let him go," said Foxx.

"But we spent so much time trapping him."

"They're hard to keep as pets," said Tom, joining them over the crate.

"Let him go and trap him again tomorrow." Foxx turned his hard stare on Tom. "That's what you call sport."

Back inside, as Rose sat at the kitchen table icing a chocolate cake, Carol asked Tom to help set the table. Two tables, actually, since Carol had sold her dining room set to make room for her mother's hospital bed. One was a sturdy wooden card table, the other a flimsy thing made of aluminum and pressboard and called a "banquet table" on the cardboard box where Carol stored it between banquets. Even brand new, the table sagged deeply in the middle.

"Set them end to end," she said.

Tom locked the last of the card table's legs and flipped it over. It stood an inch higher than the banquet table, a fact so obvious Tom resisted mentioning it. Carol snapped a long red tablecloth. It unfurled in the air, hovered briefly, then settled onto the tables. With a slight tug here and there, Carol centered it perfectly.

"Impressive," said Tom.

Carol squeezed past where he stood to smooth a wrinkle. Her butt brushed his thigh. She turned, clamped his jaw in her hand, and kissed him on the mouth.

"I so want to go upstairs with you," she said.

"That's a nice thought."

"She'll take half an hour to ice that cake," she said. "What about Foxx and Nick?"

"They caught one squirrel and let it go. They're after another."

"C'mon." She grabbed his hand and stepped toward the hallway.

"Now?" he said.

"Who is better at taking chances than us?"

They padded up the stairs, Tom reluctantly at first but with more spring in his step as they reached the top. He almost had mentioned the three grand as Carol spread the tablecloth across the tables. Now he wondered whether sex made the question even less appropriate.

Carol had planned, though not exactly plotted, this opportunity. She had tidied her bedroom and had made the bed, something she rarely bothered to do. The blinds were open, the pale sun slanting in.

"Close the door but not all the way," she said.

Tom steadied the door ajar. When he turned, Carol was kneeling on the bed. They were right now the same height. Eye to eye, nose to nose, then mouth to mouth. Tom kept his hands at his sides as they kissed. He was thinking about the three grand, and once he realized he was thinking about the three grand he knew he shouldn't be thinking about the three grand. Carol backed away at that exact moment.

"Are you all right?" she asked.

"Fine," he said. "Just nervous."

"Too nervous for this?" She kissed him again, but felt something lacking in his response and broke off. "Maybe you are. Nervous about the judge?"

"No," said Tom. He pointed down through the floor.

Carol shook her head. Then she kissed him, and this time he did respond. His tongue flicked at her teeth. He ran his hands up and down her sides, the rough spots of his fingers catching on the fabric of her top. She brushed his hands away and reversed the top over her head. She wore nothing underneath.

"How about now?" she said.

"Not nervous at all," said Tom.

She lowered his pants. He plucked the button on the waistband of her skirt. Then Nick's breathless voice called up the stairs.

"Mom, Mom, you gotta see this!"

"Now you know why I crack the door," whispered Carol. She quickly shrugged into her top and tucked it into her skirt, leaving Tom to deal with his lowered pants and the huge hard-on poking through his underwear.

"What do you want me to see?" Carol asked, her voice fading as she descended the stairs.

"We caught two, Mom. Two squirrels at once."

Tom shuffled to the window. Through the blinds, he could see Foxx standing over the milk crate with two gray shadows bouncing inside. Nick and Carol joined him, Nick gesturing wildly and Carol kneeling to peek into the crate. Tom sat on the bed. By the time his hard-on began to fade, the backyard was empty and the milk crate was flipped over. A moment later, voices floated up from below.

Tom went down the stairs slowly and quietly. As he neared the bottom, he could see into the kitchen. They were all there, gathered around Rose, who, as Carol had predicted, barely had half the cake iced. Nick spoke excitedly, and Tom, listening closely for the first time, noticed missing vowels and slurred consonants. Foxx stood behind Rose, a hand on her shoulder. Tom imagined that Rose must have liked Foxx, that she had been taken by his rough charm, that she still in her forgetfulness must ask Carol whatever happened to that hard guy with the silver hair. He knew it would take Rose years to warm up to someone like him.

Foxx turned, locking onto Tom's eyes with such force that Tom literally stopped two steps from the bottom. Foxx glanced at Carol and then back at Tom, and Tom knew that Foxx knew what Nick had interrupted.

CHAPTER 14

Carol threw them together. First she suggested that Foxx run to a deli for some last minute items, then she inveigled Tom to go along for the ride. Nick insisted he join them, too, but Carol said she needed him to stay home. And so it was just the two of them in Foxx's car.

Foxx drove the way he walked, outwardly relaxed yet with a tension that rippled just below the surface. He slouched deeply in his seat and worked the steering wheel lightly with two fingers and a thumb. His hips turned slightly to the right, as if considering whether to focus his attention on Tom.

"I saw Judge Canter coming into the courthouse early yesterday morning," Foxx finally said. "When I saw that, I thought he'd be issuing his decision in the union case."

"That's not what happened," Tom replied.

"Still working on it, huh?"

"You know I can't say."

"Well, just for the record," said Foxx, "I don't give a shit which way the decision comes out. What I want to know is, what's up with you and Carol?"

"Nothing," said Tom.

"Don't shit me, Carroway. I know something is going on. Carol was red in the face when she came outside, and then I see you coming down the stairs like you were still shaking a boner out of your pants."

"What's going on is none of your business, Foxx."

"You're half right. What you and Carol do in the privacy of a bedroom isn't any of my business. But how you treat her otherwise is."

Foxx suddenly punched the accelerator and whipped the car into a left turn, throwing Tom against the door.

"Sorry. My foot slipped." A laugh rumbled deep in Foxx's throat. "There's still a question on the table."

Tom righted himself. "It's all new. We went out last night and she invited me here today."

"How festive. What did you do?"

"Hung out. Had dinner. Watched the ball drop."

"Where?"

"With people. An apartment. You don't know them."

Foxx drove in silence for a while. The car approached a sharp left curve, and Tom braced himself. But Foxx took the curve slowly and pulled up in front of a deli.

"Carol's a good kid," he said. "Nick's a good kid, too, and she's very devoted to him, okay?"

"I know," said Tom. "She said you two had a thing."

"Yeah. We had a private thing because she didn't want anyone at the courthouse knowing her business. A good thing, too, but instant family scared me off."

"You look okay with it to me."

"I can be entertaining for an afternoon," said Foxx. "Full-time fatherhood is different, so you'd better start thinking about that because it's part of the package. And while we're on the subject of you, I still want to know what happened yesterday."

"Nothing."

Foxx smiled. "I don't know what you're into, Carroway. But if you mix Carol up in whatever the hell it is, you'll have more to worry about than some pig-faced pug."

Tom followed Foxx into the deli. He would have preferred staying in the car, but staying would have been tantamount to admitting he was scared of Foxx. They separated inside, Foxx disappearing down an aisle while Tom stopped at the counter. Above, a bulletin board displayed scratch-off lottery cards with slick-sounding names. Tom rarely had played scratch-offs. The effort of rubbing the edge of a coin more than deadened the dubious thrill of revealing whatever was hidden beneath. Besides, despite the signs trumpeting the large prizes, the payoffs were modest, designed to persuade you to buy more cards rather than walk away with any cash in your pocket.

But right now, the cards more than caught his eye; they weaved into his psyche. His heart began to pound in that special way, as when the referee would walk to center court spinning a basketball in his hands and the two gangly centers would lean in, crouched and ready to spring upward to start the game. At the very first GA meeting, Monty had told him that stress kicked him into these modes, and that car ride with Foxx was a big-time stressor. Tom slipped his cell phone out of his pocket, scrolled through the directory for Monty's number. Then he closed the phone. He couldn't call Monty, not now and not about this. Monty would insist on meeting, maybe even show up at his apartment. Tom couldn't afford the interruption with the night he had ahead of him.

He shoved the phone into one pocket and fingered the money in his other. He had forty of the thousand Bobby had given him, plus random bills that remained from what he had lifted off the judge's nightstand. He pinched one of these bills between his thumb and forefinger and closed his eyes.

Whatever comes out, he told himself.

It was a twenty.

He stepped up to the counter and pointed out the games he wanted. The young female cashier tore the games off the spools. Tom looked over his shoulder for Foxx, then began to scratch furiously, stopping only to wipe away the gray dust. He separated the winners from the losers, and, when he was finished, the twenty dollar stake had become thirty-six. He looked at the clock, extrapolating how long it would take him, at an 80 percent return rate, to turn a one-thousand stake into an eight-thousand-dollar stash. He simply did not have enough time for that nonsense.

Foxx swung the shopping basket onto the counter just as Tom pocketed the thirty-six bucks. The cashier totaled the bill and bagged the items.

"How much you win?" Foxx said as they got back into the car.

"Win?" Tom said, then realized the futility of denial. "Sixteen bucks."

"Not bad for a few minutes' work." Foxx went silent as he started the car and goosed the accelerator until the engine caught. "There's a cup Carol keeps on the shelf over the sink. Sometimes there's money in it, sometimes not. Be big of you to put that sixteen there. Anonymously, of course."

*　*　*

Dinner turned out to be a cozy affair. Foxx sat at the head of the banquet table. Nick and Rose took one side, Tom and Carol the other. Carol served. Rose ate. Nick listened wide-eyed as Foxx held forth with stories from his childhood in the Bronx, and even Tom had to admit that Foxx told a good story.

Dinner ended as Foxx told a more contemporary tale about a juror escaping from a motel during an overnight sequestering for a criminal trial. Outside, night had fallen with midwinter speed. Carol reached behind the Christmas tree to plug in the lights. Then she gathered the dirty dishes into a single pile.

Foxx opened the door of an end table beside the couch. He took out a bottle of Jameson and held it up to the Christmas lights.

"What a trustworthy household," he said. "No one's touched this in a year."

"He has many bottles in many places," Carol stage-whispered to Tom. "He knows the exact levels of each."

"Object permanence," said Foxx.

He went into the kitchen and returned with a tumbler and a bag of brown sugar. Then he stirred two spoonfuls of sugar into four shots of Jameson.

Carol nudged Tom's elbow, signaling him to pick up the pile of dishes and follow her into the kitchen.

"He seems awfully comfortable here," Tom said as he set the dishes down beside the sink.

Carol leaned against him, kissing him and then nuzzling her face into his chest. Tom caught a whiff of her hair, and he realized how quickly he had grown accustomed to certain things about her, as if they had been together for longer than a mere day. He locked his hands behind her back, wondering again whether this was the time to ask her.

"Foxx makes himself comfortable anywhere," Carol said into his chest. "That's his real gift. But you can be just as comfortable here. Even more."

In the living room, Foxx's voice rose.

"I'd better see about this," she said, pushing off Tom and leaving the kitchen.

Tom listened. Foxx had offered Nick a shot of Jameson and now explained to Carol that he had had no intention of actually letting the boy drink. He was trying to teach him good manners, and good manners included offering someone a bit of what you were having yourself. Tom shook his head, wondering whether Foxx was telling the truth or being plain disingenuous. He turned on the faucet, and that was when he spotted the cup on a shelf over the sink. Inside it was some change and two crumpled dollar bills. He pulled the money from his pocket, peeled off the sixteen bucks, and tucked them into the cup before Carol returned.

"Now do you understand?" she asked.

"I do," said Tom.

"Would you imply that a boy should have a shot of whiskey and then back away from it?"

"No. That's one thing I wouldn't do."

"Good," said Carol.

Tom ran the dishes under the water, then handed them to Carol, who loaded the dishwasher in a particular manner. Several times, he felt the words rise in his throat only to have them stick. He did not know what inhibited him more, the proximity of Foxx or the cup on the shelf. How could he play the supplicant while Foxx acted like the man of the house? How could he leave sixteen bucks in the cup and ask for three grand in return? No, there was no way he could ask Carol. He needed to dig out of this mess himself.

Carol loaded the last of the dishes, then started the dishwasher. Her hands were wet, but rather than use a dish towel she wiped them on the front of Tom's jeans.

"You seemed like you were just thinking of something very deep or very far away," she said.

"I'm not deep. And I'm not far away."

"It was him, right?"

"Yeah," said Tom, realizing she meant the judge. "Him. Yesterday. Tomorrow."

"Let's not think of that right now," said Carol. She swirled her hands across his hips until they met at his crotch. She could feel him rise beneath them. "That's better."

Tom breathed deeply.

"I wish," she said.

"I know," he said.

"Mom!"

Carol and Tom jumped away from each other.

"The cake," said Nick. "Grandma's been asking for the cake. Can't you hear her?"

Carol shut off the faucet.

"No, Nick. I didn't. Sorry."

"And Foxx wants coffee," Nick added.

"He does?" Carol smiled at Tom, a reference to just how comfortable Foxx could be. "Well, we'd better get right on that, huh?"

Tom had only a thin slice of cake for dessert and resisted Foxx's repeated offers to concoct an Irish coffee made of the sugared

Jameson and fresh whipped cream. Carol, beside him, kicked off her shoes, crossed her legs, and hooked a foot behind Tom's knee.

"I need to think about leaving soon," he whispered to her.

"When?" she whispered back.

But Tom did not answer. He continued to sit because he liked the coziness of the house: Rose scraping off the very icing she had so arduously sculpted onto the cake; Nick slouched back in his chair, a chocolate stain at the corner of his mouth as he concentrated on the video game; the pressure of Carol's foot as she reached to pour herself another half cup of coffee. Tom wanted to freeze the scene. He wanted to sit here forever, even as the Irish coffee worked on Foxx, the caffeine turning him edgy and the whiskey loosening his tongue.

"What is it about lawyers?" Foxx wondered aloud.

Carol, sensing a subtle shift in Foxx's mood, deflected the question by turning her attention to Nick.

"Why don't you play something more sociable?" she asked. "Like that game that's been under the tree since you opened it Christmas morning."

Nick moved quickly, like someone infused with a brilliant idea. He slid off the chair, dove under the tree, and rustled out Monopoly.

"Let's all play!" he said.

As Nick cleared space and opened the board, Carol pressed her foot harder into the hollow behind Tom's knee. Tom knew exactly what she meant and used his turn for selecting his playing piece to announce that he must, really must, be going home.

"I'll drive you to the station," offered Carol.

"But, Mom, you're playing, too."

"I sure am," said Carol. "I'll be the top hat. Play for me till I get back."

Tom said good-byes all around, high-fiving Nick, bussing Rose on the forehead, shaking hands with Foxx.

"We'll talk," said Foxx.

"I'm sure we will," said Tom.

Out in the car, Carol sat with her shoulders hunched and her hands under her thighs. She revved the engine, and a rattle shook the car.

"I'm sorry," she said.

"For what?" asked Tom.

"Everything. Especially Foxx."

"Don't be silly," said Tom. "I loved every minute."

"You did?"

"I did. Honest."

"I hoped you could outlast him. I thought we still might get some time alone. But I could sense him getting into one of his moods when he lectures people on what's wrong with their lives."

He wrapped an arm around her shoulder, and she leaned in to kiss him.

"We are alone right now," he said.

"In my car, in my driveway?"

"Mmmm." Tom kissed her hard. He trailed a finger between her breasts, then dipped his knuckle into the hollow of her navel.

"We need to stop," said Carol, pushing off. "You have a train to catch, and I have a game to play and an ex-boyfriend to turn out."

She shifted into reverse and backed out of the driveway.

"He won't give you any trouble, right?"

"Foxx? No way. He has his principles, and they definitely do not include fanning an old flame."

Carol pointed out landmarks as she drove: this restaurant, that store, the YMCA where Nick spent many after-school hours while she worked. Tom only half listened. Each time Carol paused, he felt the words rise in his throat.

Carol, I have a cash flow problem. I need a loan, and I don't have the luxury of going to a bank.

But then the images of the day played like a slide show in his mind—the dirty hearing aids beneath Nick's hair, Rose diligently slopping icing onto the cake, Foxx lifting the milk crate to release the squirrel, Carol kneeling on her bed—and he was more determined than ever not to ask.

"Is everything all right?" he heard her say. "I get the feeling you aren't listening to me. Did something happen I don't know about?"

"Like what?"

"Like something with Foxx?"

"No," he said. "I'm just tired. I didn't sleep so well last night."

"I thought guys slept like babies after sex?"

"Not this guy."

Carol smiled, then reached over and gently touched his cheek. He held her hand to his mouth and kissed it.

"We need to be cool tomorrow," he said. "Poker-faced."

Carol nodded. Light reflecting off the rearview mirror lit her face. She looked so pretty to him right now.

"Until we find out," he said. "Then we need to be suitably shocked."

"These last two days have been so unreal," she said, "I think we will be shocked."

She pulled into the train station parking lot.

"We'll go in at our normal times," said Tom. "Start the day as usual."

"As usual," said Carol.

Tom kissed her cheek and backed out of the car.

"Hey," she said. "Get back here and kiss me right."

The train ride plus the subway ride that followed were remarkably fast, and less than one hour after kissing Carol right, Tom was in his apartment with the motion papers open and his laptop flickering. At about the same time, Carol and Foxx, on consecutive rolls of the dice, landed on the hotel Nick had erected on Boardwalk. Neither of them could pay the rent, and the game ended with Nick as the winner.

Nick put the game away and went upstairs to bed, too tired to be upset about returning to school tomorrow. Rose already was dozing in her hospital bed with television images dancing on her glasses. Carol emptied the dishwasher. Foxx poured the last of the coffee into his cup and heated it in the microwave.

"So you and Carroway now, huh?" he said.

"You noticed."

"Noticed. Asked him point blank. Got him to admit it."

"You make it sound like he's committing a crime," said Carol.

"Your spin, not mine." Foxx gauged the heat of the coffee, then tipped in a drop of milk. No Jameson now. No whipped cream. "I'm surprised you'd get involved with another lawyer."

"I'm not involved yet. And I don't have a thing against lawyers."

"You told me you did," said Foxx. "Never again, you said. Not after the last one."

"I was overreacting to my past," said Carol. "Now I can look back and understand that I didn't mean exactly what I said. What I meant was that I didn't want a lawyer with a secret life."

"How do you know Tom doesn't have one?"

"Because I know him pretty damn well after five years of living in each other's pockets," said Carol.

"That sounds sexy."

"That's how the judge describes working in a chambers."

"Then maybe you can tell me who beat up Tom yesterday and why," said Foxx.

"Beat him up? What are you talking about?"

Foxx told Carol about the wise guy with the small-time prize-fighter look who came into the courthouse and left with Tom. He explained how he found Tom slouched on a bench near the bottom of the courthouse steps, gasping as if he'd had the wind knocked out of him. The guy was gone, and Tom refused to say what had happened.

Carol remembered returning to chambers from the bank and remarking that Tom looked red in the face. He joked about having been punched in the stomach, then quickly explained that he had gone to the coffee shop and had taken the stairs back to chambers. She had other things on her mind, of course, like the judge lying dead in the other room, so she accepted the explanation because it was believable, and, because she believed him, what he told her had been the truth.

"I don't know what you're talking about," she said now.

Foxx turned away, smiling. It was the smile she always resented, the smile that said, not only that I know more than you but that I know better than you.

"Watch yourself," he said.

"I always watch myself," she replied. "And I suppose you warned him."

"You know me pretty well, don't you?"

"Yeah, Foxx. I know you too well."

Tom finished rewriting the decision just after 2:00 A.M. It was not just the recasting of the decision to reach the opposite conclusion that was so difficult—there was the journey to get there, too, stretching some legal points and eliding over others. But it was done. He had preserved the first page and the signature page, and the seven new pages perfectly picked up and left off between them.

He didn't expect to feel happy or exhilarated. But he did expect to feel satisfied, and he wasn't even that. He was just plain tired, though with a background buzz from the coffee he had brewed as soon as he walked in the door. He bound the motion papers together with two thick rubber bands and packed them into his briefcase. He rarely carried the briefcase, but he needed some way of getting the papers into chambers, and the Redweld was just too open. No matter how early he arrived, there was always a chance he would run into someone. With his luck, it would be Foxx.

He shut off the lights and got into bed. The sheets felt cool, but his body heat quickly warmed them. From outside came the muffled sounds of the city: the whoosh of traffic, the whine of a distant siren, the yip of a dog. He tried to imagine his encounter with Dominic tomorrow, but the imaginary conversation went out of control and his heart began to pound. Screw it, he thought. He needed something else to fill his mind or he never would drop off to sleep. And he needed to sleep, even for the short amount of night that was left to him, because he needed to be as sharp as possible.

So he thought of Carol, and his reaction was predictable and immediate. He rolled onto his back and loosened his underwear to make room for his burgeoning hard-on. They had started so fast, like tumbling over a waterfall together. Now, and for the next few days, till they got clear of the judge's death and he got clear of Dominic and his boss, they would be running through whitewater rapids. But after that, if they could hold on—if he could hold on—they would find themselves in a slow, beautiful, meandering river.

Meanwhile, he needed to keep Carol out of his deal with Bobby Werkman. He needed to protect her and to be around afterwards to continue their relationship. She might eventually suspect that he had changed the outcome of the judge's decision, and he would need to come up with some kind of explanation. Till then, though, he resolved not to tell her any lies.

At about the same time that Tom dropped off to sleep, Carol was trying to drop off, too. She had not expected to be up so late, but she had not expected an argument with Foxx. She realized now that she was wrong about him. He was not so principled that he would not try to fan an old flame. He definitely had tried, and the timing was so, so suspect, being totally a reaction to Tom's interest.

Well, she was not about to let Foxx ruin something good.

The judge had been her lifeline, problematic as he was. But over the last month, she felt that she and Tom had grown closer. The dinner only had confirmed her feelings. She had not planned it as a litmus test. She would not have planned it at all, of course. But after watching Tom and Foxx bounce off each other all day and deep into the night, she knew that she preferred Tom's quiet strength and steady rudder to Foxx's philosophical rants and entertaining unpredictability.

That story about the guy who punched Tom troubled her. But there had to be a reasonable explanation. There had to be.

PART THREE

January Second

CHAPTER 15

Foxx bolted up at the sound of the alarm. His bedroom was dark except for the red numbers on his digital clock and the twinkle of lights on the distant Throgs Neck Bridge. He slapped at the snooze button, knocked over the clock, righted it, and slapped again. Still, the alarm clock tweeted.

"What the hell," he muttered.

Last night's parting argument with Carol wound back into his head, the replay sharpening his senses. It wasn't his alarm that was ringing. It was his phone. And it wasn't the landline, the one listed in the City Island phone book under the single name Foxx. It was his cell phone, the one he always kept hidden, the one he never answered in front of anyone, the one he thought of as the Batphone. He whipped off the blankets, tracked the ringing to his jacket draped over the back of a chair, and squeezed the phone out of an inside pocket. The phone had rung five times; two more and it would kick into voice mail. He took a quick peek at the sky, imagining the Bat Signal rippling on the underside of an ominous cloud deck. Then he answered.

"Foxx? Bev. I want you to look in on Judge Canter." She let that sit a beat before she continued. "It's early, I know. But that's why I'm calling. I want you to look in on him at his apartment."

Foxx lifted a foot onto the chair and pushed himself forward to stretch his hamstring. It was six forty-five, dark as night, the sun not only still on the other side of the world, but way under it, too.

"You're in the office already?" he asked.

"New year, old problems. Canter shouldn't be one of them, but then there's that case. I thought you said he would issue his decision on New Year's Eve."

"So I was wrong. Sue me," said Foxx. "Am I getting comp time for this?"

"You're funny, Foxx. You know that?"

"Haven't been told that . . ." He thought of his last words to Carol and a pang of regret curled in his stomach. ". . . lately. Want to give me a hint?"

"City hotline got a noise complaint from a neighbor. We got a buzz because the judge and this neighbor have a running feud. Apparently, the judge objects to the neighbor playing big band music."

"So you mean the judge made the complaint."

"No. The neighbor. Probably in retaliation for all the complaints Canter has made against him."

"Ask me, the judge seems like the big band type."

"Not twenty-four seven."

"Why are you involved?"

"Because of the case. Because the neighbor described the noise as sounding like a wrestling match."

"You think Bobby Werkman tried to wrestle a decision out of him?"

"You really are funny, Foxx. I'm surprised I'm the first to tell you."

"Latest," said Foxx. "Not the first."

Foxx found the super's name in the apartment house directory and leaned on the intercom.

"It's early," came a gruff voice over the speaker.

"Seven-thirty. Time to get up."

"Who is it?"

"Inspector General's Office," said Foxx.

The lock snapped back, and Foxx went inside. The super met him at his apartment door, hopping on one foot while he pulled up his jeans. These reactions never failed to amuse Foxx. No one knew what the Inspector General's Office was. No one knew that the actual Inspector General was a slip of a woman with an interesting body (in Foxx's estimation) and a mind that was always five steps ahead of the game (again in Foxx's estimation). No one knew that the Inspector General had jurisdiction only over the state court system and its employees, and that when confronted with the type of request that Foxx was about to make, most people simply could say "Go screw." But most people just assumed they needed to cooperate. And so the super led Foxx into the elevator and up to the sixth floor, where he knocked on the judge's door.

"Judge Canter," he called. "Sir, are you there?"

He and Foxx stood quietly, listening for any sound inside. Music played from down the hall, but at such a low volume Foxx could not tell whether he heard it or imagined it due to the power of suggestion.

"Judge Canter," the super called again as he fit a key into the lock, "we're coming in."

He pushed the door just enough for it to swing slowly open. The apartment was quiet, the air perceptibly cooler than in the hallway.

The super flicked a light switch on the inside wall, then stepped aside. Foxx crossed into the living room as far as the coffee table, where two remotes lay perfectly parallel atop the TV page of *The New York Times*. Foxx leaned down to read the date. December 31. Papers lay in neat piles on the small table in the dining area. Foxx looked at these, too. There were federal and state tax return booklets, Emigrant Savings Bank statements held together with a rubber band, a pile of sealed and stamped envelopes beside a pile of invoices. The accouterments of a man who ran his life in hard copy.

The super waved Foxx into the bedroom. The bed was partially made, the covers pulled up but not smoothed, the pillows skewed. Foxx lifted the covers and caught a fleeting whiff of something. Sleep, he might have called it, laced with an old man's smell. He dropped the covers down. The nightstand was empty except for the alarm clock. No glasses, no wallet, no money clip, just a pewter plate with a thick layer of coins.

The bathroom was slightly more humid than the bedroom. The shower curtain liner was dry, but the faucet dripped hot water. A thin ring of rust surrounded the drain. Foxx tightened the hot water tap, but the water still dripped. He opened the medicine cabinet. A razor and a toothbrush stood upright in identical, soap-stained plastic cups. Both were dry to the touch. A tube of toothpaste was rolled to squeeze out the last drops. A comb stuck in a brush. On the top shelf stood a line of medications for blood pressure, cholesterol, and acid reflux. Behind them stood another, smaller bottle for erectile dysfunction. Foxx took that bottle off the shelf. The prescription, for twelve pills, was several years old. He shook the bottle, then opened the top and knocked the pills onto his palm. He counted three.

Foxx put the bottle back on the shelf and went out to the living room. The super waited by the door.

"I want to see the neighbor," said Foxx.

The super locked up, and they went next door to the neighbor's apartment. Music really was playing, and as soon as the super knocked the volume diminished to nothing.

The neighbor was a big florid man. He wore baggy red flannel sweatpants and a blue flannel sweatshirt with the sleeves roughly cut away.

"I'm from the Inspector General's Office," said Foxx.

"Which general and what do you inspect?" said the neighbor.

Foxx showed his ID.

"The Office of Court Administration," the neighbor said, squinting at the ID as he steadied Foxx's hand. "What a hoot this is. He complains about my music and that jackbooted city agency comes down on me. I complain about him, and he tattles to the Inspector General of the courts. Well, I don't work for the courts. I don't need to talk to you."

"I'm not here about you. I'm here about him."

"So talk to him."

"He's not here," said Foxx. "You complained about a wrestling match?"

"That's the only way I can describe it," said the man. "Lots of banging and thumping. No voices."

"None? What time was this?"

"Between seven and eight o'clock last night."

"How long did it last?"

"Not very. But it was so intense the pictures on my wall

were trembling. It stopped right after I called the complaint line. I heard his door close and lock and after that there was nothing but silence."

"Close and lock," said Foxx. "From the outside or the inside?"

"Outside. I heard the tinkling of keys."

Foxx turned to the door and saw that it opened to give a clear view down the hallway to the elevator.

"Did you watch him leave?"

"Oh no," said the man. "He would accuse me of spying."

A pole lamp with three lights in cylindrical casings stood beside Nick's bed. Carol steadied the pole with one hand while she aimed one of the lights at the ceiling and twisted the switch. Nick rolled onto his stomach and folded a pillow over his head. Then he peeked out.

"Mom?"

Carol brushed the pillow off and spoke directly into Nick's ear.

"I have to go into work early." She moved the phone to the closest edge of the nightstand and raised the ringer control to the highest volume. "You have all clean clothes in your drawers. Dress warm. I'll call you from the train to make sure you're up."

Nick whipped off the covers.

"No. Stay," said Carol. "It's too early. You can sleep another half hour."

"I'm not tired."

But life was tiring for Nick, Carol thought. Even with hearing aids, there was a constant need to concentrate, especially in situations like a holiday dinner with several people speaking at once. Fatigue seemed to engulf Nick quickly at the end of the day, and Carol preferred that he surrender rather than fight it.

"Are we going to have people over again?" he asked.

"Did you have fun?"

Nick had a particular way of nodding his head, two discrete forward bows.

"What did you think of Tom?"

"He's okay."

"Only okay?"

"He's not like Foxx," said Nick.

"No," said Carol. "Nobody is."

Foley Square very early on a winter's morning: little traffic, few pedestrians, no lines at the coffee carts. From the sky overhead to the pavement beneath Carol's feet, the pervading color was gray.

Carol chugged up the front steps, loosened her scarf as she pushed through the revolving door, hung her ID in front of her chest before she passed the information desk. At the bottom of the promenade, beyond the last magnetometer, Jerry Elliott sat at a desk with his head thrown back and his eyes closed. Carol hurried past without waking him.

The sight of the *Law Journals* wedged into the mail slot gave Carol only a fleeting sense of normalcy. Today would be the most abnormal of days. But for now, she placed one copy of the *Law Journal* on the judge's desk, measured out the coffee, filled the coffeemaker to the top. The routine, even the fluorescent buzz, comforted her momentarily. Then she sat down to wait for Tom.

This time, Tom did not duck behind a coffee cart or skirt Foley Square. He angled across the street and walked straight to Dominic.

"You're early, Carroway. I like that."

Tom dropped his briefcase between his feet, pressing his heels into the sides. He scooped the wad of cash from his rain-coat pocket and handed it over. Dominic held it close to his chest. He counted it quickly, his smile ratcheting down into a frown and then a scowl as the denominations diminished into twenties and tens.

"This is only a grand," he said. "Where's the rest of it?"

"In here," said Tom. He tapped one heel against the briefcase.

"Open that up so's I can count it," said Dominic.

"It's not cash. It's something I will turn into cash."

"You hocking something?"

"No. Selling."

"Let me see."

Tom expected Dominic to ask to see what was in the brief-case. In his imaginary dialog, the one he finally managed to complete on the downtown subway, he sighed and then opened the briefcase. So now, in real time with the real Dominic, he sighed, lifted a foot onto the lip of the fountain, and opened the briefcase on his knee.

"That's a pile of paper."

"But a valuable pile of paper," said Tom. "The same person who gave me that grand is giving me four more once I'm fin-ished with this paper."

"I don't get it," said Dominic.

"It's a judge's decision. I write them for a living."

"And you're getting paid five grand to write this decision? That's how you get paid? Like piece work?"

"Never mind how I get paid. I'm getting five grand for this. That's all you need to know."

"Oh," said Dominic. The idea of selling a judge's decision seemed like a revelation to him, a peek into a world with possibilities he never had considered. "But there's something else I don't get."

Tom expected more doubt. It was at this approximate point in his imaginary dialog that he sighed for the second time. And so he sighed now.

"Four and one makes five," said Dominic. "You owe eight."

"I know. I have more stuff to sell."

"More of these?" Dominic riffled the papers.

Tom closed the briefcase and set it down between his heels again.

"No," he said. "World War II artifacts."

"I don't see them."

"They're in storage. I need time to get them to a dealer."

"You mean a pawn shop."

"I mean an antiques dealer."

"I told you the money was due today," said Dominic.

"I know what you told me. But I gave you one already and I'll have four more for you by ten o'clock. Your boss will wait a day or two for the rest."

"How do you know?"

"Because you're going to call him. Because you're going to tell him it makes more sense to wait for all the money than to kick my ass and only get part of it."

"How do you know it doesn't make more sense for me to kick your ass and get all the money?"

Tom bit back a smile. He had imagined Dominic saying that exact line.

"Make the call," he said.

"Make the call," mimicked Dominic. "Carroway, I don't know what's gotten into you."

But he flipped open his phone and walked away to make the call. The call lasted less than a minute, and Tom, who had foreseen a longer and possibly animated discussion, felt the first crack in his bravado as Dominic returned looking grim.

"You got two days," said Dominic. "But on the four, you got till ten. Otherwise, take a good look at your ass now because by ten oh five you won't have one."

Courtesy of the IG's office, Foxx had a passkey to every chambers, courtroom, and back office at 60 Centre Street. He planned to root around Canter's chambers for any clue to the judge's whereabouts, but finding the light in the transom changed his plan. He held his breath, listening carefully but hearing no sound inside. He backed away and looked up and down the corridor. The doors into the two other rooms of Canter's suite were security doors without transoms, so there was no way to tell if there were any other lights on. He leaned back to the door and listened again. Still no sound except for a faint electrical buzz. He carefully turned the knob enough to confirm that the door was unlocked.

He stepped back again. Someone was there. Carol never left home before seeing Nick get on his school bus, and Tom always arrived at the courthouse around nine-thirty. So most likely, it was Canter himself. Foxx knocked hard enough for the judge to hear at his desk in the inner office. The door opened immediately.

"Carol," he said.

"Foxx!" she said. She held the doorknob with one hand and braced herself against the jamb with the other.

"Is the judge in?" said Foxx.

"He's never here this early."

"Neither are you," said Foxx. "Nick got on the bus himself?"

"Our New Year's resolution," said Carol. "What do you want with the judge?"

"I want to make sure he's all right."

"Of course he's all right. Why wouldn't he be?"

"When did you last see him?"

"New Year's Eve. When do you think? And you didn't answer my question. Why wouldn't he be all right?"

"That's confidential," said Foxx.

"Confidential? You had lots to say about Tom last night, and now you come here implying there's something wrong with the judge, but you conveniently say it's confidential. Are you trying to destroy every male relationship in my life?"

Foxx let Carol shoo him out of chambers. He could not remember everything he said last night. But it must have been bad. Real bad. He walked to the next angle in the corridor and pulled out his cell phone.

"What did you find?" said Bev.

"I missed him at his apartment, and he hasn't gotten to chambers yet," said Foxx.

"Find anything at his apartment?"

"No sign of any wrestling match. The neighbor couldn't add anything. Heard someone lock up and leave, but didn't look to see who."

"But," said Bev.

"Did I imply a but?"

"Not in words."

"I don't have the words," said Foxx. "It's a feeling some-thing's up."

"Find the judge," said Bev. "Don't do anything else till you do."

CHAPTER 16

Tom had no sensation of climbing the front steps. He was floating, confident, charged up. He had looked his enemy in the eye and it was the enemy who had blinked. He wasn't quite finished yet. There was the decision he needed to print. Then there was the person Bobby would send to chambers to verify that the decision was rewritten and filed. Then he needed to bring the money out to Dominic. Then he needed to arrange selling those antiques. And at some point during all this the judge was going to be found dead. What a day this would be. But yes, yes. His plan was going to work.

He pushed in through the revolving door. Only a few people were in the lobby. The officer at the information desk lifted his eyes from his newspaper and lowered them once he recognized Tom. At the bottom of the promenade, at the end of the empty magnetometer lines, Jerry Elliott leaned against the wall. Tom cut to the right, toward the judges' elevator. The candy stand was open, the aroma of coffee spilling out into the lobby. As he walked past, he saw Derek Moxley at the counter. The call to Moxley on New Year's Day had been a mistake that luckily fell into the "no harm, no foul" variety. He was glad he had hung up before Moxley took the line, relieved that he had contacted Bobby Werkman instead. It was cleaner and more direct to deal with the litigant rather than with the lawyer. When all was done, he and Bobby could shake hands and part ways and never speak to each other again. With Moxley, knowing looks and snide hints would have dogged him for the rest of his career. Because as long as Tom stayed with the court system, there always would be Derek Moxley. Yes, he had been smart to chicken out on that phone call. Still, he quickened his pace to get around the corner and out of sight before Moxley spotted him.

Carol was shaking, literally shaking. She had poured herself coffee, but it tasted harshly metallic and after two sips she dumped it down the wash closet sink. Now she sat behind her desk with her red coat draped over her shoulders. She took a deep breath and held it, hoping to calm her quaking muscles. Why would Foxx come to chambers so early in the morning to ask about the judge? She had been with Foxx all day yesterday, and the conversations, even their argument, never once touched on the judge. This was a bad sign, a really bad sign.

But maybe, she hoped, Foxx had come by because he regretted their words at the end of last night. He had seen the light in the transom and popped in to apologize. This logic made perfect sense except for two small details: One, Foxx reacted with genuine surprise when he saw her, and, two, Foxx rarely apologized. Which meant he probably *had* been looking for the judge. And so when she resumed breathing, she also resumed shaking.

The door opened, and Tom pushed in.

"Carol," he said, and then smiled. "What are you doing here so early?"

"Couldn't sleep," she responded.

"Neither could I," he said, letting the door close. He crossed in front of her desk, set his briefcase on the floor beside the conference table, and opened his arms toward her. She got up from her chair, letting her coat fall from her shoulders. They hugged.

"Kiss me," she said.

He did, but quickly pulled away.

"You're cold," he said.

"Freezing." Her laugh was more of a shiver. "You know how long it takes for the heat to come up after a day off."

He sniffed. "You made coffee."

"Everything as usual. That's what you said."

"Except we're both way early." Tom held her by the shoulders. "Something's bothering you."

"Today . . ."

"Today will go fine," he said.

"No, Tom, it's not just today. It's Foxx."

"Did something happen after I left last night?"

"He came by here looking for the judge. He asked if the judge was all right. Then he asked when I last saw him. I told him, of course the judge was all right. Why wouldn't he be? I told him I last saw him on New Year's Eve. When did he think I last saw him?"

"Did he say why?" asked Tom.

"He said it was confidential. So I told him that I wasn't going to let him ruin every male relationship in my life."

"What did he say to that?"

"Nothing," said Carol. "I chased him out. I've been shaking ever since."

Tom pulled a chair out from the conference table and sat. Several things ran through his mind, but his priority was to calm Carol's fears.

"It must have been a coincidence," he said. "Think. We were so careful. No one saw us. If anyone did, we'd know by now. Did Foxx mention the judge yesterday?"

"No," said Carol.

"So what could have happened since last night that would have Foxx looking for the judge?"

"I don't know."

"Then it probably was a coincidence. Unless it was for a whole other reason."

"That's what I've been telling myself." Carol went behind her desk but did not sit down. "Something did happen last night. We had a big argument."

"About me?"

Carol nodded.

"It's an old argument, and it really wasn't so much about you as it was about me. I knew it was coming when he asked that question about lawyers."

"I wondered whether that was rhetorical or pointed," said Tom.

"It was pointed," said Carol. "Anyway, I can handle Foxx's philosophical rants. But he told me something else that's been bothering me all night. He said that on New Year's Eve some guy punched you and left you on a park bench. He said you denied it, but that he knew something was going on and that I should watch out."

Tom stared at the floor for a long moment.

"My God," he muttered.

"You mean Foxx was right?" said Carol.

Tom took a deep breath. "I had an argument with a client."

"How could you have a client?"

"Because I've practiced a little law on the side."

"But you're not supposed to."

"I don't consider what I do practicing. It started with friends, and then friends of friends. Mostly drawing up wills. I don't charge much because the wills are simple. I avoid anything complicated."

"This was over a will?" said Carol. "The guy isn't even dead."

"It wasn't over a will. A few years ago, when real estate was flying high, this guy called me and asked if I would represent him on a condo deal. He was this tough-looking fireplug type of a guy. Said he was a professional boxer. The loan was a big one, and it was adjustable. I told him it was a crazy loan, and he said he had loans before and always paid them back. He said he needed a lawyer, not a financial advisor. So we closed the deal, and now he's lost the condo and he's mad at me."

"But you tried to talk him out of it," said Carol.

"Yes, and why should facts get in the way?" said Tom. "He's been threatening me for a while, mostly off the wall stuff that I ignored. But a couple of weeks ago, he started saying I should give him back my fee for the closing."

"That's ridiculous."

"And that's the way I treated it until he threatened to file a complaint with the disciplinary committee. So I decided to pay him. I'd get him off my back and, if he did file a complaint, at least I could say that I didn't take a fee.

"I charged the guy seven-fifty for the closing. He wanted

that plus interest, and I said fine. It was worth the extra money to send him away. But the problem was I got down to the end of the month and all I had was five hundred to spare. He got mad and reacted the way you'd think a boxer would react. He threw a punch."

"So Foxx didn't make that up," said Carol.

"Foxx guessed lucky," said Tom. "He didn't see a thing."

"Tom," she said. "I'm so sorry."

Foxx usually worked the first magnetometer shift. Staring at lines of people eased him into the day and often foreshadowed problems that cropped up later. After slowly changing into his uniform and quickly downing a cup of coffee, he got to the mags with a minute to spare.

"Well if it ain't the Foxx-meister," Jerry Elliott said as he shouldered his duffle bag.

"Where are you headed, Jerry?"

"Comp time. Where else?"

"You have your pillow and blankie?" said Foxx.

"Funny, Foxx, real funny," said Elliott. "But as a matter of fact, I'm going to spend some time on personal improvement. Just like you told me."

There was still the stack of decisions that the judge had signed on New Year's Eve. Normal process was for Carol to photocopy them in the library, log them on her motion charts, then cart them to the Motion Office, where they were officially recorded on the court's computer system. So at nine o'clock, after assuaging Carol's worries enough for them to kiss and embrace, Tom suggested that she process half of the decisions.

"Why not all of them?" she asked.

"It will look more natural," Tom replied.

Carol went into the middle room and pulled decisions from their folders while Tom fired up his computer. He could hear the slaps of the thin motion folders and the thuds of the thick ones as Carol dismantled the pile and created another. His computer finished booting, and he opened his applications in their usual order: e-mail, case management, word processing, and the court's intranet. Carol came out from the middle room, fanned the sheaf of decisions, and left for the library. As soon as she closed the door, Tom popped his flash drive into the USB port. His laptop had a different version of the same word processing program, and he needed to make sure that the new decision paginated the same. Foxx's visit crept into his head, but he pushed it back and quickly scrolled through the decision. Everything looked exactly right. He clicked the print command and circled the conference table to lift the pages from the printer tray. Then he pulled the papers from his briefcase, sandwiched the new seven pages between the original first page and the judge's signature page, fit them all into the motion folder, and bound the whole package with two thick rubber bands.

He carried the motion folder into the middle room and stuck it in the untouched pile of motion folders. He originally had nixed the idea of slipping the new version of the decision into the motion folder and allowing Carol to process the decision because he did not want to involve her in his scheme, even unwittingly. But her surprise appearance this morning forced him to change his plans on the fly, and having Carol do her job was the better, safer course. If anyone investigated chambers procedure, nothing would stick out as odd.

Carol returned a few minutes later.

"Anything yet?" she asked.

"No." Tom checked the clock on the computer. It was nine fifteen. "That's why I'm not too worried about Foxx. If someone found the judge, we would have heard by now. So I think we're in the clear. We can wait till ten thirty before we start to worry about the judge."

Carol went into the middle room. Tom could hear rubber bands snap as she attached the decisions to their motion folders, then the metallic roll of the file cabinet drawers as she tucked the copies into their alphabetical places. He took the pages he had removed from the union decision and was about to rip them, slowly and silently in long thin strips, when the door opened and Jerry Elliott stepped inside. Elliott was out of uniform, wearing a dull green parka with a fur-lined hood and the zipper down low enough to reveal a tee shirt underneath.

"What's up, Jerry?" said Tom, quickly tucking the pages under the keyboard. Something in Elliott's demeanor struck Tom as strange. His hands were balled into fists and his arms were folded across his chest.

"I need you to come with me," said Elliott.

"Me?" said Tom. "Where?"

"I can't say where."

In the middle room, a file cabinet drawer rolled shut. Carol stood in the doorway.

"Aw, Christ," Elliott muttered, then said to Carol, "What the hell are you doing here?"

"I work here, Jerry. What kind of hello is that?"

Elliott fixed his gaze in the middle distance, somewhere between Carol in the doorway and Tom seated at the conference table. His mouth moved, though no sound came out. Carol looked at Tom, and Tom looked at Carol. Tom could not believe that Elliott was the person Bobby Werkman would send to chambers. Besides, it was forty-five minutes earlier than Bobby had promised.

"Guess I'll bring both of you," Elliott said to himself.

"Where?" asked Carol.

Elliott shifted his gaze, but still avoided eye contact with either of them.

"I can't say," he replied.

"What's this about?" asked Carol.

"I'll bet he can't say that, either," said Tom.

Elliott cut Tom an unfriendly look that seemed all the more venomous because it was so unlike his usually pleasant face.

"You're right. I can't say," he said. "Get your coats and let's go."

"I am not going anywhere," said Carol.

Elliott slowly opened one fist, stuck his hand into his pocket, and drew his pistol.

"Hey, Jerry, whoa," said Tom. "Take it easy."

Elliott swung the pistol toward Tom.

"Okay," said Tom. "Just tell us what you want."

"I already told you, I want you to come with me."

"But, Jerry, just tell us where."

"You'll find out," said Elliott. "Now get your coats and let's go."

Without taking their eyes off Elliott, Tom and Carol put on their coats.

"Lemme have your cell phones, too."

"Jerry," said Tom.

But Elliott shook the pistol, and they handed over their cell phones.

"Okay," said Elliott. "We're going out the door and past the security desk to the first set of stairs. We are going to walk down to the basement and exit to Worth Street. Don't talk to anyone on the way. If you see someone you know, you say hi. Nothing else. Understand?"

They walked in front, Elliott following. Tom could tell from the sound of Elliott's shoes squeaking on the terrazzo floor that he was far enough behind them that a casual observer might not think they were together. The corridor angled and midway through the next segment they passed the fifth floor security desk. Several people waited in the foyer: messengers, lawyers, a woman with the desperate look of a litigant—the normal mix of people for a normal weekday morning. The officer at the desk did not look up from her newspaper.

At the next angle, a small alcove led to the internal stairs. Tom grabbed Carol's elbow to stop her from going down.

"Jerry," he said. "Judge Canter will be in soon. He'll wonder where we are."

Elliott said nothing, just stared at the floor.

"You saw the people waiting at the security desk," said Tom. "They could be waiting for Canter. He doesn't like to deal with them. He gets very nervous when we're not around."

"I really don't give a good goddam," said Elliott. He jammed his pocket against Tom's back hard enough for Tom to feel the muzzle of the pistol.

They descended the stairs without another word. Outside, a black Crown Victoria with deeply tinted glass was parked near the Worth Street entrance. Elliott opened the back door, told Carol to slide in first, then Tom. Elliott jumped into the driver's seat, and the car glided into traffic.

Tom and Carol each looked out their own window as the Crown Vic picked its way through the crowded streets of Chinatown. Carol sat bolt upright, her knees pressed together, her hands clutching the front edge of the seat. Tom leaned forward, his elbows on his knees, his thumbs hooked together. The Crown Vic headed out of Chinatown and toward the East River. As it swung north on the FDR Drive, Carol nudged Tom's arm.

"This is about the judge," she whispered.

"But we're the only ones who know."

"Not anymore. That's why Foxx came by asking about the judge. This is connected. I know it. And we're headed toward the judge's apartment, aren't we?"

Tom sank back in the seat, tacitly admitting that Carol was right. Not one hundred percent right, but right enough. They weren't the only two people who knew about the judge; Bobby Werkman knew, and so did Anton Vuksanaj. Where did Jerry Elliott fit into the picture?

Elliott sped up, moved left, passed the exit that would have taken them to the judge's apartment. They sped north, skirting midtown.

They could be going anywhere.

CHAPTER 17

The room was small and warm, thickly carpeted, painted in earthtones, furnished in rich leather and deep mahogany. On a desk in a corner, six TVs were stacked three on three. Five of the screens were blank.

Bobby stared over Vuksanaj's shoulder. The single live screen showed a high-angle view of a brightly lit room. Carol sat in a chair, her red coat still buttoned around her and her hands thrust into the pockets. Tom paced, foreshortening dramatically as he passed beneath the camera.

"They're talking," said Vuksanaj. He pressed a button, and static crackled. "It's not the best audio."

"I'll be sure to share your opinion with my uncle," said Bobby.

"Tom," Carol said on-screen. "What do you think is going on?"

Carol's words arrested Tom. It was not just the words themselves, the first she uttered since getting out of the car, but the slightly inflected stress on *you* that implied he knew more than she.

"I don't know," Tom answered. He spoke softly and slowly

because he wanted her question to sink into silence rather than provoke any discussion. And in truth, Tom knew nothing about this turn of events.

"This is about the judge," said Carol.

Tom shrugged, still not comfortable with her tone. Thoughts swirled through his head: Foxx's visit to chambers early in the morning, Elliott taking them at gunpoint, this cold, antiseptic room with a camera in the ceiling. He felt they were being observed.

"You said no one saw us," said Carol.

"Maybe I was wrong."

He had been relatively calm until they crossed the Queensboro Bridge and descended into one of those gray, industrial sections he saw only from the other side of the East River. He tried to hold onto the trail, memorizing turns and noting street names. But he quickly became hopelessly lost. And then the street widened, and the warehouses and factories fell away, and Elliott swung into a parking lot behind a huge brick building with a façade like a Greek temple and the name O'Rourke cut into the stone pediment. He ordered them to get out and shepherded them to a side door where a freight elevator took them down to this room.

"Tom." Carol stood up from the chair and opened her arms. "Hold me."

Tom hugged her tentatively because his mind was distracted and his heart was disengaged. Carol squirmed herself free and took off her coat.

"Hold me like you mean it," she said.

"Bring in Carroway," Bobby told Vuksanaj.

He watched Vuksanaj leave the room, opened the desk

drawer for one more look at each of the photos, then closed the drawer as Tom walked in. Tom immediately noticed the TV screen, which showed Carol pacing in the white room.

"My uncle's a technology nut," said Bobby. "Irish side of the family. Neddy O'Rourke. He buries ninety percent of the people who die north of Queens Boulevard, even the Greeks."

"Why do we need a funeral home?" asked Tom.

"To help you and Carol keep your jobs."

"We did that," said Tom. "We got to midnight."

"You might think you did," said Bobby. "You might think you were safe once the old year rolled into the new. But it's more complicated than that, so I took custody of the judge."

"The judge is here? How?"

"Never mind the details. The important thing is that with me involved you get the benefit of my political connections and my uncle's mortician skills."

"Why do I need them?"

"Because, Tom, you didn't think your plan through. This is a judge we are talking about. There are things like autopsies and ME reports and determining time of death by looking at stomach contents. Do you think the notion that the judge died on January first would have survived a routine inquest? Do you think no one would have noticed that someone moved the body? Do you think when people started inquiring, Tom, you would have the answers? I don't think so."

"Why didn't you tell me all this yesterday?" asked Tom.

"I needed to think things through," said Bobby. "Anyway, we're back to a simple version of our plan. I get my decision and you, with my help, keep your jobs."

"What about my payment?"

"There won't be any payment."

"But we had a deal."

"C'mon, Tom. You're a law clerk. You've written hundreds of decisions on contract disputes. You know how things go. And we still have a deal. Decision for jobs. Simple quid pro quo. A contract any judge would uphold, dead or alive. So is my decision finished?"

"Not yet," said Tom. "I ran into some problems."

"What kind?"

"I'm having trouble making it fit, legally and between the pages."

"How much time do you need? An hour? Two?"

"No time. I told you yesterday, if I'm not getting five, I might as well do it for nothing. If I'm getting nothing, I might as well not do it at all. But remember, I'm holding the original."

"Is that a threat? Because if it is, you don't bring it off very well. Besides, Anton can sniff it out, and where would you be then?"

Bobby looked at Carol pacing on the TV screen.

"She doesn't know you called me."

Tom said nothing.

"And you want to keep it that way."

Tom said nothing again. After a moment, Bobby took out his cell phone and stabbed out a text message. On the screen, Vuksanaj entered the white room. He sat on the chair, folded his arms across his chest, and watched Carol continue to pace.

"Here's my final offer," said Bobby. "You give me my decision, you and Carol both keep your jobs and she never finds out about our deal."

Tom wanted to say *fuck you,* but the words died in his throat.

* * *

Vuksanaj disappeared from the screen, fetched Tom out of the office, and returned him to the white room with a push that sent him stumbling. Tom caught himself before crashing into Carol. They clutched tightly, Carol whispering a string of worries and fears into his ear. Tom only half listened. He needed to get a grip on himself.

"It's Bobby Werkman," he finally whispered back.

Carol broke their clutch, but held onto Tom's arms.

"The head of the court officer's union?"

Tom nodded.

"But how does he know?"

"He didn't tell me. I don't know. Maybe a court officer got suspicious about what we were doing on New Year's Eve and reported it to Bobby."

"But if someone knew the judge was dead, why call the union instead of the police?"

"Because of the case. Bobby wants me to rewrite the decision to come out in favor of the union."

"He can't make you do that."

"Yes he can, Carol. Unfortunately, he can."

"That would be breaking the law."

"We've already broken the law by hiding the judge till midnight. He's using it against us."

"So we come clean. We go to the police and tell them what we did and why we did it."

"Carol," said Tom. "It's gotten way too complicated for that. This funeral home is owned by Bobby Werkman's uncle. They have the judge in the morgue."

"How did they do that?"

Tom closed his eyes and lifted his glasses to squeeze the bridge of his nose. "He didn't say. It's really beside the point anyway."

"Well we're not going to cooperate. It'll just make everything worse. You're not . . ."

Vuksanaj stuck his head in the door and pointed at Carol.

"Bobby wants to see you," he said.

Bobby stood up for Carol as she entered the office and actually bowed toward her.

He wants to charm me, she thought. Fat chance of that.

"Hello, Carol, please sit down."

And Carol, despite her plan to resist, did sit down. The desk was at her elbow, and she saw Tom pacing the white room on the TV screen. He's been watching us all along, she thought.

"How did you find out about Judge Canter?" said Carol.

"Let's just say that nothing happens in any of my courthouses that I don't know about. Not even the fall of a sparrow."

"You sound like you think you're God."

"Hardly," said Bobby. "Just a humble civil servant fighting for the good of my union brethren. I understand what you and Tom tried to do. These are tough times. Jobs are scarce, and it's no time to be a single woman with her own mother and son to support."

Carol started to speak, but Bobby raised a hand.

"Please. I know the people in my courthouses, too."

"Tom is not going to write that decision for you."

"He will," said Bobby. "Because it's in his best interest to write it. Just like it's in your best interest to help us all get through these next few hours. Your plan to save your jobs was clever but wouldn't have worked. I can make it work, and in a few hours we'll all walk away with what we want. Me with my decision, you and Tom with your jobs for another year."

"I'm not going to help you," said Carol.

Bobby smiled, then opened the desk drawer and dealt out the three photos.

"My director of security has resources even I didn't realize," he said. "They're scanned into my laptop. One click of my mouse, and they can go wherever I want. But it's just one pair of eyes you care about."

Carol looked at the photos, then pushed them away. She bit her lip, trying to keep the corners of her mouth from turning down. Bobby scraped the photos together, gave the top one a long look, and slipped them into his shirt pocket.

"You've slimmed down since then," he said. "I think I prefer you zaftig."

CHAPTER 18

Foxx never spoke about the incident that landed him in front of the Inspector General. It had happened years earlier, when he worked Bronx Supreme. He did not contest the charges, did not even notify the union, which, after learning about the investigation in back channel fashion, sent a lawyer to represent him. Foxx refused the help. His attitude was, I did what I did and I'll suffer the consequences.

The consequences were a four-week suspension without pay. It was spring. City Island was in bloom. Tourists and suburbanites filled the waterfront restaurants on weekend evenings. Foxx's cottage was on the back end of the island. From his front porch, enclosed with jalousie windows, he could see the barges on the Sound and the bridges to Long Island. He needed something to do those four weeks, so he bought a scraper and some paint and spent the month scraping and repainting the cottage.

The night before he was to return to work, the phone rang. It was the IG herself. She told him that his days at Bronx Supreme were over. Tomorrow, he would report to the New York County

Courthouse at 60 Centre Street. But before that, he needed to meet with her at Central Administration.

The office was at the extreme southern tip of Manhattan. Foxx found the streets crawling with stockbrokers and investment bankers, two of his least favorite types of people. His case had been investigated by a staff attorney in the IG's office. He had seen the IG herself only at the end, when she personally imposed his suspension. She was a small neat woman whose obvious intelligence—he liked to describe it as a light in her eyes—struck him as immensely sexy. He felt that same surge of attraction when they met that second time and she handed him a cell phone.

"You call me whenever you see something you think I should know," she said. "And I'll call you whenever I think there's something you should look into. Think of it as undercover work."

"I was thinking of a different type of undercover," said Foxx.

"Don't get your hopes up," said the IG.

Only two people at 60 Centre Street knew about the arrangement: the captain and the lieutenant. The sergeant, who doled out the assignments at the start of each four-week term of court, knew only not to assign Foxx to any specific post. Except for his early morning gig at the mags, Foxx was a permanent floater, alighting on different posts at odd times.

Foxx left the mags shortly after ten, noting that Elliott had not returned from his hour of comp time. His next stop was to relieve the officer at the fifth floor security desk. He found six lawyers milling in the small foyer. According to the officer, none was waiting for Judge Canter.

Soon after Foxx sat down at the desk, a messenger arrived and handed Foxx a manila envelope.

"For Judge Canter, huh?" said Foxx.

He picked up the phone and called chambers. The phone rang four times, then kicked into voice mail.

"Leave it," he told the messenger. "I'll see that it gets there."

The officer returned ten minutes later, and Foxx relinquished the desk.

"Got a hand-delivery for Canter," he said. "No one's answering the phone in chambers."

"The secretary and the law clerk must not be back yet," said the officer. "They went out about nine."

"Out out?" said Foxx.

"They had their coats on."

"Did they say where they were going?"

"Not to me. Should I have asked?"

Foxx picked up the envelope. "The guy who dropped this off seemed pretty uptight about it getting to chambers. I told him I'd deliver it myself."

The light was on behind the transom, but the door was locked. Foxx listened and, hearing no sound inside, unlocked the door with the master passkey. He pushed in, calling Judge Canter's name, since it was possible the judge could be sitting behind a locked door and refusing to answer the phone. But chambers was empty. The officer had not mentioned seeing the judge leave, just Carol and Tom. Maybe the judge had phoned them from somewhere, and they went to meet him.

Foxx looked around anyway. Carol's computer was on, but when he nudged the mouse the monitor showed only the computer desktop. She had not opened a single program. He went around the conference table. Tom's computer was on, too, and had a flash drive stuck into a USB port. Several pages of printer paper, folded in half, were under the keyboard. Foxx nudged the mouse, and the monitor hissed as it brightened into a page of typescript. He leaned closer to read and immediately recognized the recap of last summer's contract negotiations between the court officers union and the Office of Court Administration. This was the decision in Bobby Werkman's case to reinstate overtime pay.

Foxx scrolled through the decision. He had carted thousands of decisions from judges' chambers to clerks' offices, and so he was familiar with their format. The first page showed the parties' names in a rudimentary graphics box and, below that, listed the names and addresses of counsel. Below counsel came the judge's name, and below that the decision itself began. The decision could be any length, but the last page always included a signature line and a line for the date. This decision was seven pages long, but began in mid sentence on page two. The last page ended in mid sentence, too, but said enough to show that the decision ruled in the union's favor.

Foxx scrolled back to the top, then slid the folded pages out from under the keyboard. There were seven pages in all, and they started with the exact same language as the pages displayed on the computer. Someone taking a quick glance might have assumed the pages to be simply a hard-copy version. But Foxx assumed nothing. He skimmed these pages and saw facts recast with a different slant and legal reasoning that reached a different conclusion. In this version, the union lost.

Foxx slid the pages back under the keyboard. He knew enough about how Judge Canter's chambers operated to know where to look next. The table in the middle room had two stacks of motion folders, one face up and the other face down, as if Carol had stopped working on them halfway through. The folders in the face down pile had originals and two photocopies of the decision rubber-banded on the outside. The face up pile had only the originals. Foxx found the union case folder in the face up pile and quickly saw which version of the decision was attached.

On his way out of chambers, Foxx took the hand-delivered envelope he had dropped onto Carol's desk. He went back to the security post and gave it to the officer.

"Chambers is locked," he told her. "Better keep this here."

The officer did not question Foxx; no one ever questioned Foxx. But Foxx had a number of questions for Tom, for Carol, and for Judge Canter, too, if he ever found him.

Dominic paced beside the fountain, dividing his attention between the courthouse steps and the hexagonal stones at his feet. His reptilian mind did not understand the imprecision of common speech. He could not imagine that the payment Tom awaited might arrive late or that Tom might take a few extra minutes to make his way out of the courthouse. For him, ten o'clock meant ten o'clock. Sharp. Precisely. On the dot.

Dominic crossed the street and looked up the courthouse steps. There were twenty-nine of them. He had counted them once, the way he counted everything—money, breaths, the combinations of lefts and rights as he worked the speed bag. These were awkward steps to climb. The risers were too short and the treads were too deep for you to get any rhythm. You chugged rather than glided. And Dominic liked to glide. Back when he fought, his manager had billed him as the Gramercy Glider.

Should he climb the steps now or not? Not, he decided. He would need to clear security, and once he got through he wouldn't know where to look. The building was massive, and he didn't know where Carroway worked except that he worked for some judge. So he stayed below and looked up. Carroway wore his usual gray raincoat today. And black pants. Dominic would spot him in a second.

But more minutes passed, and Dominic drifted to the north side of the steps, edging into the small park where he'd punched Carroway in the gut. This was brilliant, he thought. He would wait for Carroway to come all the way down the steps, then call him over. Carroway would think, hey, maybe he'll punch me again. And maybe he'd be right.

Dominic counted ten men wearing gray raincoats coming down the steps in the next five minutes. None of them were Carroway. He lifted a foot onto a bench and stared down Worth Street toward Chinatown, remembering a proverb about a watched pot never coming to a boil. A black car pulled to the curb near a street-level door that was the color of bronze. A big, shambling guy wearing an Eskimo parka got out of the drivers side and then two other people got out: Carroway and a woman. And not just any woman but the good-looking head from New Year's Eve. They all three walked to the bronze door. The shambling man swiped a card through a slot then yanked back the door. The woman went in first, and before Carroway followed he glanced into the park. Dominic reacted quickly, pummeling the cold air with a three-punch combo.

CHAPTER 19

Anyone who walked into the empty robing room would have thought Foxx was cooping. The lights were out, the blinds of the single large window were closed against the weak January light. Foxx's feet lay on the judge's desk, and his chair was tilted back at a forty-five degree angle. He seemed to be asleep, but in fact he was performing his version of transcendental meditation, which involved closed eyes, slowed respiration, upturned palms, and the rhythmic repetition in his mind of a single syllable. When it worked well, he imagined himself rising and hovering, supine, just below the ceiling. Once, he felt something strike his nose and saw a tiny smudge on the ceiling directly above his head. The idea that he actually had levitated himself haunted him for years, but had since taken on the aspect of a recovered memory: neither true nor false.

But sometimes meditation did not work because Foxx could not control his thoughts. And he could not control them today. Images of Carol and Tom, Tom and Carol filled his head. Then other thoughts swept in: Judge Canter, the dopey pug who punched Tom, the two versions of that decision.

The phone rang on the desk. Foxx swung his feet and let gravity pull his chair forward. The readout on the phone showed the number of the fifth floor security desk. Foxx answered.

"They're back," said the officer.

"All of them?"

"Law clerk and secretary."

"No judge?"

"Didn't see him."

Foxx hung up and lifted his feet back onto the desk. Tilted the chair. Closed his eyes. Cleared his head. Turned his palms up.

Maybe he would touch the ceiling this time.

Elliott unlocked the door to chambers and stepped back to allow Carol and Tom to enter first. Carol moved slowly, and Tom, following impatiently, stepped on her heel as she turned past the corner of her desk.

"Sorry," he said.

She did not answer, only turned and gave him an odd smile. A curtain seemed to have dropped between them, and under any other circumstances, this sudden turn would have bothered Tom. He had experienced it many times before with many different women. There would be a word or a comment or a gesture, maybe even just a stray thought, and what had been going so well, like a jet streaking across a bright blue sky, fell into a tailspin. He was not the type of person who could yank back on the stick and be joyful. He usually just turned morose, spinning in silence until the ground rushed up to meet him. Carol was different. He liked her a lot, even believed that he could fall in love with her. But first he needed to save himself, and Carol's distant silence, which began when she returned from her meeting with Bobby Werkman, could be an advantage.

Tom shrugged his raincoat onto a chair, then went quickly into the middle room and took the union case motion folder from the pile where he had buried it not two hours ago. A weird sense of relief coursed through him, connected with the realization that Carol was no longer an unwitting tool in his scheme.

He brought the folder to the conference table. Using his computer as a shield, he pulled the middle seven pages from the "new" decision and joined them with the original seven pages still under the keyboard. Then he started ripping the lot.

"Hey, what the hell are you doing?" said Elliott.

"Ripping up the old decision," said Tom. "Unless that's the one you want me to file."

Elliott said nothing.

"I know what I'm doing, Jerry. I may not like what I'm doing, but I know what I'm doing."

Elliott pulled a chair out from the conference table and sat opposite Tom.

"You going to sit there?"

"Bobby said to watch you."

"Then don't watch too closely, Jerry. You'll destroy my concentration."

Tom turned to his computer and closed the file he had left open earlier this morning—the middle seven pages of the new decision. He opened a blank document and then asked Carol to send him the version of the decision the judge had signed on New Year's Eve. Carol obeyed without a word, her every movement slow. Finally, an e-mail message popped onto Tom's screen. Tom opened the file attachment and pretended to read the decision through. He pulled a legal pad onto his lap and scribbled notes. After enough time had passed, he stood up with the legal pad under his arm.

"I need to go to the library," he said.

"What for?" said Elliott.

"Legal research."

"Don't you use the computer?" said Elliott.

"I'm old-fashioned. I use books."

"I don't know if I should let you go."

"Bobby wants me to rewrite this decision, and you don't know if you should let me?"

"He said to watch you."

"So watch me," said Tom.

"But I need to watch her, too. I can't do both if you go to the library."

"Then you need to choose," said Tom. "Carol or me."

Elliott took out his cell phone.

"Who are you calling?" asked Tom.

"Bobby."

"You're really going to call Bobby and ask him if you should let me go to the library so I can rewrite his decision? Okay. I'll wait."

Tom sat down and folded his arms across his chest. He flicked a glance at Carol, who stared into space, then back at Elliott, whose finger hovered over the cell phone's keypad.

"Maybe I better not," said Elliott.

"Good choice," said Tom. "Because you know what he would have told you? He would have told you there's no way I'd do anything stupid because we're all in this together."

Tom got up and stepped around the conference table and left chambers.

Elliott clipped the phone back onto his belt.

"Is he always like this?" he asked.

Carol turned toward Elliott, her eyes moist.

Tom stood in the library stacks and browsed through a book, making sure the librarian laid eyes on him. Then he silently exited through the side door. He decided against taking the judges' elevator and instead took the stairs all the way down to the first floor. The stairs landed not far from the coffee shop. It was too much to hope that Moxley would be standing at the counter again, three hours later. And because Tom dared not to hope, he was not disappointed.

Moxley was a lawyer, but also was a schmoozer who prided himself on his back office connections. Tom found him in a tiny room behind the large Motion Part courtroom. Moxley was sitting on a desk, his suit jacket off and his shirtsleeves rolled up to his elbows. Three clerks sat on chairs. They all were laughing about something, and the distinct smell of Scotch hung in the air. One of the clerks spotted Tom first. He stopped laughing, and the others followed until the only person laughing was Moxley.

"Hey, Tom, what's up?" said the clerk.

Tom said nothing, just pointed at Moxley, who by now had stopped laughing as well.

"Me?" said Moxley. He jumped off the desk and slapped down his sleeves. "Hold that thought, guys, I'll be right back."

Tom led Moxley out of the room, through the main office, and into a quiet alcove off the rotunda.

"I want to do business," he said.

Moxley cocked his head and squinted one eye.

"That conversation we had a long time ago." Tom paused to

let Moxley recollect. "You said we might be able to do business some time."

"I remember, Tom. I remember everything. And I remember that you made it clear you weren't interested."

"Times change. Problems crop up."

Moxley cocked his head again, this time adding a smirk to his squint.

"The incorruptible Tom Carroway descends from the rarified air of chambers to cavort with baser men. What kind of problem?"

"Money with consequences."

"Physical consequences?"

Tom nodded.

"How much to avoid these consequences?"

"Ten."

Moxley whistled. "Not a whole lot of things with that kind of value lying around."

"The *Berne* case does."

Moxley tugged at his sleeves, smoothing out the wrinkles.

"We've been waiting a long time for that decision," he said.

"I'm having trouble with it," said Tom. "Your papers focus on the extent of the plaintiff's injuries, which isn't relevant to whether the court should allow you to serve a late notice of claim. You know that."

"Sympathy has its role. What does the judge think?"

"He hasn't expressed any opinion."

"And you can go any way you want."

"It's one of the areas he lets me handle. He'll sign whatever I put before him."

"Ten would be a stretch, even to keep a big case like that in court," said Moxley. "Seven and a half might be closer."

Tom resisted the impulse to snap.

"And I can't give you a definite answer right now. I need to run it by some people."

"I can have it for you today."

"It won't happen so fast."

"Tomorrow?"

"Whoa, Tom. Your problem isn't my emergency."

"But you'll let me know," said Tom. He lifted his hand to shake.

"I will," said Moxley. He turned, leaving Tom's hand to dangle in the air.

"Does he always take this long in the library?" said Elliott.

"Longer," she said. "When he's working on something big, he can spend a whole day doing research."

"Damn." Elliott got up from his chair. He listened for a moment at the door, then cracked it to peek down the corridor in the direction of the library.

"Tom needs to rewrite the whole decision," Carol said when Elliott closed the door. "You think he just changes a word here and there?"

She could see he was not listening and realized that what she was trying to explain was beyond his comprehension. Elliott settled back onto his chair while Carol began deleting old e-mails, something she did when extreme nervousness coincided with idle moments. She wanted Tom to hurry back. More than that, she wanted the Tom who had existed in her mind, the Tom she kissed on Christmas Eve, the Tom who accepted her invitation to New Year's dinner, even the Tom who conceived the plan to get to midnight. It was sad to see how the situation had changed him from an affable, confident person into someone who spoke to Elliott in such a sarcastic, mean-spirited way. A sudden loss of power could change someone, and how quickly and completely Tom had knuckled under to Bobby made her wonder what Bobby had on him. She didn't want to ask, not now, anyway. Because now she just wanted Tom back here without any conditions. She wanted him in command, the way he always was, running the day-to-day business of chambers. Without him, she worried what she might do or what she might say. She worried that if the security desk called, or if a lawyer strolled in with an order to show cause for the judge to sign, she might blurt out, "The judge is dead!"

As if conjured by her thought, the phone rang. Elliott jumped up from his chair.

"Who is it?" he asked.

For a moment, the numbers on the readout looked as tangled as a bowl of spaghetti. Carol blinked, and the numbers realigned themselves into a familiar sequence.

"It's home," she said. "My mother."

Elliott considered this information for another ring, then told her to answer.

"Mom?" said Carol. But it was Nick. "What are you doing home, young man?"

"I had a real bad headache and was feeling hot and cold, so I went to the nurse and she took my temperature and told me I had a fever."

"Slow down, Nick. How did you get home?"

"The nurse called Grandma and Grandma called Mr. Pollio next door and gave him a note that said it was okay for him to pick me up."

"How do you feel now?"

"Still have a headache."

"Did you take anything?"

"No."

"Let me speak to Grandma." Carol could hear the TV audio increase in volume as Nick walked the phone toward the dining room. She wondered how much of the headache was real and how much was a reaction to today's break from their morning routine.

Rose got on the phone, and Carol thanked her for sending the neighbor to pick up Nick, and explained where she kept the medicine and exactly how much to give. Rose said the boy looked all right. He might have been homesick or tuckered out from the holidays.

"Things aren't easy for him," she added.

Carol resisted countering with her usual mantra that things will be even tougher for him later if he doesn't toughen himself now. But instead she just thanked Rose again and hung up. She realized, as she went back to deleting more e-mails, that she had not blurted out that the judge was dead. She had not thought of the judge at all.

CHAPTER 20

Tom burst into chambers. He slapped his legal pad onto the conference table, then plopped himself at his computer, alternately pounding the keys and stabbing the mouse. Elliott looked up over his newspaper.

"Something wrong, Tom?" he asked.

"I need to talk to Bobby."

"Bobby?"

Tom shoved the mouse across the conference table. It fell off the far edge and swung on its cord.

"Yeah, Bobby. I need to talk to him. What part of that don't you understand?"

"Well, gee, Tom, I'm not sure if . . ."

"Are you saying you can't contact him?"

"Only if it's important," said Elliott. He glanced at Carol for support, but could not catch her eye.

"It's about the decision being all fucked up. Is that important enough for you?"

Elliott unhooked his cell phone from his belt. He held it away from him, his lips moving silently as he pressed a button and watched a series of contact numbers scroll up the tiny screen. Tom smiled at Carol, but her eyes quickly slid off his. Something definitely had changed in her, and he was not sure what word precisely described it: docile? disconnected? resigned? He ran back through the morning, trying to recall any possible way she could have learned about his original deal with Bobby. He couldn't think of any.

Elliott handed Tom his cell phone.

"What's so important?" asked Bobby.

"I have a problem with the decision," said Tom.

"Not making it fit?"

"No. Something else."

"And you just see it now?"

Tom tightened the phone to his ear. Bobby was speaking loud, practically yelling, and Tom did not want his words to leak out into the air.

"It's not that easy to take a decision that makes perfect sense and just reverse it," said Tom. "It's not like flipping negatives into positives."

"Well, you're going to need to explain it to me because you said you only needed an hour or two."

"There's this one argument . . ."

"No. Not over the phone. Give me back to Elliott."

Tom handed the phone across the table. As Elliott grunted at Bobby's rapid-fire instructions, Tom caught Carol's eye. He shook his head sadly as if to say, what a mess. Carol shook her head, too. But he could not read what she meant, whether it was her own sadness, or pity, or a smoldering anger.

Bobby told Elliott they were to meet at a restaurant in Chinatown. With Elliott leading, Tom and Carol descended a set of internal stairs to the basement. They met no one along the way and spoke not a word except for Tom's whispered, "I'm sorry," on the landing between the second and third floors. Carol quickly squeezed his hand, and for the moment at least he felt he still had a girlfriend.

They went out the back door, which opened into a narrow courtyard between 60 Centre Street and the federal courthouse. The clouds had rolled in, ending the sun's cameo appearance for the day, and a sharp wind tore between the buildings. As they skirted the basketball courts on Mulberry Street, Tom looked back toward the courthouse. At the front corner of the building, Dominic bounced lightly on his feet.

They crossed Mulberry and climbed a short, uphill street into the heart of Chinatown. The air smelled of fish. Water rushed down the curbside as if oblivious to the sub-freezing temperature. Elliott hooked a sharp right and led them down a steep set of steps to an underground restaurant. A waiter ushered them through the main dining room and into a back room where Bobby Werkman sat in a booth with Vuksanaj. Bobby moved in close to the wall. Vuksanaj slid out of the booth and told Tom to move in opposite Bobby. Carol sat beside Tom, and Elliott sat beside Bobby. Vuksanaj squeezed in next to Carol, his thigh pressed against hers.

"What's this big problem?" asked Bobby. He had changed into a shirt and tie since the funeral home, but already the tie was loosened, the shirt unbuttoned at the neck. One hand squeezed a napkin into a tiny wad.

"The contract allows OCA the option of suspending overtime pay and replacing it with comp time by administrative order," said Tom. "Your lawyers argued that OCA's interpretation of the contract was arbitrary and capricious, therefore the court should annul the administrative order that suspended overtime on January one. OCA made two counterarguments. One, the order was not arbitrary and capricious. Two, overtime pay isn't a vested property right, like a pension. And because overtime pay isn't a property right, OCA can do whatever it wants. The first argument is one of those questions that could go either way. The second isn't, and that's what the judge's decision is based on."

"My lawyers made a property right argument," he said.

"They tried, but they sloughed over it," Tom replied.

"You can slough over it, too," said Bobby.

"No I can't."

"I don't care about a perfect decision. I don't care if the decision gets reversed. The election will be over by then."

"But you need a perfect decision," said Tom. "Think about it. You have a ruling with shoddy reasoning and a judge who turns up dead a day later. You think that's not going to set off any alarms?"

Bobby passed the napkin back and forth between his hands, squeezing it into a tighter and tighter wad. Carol shifted in the booth.

"Can I go to the ladies' room?" she asked.

"Yeah," said Bobby, distracted.

Vuksanaj slowly got out of the booth, giving Carol barely enough room to slide past. He started to follow her, but Bobby called him back.

"She's fine. She's not going anywhere." He turned his attention back to Tom. "My lawyers were going to deal with this in their reply papers."

"Yeah, well, it's a little late for that now."

Bobby tossed the wadded napkin onto the table.

"So why did you call me to talk?"

"Because I can write around this problem, but I need time."

"How much time?"

"An extra day."

"What are you, dicking me around? This went from being finished this morning to being finished this afternoon, and now it's tomorrow."

"Then let's forget about the whole deal. You put the judge back in his apartment. I'll destroy the decision. I'll take my chances on keeping my job, and you take your chances with a new judge. Good luck with that."

Bobby looked at Vuksanaj, who mouthed something Tom could not read.

"And what do I get for this extra day?" Bobby asked.

"You get that perfect decision," said Tom.

Carol truly needed to pee, but that was only the second reason she needed to get out of the booth. The first was her utter disgust at listening to Tom using his fine legal intellect in the service of Bobby Werkman. She turned the corner into the main dining room, which had filled up since they arrived. She spotted the light above the ladies' room door in the back corner of the dining room, but never got there because a hand grabbed her wrist and pulled her into a booth.

"Tired of your company?" asked Foxx.

Carol pried Foxx's fingers off her wrist and straightened herself in the seat. "I'm going to the ladies' room."

"Good. That gives us a couple of minutes before you need to get back."

"What are you doing here?"

"Saw you and Tom and Elliott leaving through the back door," said Foxx. "So I followed."

"Why?"

"You know why. I'm looking for Judge Canter."

"Still?" said Carol.

"Don't snow me, Carol. Something's going on with him, and I think you know."

"I told you this morning. He's all right."

"Then let me tell you what I didn't tell you this morning. We got a call during the night. Someone picked up a noise complaint from Judge Canter's neighbor."

"Court officers get calls about noise complaints now?"

"That's not important. I went to the judge's apartment before seven this morning. The judge wasn't there and he hasn't turned up at the courthouse, either. But you and Tom left chambers this morning. And now you and Tom and Jerry Elliott come here to meet Bobby Werkman. So I get to thinking not only about where the judge is, but what's going on behind his back."

"There's nothing going on," said Carol.

She started to get up, but Foxx grabbed her wrist again. She shook him off and got out of the booth. And then she sat back down.

"He's dead," she said. "He died two days ago in chambers. Tom said if we could make it look like he died on New Year's Day we could keep our jobs for a year. So we brought him to his apartment and stayed till midnight. This morning, we were going to report that we couldn't reach him, but then Jerry came in and pulled a gun on us and took us to a funeral home in Queens. Bobby Werkman stole the judge's body and he's forcing Tom to rewrite the decision in his case. Tom's been working on it, but he's having problems. That's what they're talking about."

Foxx looked at his watch. Carol's story didn't explain the two versions of the decision he saw earlier in the morning.

"Who's the guy with the spiked hair?" he said.

"Name is Vuksanaj. He's a real creep."

"You need to get back," he said. "Don't tell anyone that we spoke. Not even Tom."

"What do I do?"

"Nothing till you hear from me."

Foxx stayed in the booth as Carol went into the ladies' room. A few seconds later, Vuksanaj planted himself in front of the ladies' room door. When Carol came out, he took her by the elbow. Foxx lifted a menu in front of his face as they passed.

Carol sat back down next to Tom, and Vuksanaj shoved in beside her. The booth was silent, as if everyone was all talked out and they were waiting for her to return. Bobby slouched in the corner, one arm thrown over the back of the bench seat. The napkin he had crushed into a tight wad was now broken apart. Little gray spirals littered the table.

"We have a problem," said Bobby. "Tom has a solution, but it will take some time to put it together. That means the judge's death needs to stay a secret for another day. It also means that you all will be spending the night together at Tom's apartment."

"I can't do that," said Carol. "My son's sick."

"I'm sorry," said Bobby. "But neither of you leave my sight until the decision is filed."

"Do you think I care enough about your decision that I would tell anyone?"

"That's not a gamble I'm going to take."

"I'm not staying," said Carol. "I'm going home."

Bobby lifted his arm off the back of the bench seat and leaned forward.

"I understand how important your family is to you, which is why I know you'll stay at Tom's apartment." Bobby arched his eyebrows suggestively. "Now get out of here. Tom needs to work, or we'll be here two days."

CHAPTER 21

This was turning out to be one long-ass day for Dominic. Cold and boring, too. He figured he would catch Carroway early and either separate him from his money or his jaw from his skull. But here it was, afternoon—after*noon* for chrissake—and he still was camped out in front of the courthouse.

He crossed the street and sat on a bench that faced straight up the courthouse steps and through the columns to the revolving door. He thought about the story Carroway had told him, the briefcase full of papers as worthless as Monopoly money, the real grand rolled up and stuffed into one of the pockets inside his jacket. He knew something was up when he was counting that money and the hundreds dropped off to twenties too quick. He should have slugged Carroway right then instead of giving him the chance to run his mouth. These lawyers, they all thought they could talk their way to the truth no matter how many lies they told. That was another thing he believed, just as true as the watched pot that never boiled.

And what the hell was Carroway up to today anyway? He was supposed to be a law clerk for some judge, but he was spending more time out of the courthouse than in it. The trip in the black car, and then the walk to Chinatown. Was that big dumpy guy some kind of bodyguard? He doubted it, and he was a poor excuse for one anyway. That good-looking head must be Carroway's squeeze, which opened up a range of possibilities once he got to Carroway. Maybe he'd take out some of Carroway's debt in trade. Maybe he'd make Carroway watch.

He sat for a while. He wasn't cold yet but he felt he was on the verge of cold, and if it got under his jacket he would just feel colder and colder. He stood up and bounced on his feet for a while. The bench was right at the edge of a park, where the dead brown grass ended and the cold gray paving stones began. There were some weird-looking, twisted bushes running along the perimeter. In the frozen ground, among the gnarled roots, there were dark holes. And popping out of one of the holes and running across the roots to dive into another hole was a rat. Dominic shivered like a goose just walked over his grave.

He walked to the gyro cart at the corner. The guy inside didn't look Greek, whatever a Greek looked like. He looked A-rab. They were all A-rabs in these carts these days. If there were carts selling corned beef and cabbage on Fifth Avenue on St. Patrick's Day, there would be A-rabs inside them. At the moment, he couldn't give two shits. He was hungry and that shiver from seeing the rat had let some cold air under his jacket. A gyro would beat it back.

He paid the A-rab in the cart and brought the gyro back to the bench. He wanted to keep one eye on the revolving door of the courthouse, but instead he kept looking over his shoulder at the rat hole. Another shiver rattled his body. Back in the day, when he was the Gramercy Glider, he wasn't afraid of nothing. Ten, twenty rats running around these ugly-ass bushes wouldn't have fazed him. But he wasn't the Gramercy Glider anymore. He was Dominic, a has-been boxer working for a midlevel loan shark. And rats were still rats.

The gyro meat was full of gristle. He got up from the bench and walked to the closest rat hole and opened the pita. The meat hit the hard dirt and steamed in the cold. He went back to the bench and rolled the pita tight as a cigar and tore off a huge damp mouthful. Up the courthouse steps, the revolving door spit out several people who weren't Carroway. Over his shoulder, something gray and sleek dragged the meat into a hole.

He stuffed the last of the pita into his mouth and chewed. Here he was, freezing on a bench in Foley Square and feeding the rats. Carroway would pay for this, too.

Inside chambers, Tom stacked several small piles of papers and books into two large piles. Elliott, seated on the other side of the conference table, looked up.

"What the hell are you doing?" he said.

"I'm moving into the judge's office," said Tom. "I need to concentrate."

He transferred the piles in two trips, placing one on each side of the judge's blotter. Then he went back to the outer office.

"I'm going to close the door," he said. "Anyone calls, the judge does not want to be disturbed. Anyone insists on talking to him, transfer the call to me. Anyone insists on seeing him, I'll handle it."

"I think that covers every possible scenario," said Elliott. He smiled at Carol, who did not smile back.

Tom closed the door, wedging it tightly enough into the frame that it would not pop open. When he turned around, the sight of the judge's huge desk filled him with awe. Over the years, he and the judge had held hundreds of discussions over that desk. Their relative positions always had been the same— Tom on this side and the judge on that side—to the point where Tom began to associate the other side of the desk with judicial power. In his glib moments, Tom would joke that the judge, like Superman, had powers and abilities far beyond those of mortal men. He wasn't completely joking, though. A judge, like a priest, was invested with the power to transubstantiate a piece of paper into an order people disobeyed at their peril.

Tom walked to the side of the desk, paused a moment, and then stepped behind it. Thunder did not rumble across the sky. The lights did not flicker. The columns on the front portico did not crumble. He sat in the judge's big soft catcher's mitt of a chair and bellied up to the desk. He spread his hands on the blotter, feeling the slightly fuzzy texture in each of his finger-tips. He took a deep breath, trying to invest himself with the will to do what he needed to do. For a brief moment he sensed a presence, not just a ghost or a memory but a physical presence complete with Canter's distinctive odor. He turned the chair around, looked up at the shelves of green-bound state reporters looming above him. And then the presence vanished.

"Wow," he breathed. "What the hell was that?"

"I need to call my mother," said Carol.

"Didn't you just talk to her?"

"Like about two hours ago. And that was about my son, not about me not coming home tonight."

"Hey, don't look at me," said Elliott. "Not my idea."

"You're the only one I can look at," said Carol. "Unfortu-nately."

"All right, all right. Call her."

Carol punched the number on her desk phone and leaned back so her monitor blocked Elliott's face.

"How's Nick?" she asked when Rose answered.

"He took some medicine," said Rose. "He's on the bed with me, sleeping. He feels cool."

"Good. Don't you get sick, too."

"I won't," said Rose.

"Ma, I got some bad news. I won't be home tonight."

"Why not?"

"The judge is still working on that big case. I need to be here so late I might as well stay over. You don't mind, right?"

"Like those other nights?" asked Rose.

"Ma, the other night was New Year's Eve. I came home. I just came home late."

"No, I mean *those* other nights. A while ago."

Those nights, thought Carol. She remembers nothing else I tell her, but she remembers those nights?

"Ma . . ."

"I don't know what it is with him. How he can make you do those things."

"I'll talk to you later, Ma," Carol said.

After Carol ended her call, a quiet descended on chambers. Tom worked silently behind the door to the judge's office. Carol leafed through the *Law Journal,* pretending to skim the articles and court notices. Elliott pushed back his chair and looked again at the crossword puzzle. January second was not much different from December thirty-first. The courthouse was quiet and virtually empty, with officers, clerks, even judges taking an extra day off.

Elliott filled five spaces in the puzzle, then quickly erased three he figured to be wrong. He tossed the paper onto the conference table, glanced once at Carol, then closed his eyes. That buzz from the lights was annoying at first, but now felt comfortable, like white noise to help him sleep. And sleep wasn't a bad idea, figuring tonight would be a long one. He wasn't sure what pleased him more, Bobby's confidence in him or the prospect of babysitting Carol.

After an hour of uninterrupted work, Tom heard a faint knock on the door and looked up to see Carol peeking in. At first he thought someone must have asked to see the judge, and he was too deep in his concentration to have heard. But if someone had come to chambers, he would have heard voices. So, no, there was no one asking for the judge. This was Carol wanting to see him.

"Can I come in?" she asked.

"Of course," said Tom.

"How's it going?" She used her hip to insinuate herself between two chairs on her side of the desk.

"It's going," said Tom.

"I was wondering if you could finish today."

"No. It's just too complicated."

He riffled OCA's opposition papers, which were over an inch thick. Carol was silent.

"Sorry," he said. "This should have been so simple. Get to midnight. Save our jobs."

"Live happily ever after," she said.

"That, too," he said. "Things sure have hopped the tracks."

"We'll get out of this. Somehow."

"Somehow," said Tom. "That's the same as saying the devil is in the details."

Carol smiled. It was an odd smile, at once indulgent and knowing.

"Sorry," said Tom. "I should have asked. How's Nick?"

"He's fine. A twenty-four-hour bug, or just fatigue. Nothing serious."

"I always hated the first day back at school after a vacation," said Tom. "Are you okay?"

"Distraction is my normal state. A piece of me always is somewhere else."

Tom glanced past Carol and through the avenue of doors that connected the three rooms. Elliott watched them from his chair.

"Not the other night," Tom said, his voice low.

"That's what I liked about it," said Carol.

"But tonight?" asked Tom. He remembered Carol's insistence about getting home on New Year's Eve.

"They'll need to survive on their own," said Carol. She left the office, closing the door behind her. Tom exhaled deeply, realizing only then how tense he had been. He rearranged the papers on the blotter and returned to writing the *Berne* decision.

Elliott always had seemed like such a harmless dope to Carol, which only served to make this morning's kidnapping more surreal. Now, listening to his involuntary grunts as he leaned forward to rub his arches, she wondered what he knew about her. She threw him a glance, catching the tail end of a hard stare before he quickly refocused on his feet.

"Why are you involved in this?" she asked.

"Bobby's my union president. He asked me to help."

"He's the union president for hundreds of court officers. Why did he ask you?"

Elliott stopped rubbing. His eyes drifted away from her, then back.

"We worked together a long time ago in Westchester Supreme. He was a new kid, and I was part captain in the criminal court. I showed him the ropes."

"He doesn't have anything on you?"

"Anything like what?"

"Something to force you to help him," said Carol.

"Oh no. Nothing like that. He knows I'm loyal. He knows I'd go to the mats to help him."

"Did he tell you about me?" asked Carol.

"You?"

"And Tom, and the judge. He says he knows lots of things about people who work in the court system and that must be partly true. He figured out the judge was dead, right? So he must know things."

"Well," said Elliott. "He called me yesterday afternoon. Told me he needed my help. Didn't tell me anything else till this morning."

"So he knew as early as yesterday afternoon," said Carol. She thought about what she had been doing at the time: fixing dinner, glancing out the window at Nick and Foxx in the backyard, waiting for Tom to show up. She had been nervous, fearing that Tom might turn into an uncooperative dream character and simply not appear.

"Vuksanaj is his director of security. He has ways of finding things out about judges."

"He snoops?" asked Carol.

"I don't know if snoops is the right word," said Elliott. "But I heard he keeps this loose-leaf binder full of information. Keeps it even from Bobby. He calls it The Book of Judges."

"What kind of information?"

"Mostly public information. But some private and some confidential."

"Does it have information about a judge's staff?"

"I guess it would," said Elliott, "if there was a connection."

"Like a picture?"

Elliott shrugged.

"Did Vuksanaj have any information about me?" Carol said, then added quickly, "Or Tom?"

"I can't say."

"Oh, come on, Jerry. You keep saying you can't say anything. But you know, right?"

"I can't say now," he said. "Maybe when this is over you and I can have a beer."

"Really?" said Carol. "You think that when this is over I'd even consider having a beer with you?"

Foxx stood among the columns at the north end of the courthouse portico. Only one other smoker braved the cold, a clerk who stamped his feet as he sucked down his cigarette to the filter. Foxx took a slow drag. He was down to six a day, and he spaced out his drags as if each one would be his last. One day, he would take that last drag, though that day was still far off in the hazy future.

Foxx peeked out from behind a column. Across Centre Street, that pug still sat on a bench. Foxx had noticed him at the fountain early this morning, when Canter was the only player he had on his mind. He had checked the exterior at odd intervals, seeing him sometimes on this side of Centre Street, sometimes on the other, more than once in the tiny park where he had punched Tom on New Year's Eve. He had been standing on the same bench, staring balefully, Foxx imagined, as Tom, Carol, and Elliott returned from meeting Bobby Werkman in Chinatown. Whatever business he had with Tom, he wasn't letting go.

Something buzzed in Foxx's belly. His cell phone, he finally realized. As long as had been carrying the phone, he still mistook its vibration for a stomach growl. He confirmed the call was from Bev, then dropped the phone back into his pocket.

Down below, the pug got up and shook out his legs one at a time. He lifted one foot and then the other onto the back of the bench to stretch each hamstring. Foxx flicked his cigarette over the side of the abutment, watching it arc slowly to the pavement below. His stomach growled, a real one this time, but he pulled out his cell phone anyway. He had one new voice mail.

He listened. It was Bev's voice saying she was about to go into a meeting and wanted to know whether he had located Judge Canter. Foxx grinned at the fortunate turn of phrase. He waited five minutes to make sure Bev was into her meeting, then called back. Her phone immediately kicked into voice mail.

"I've located Judge Canter," was all he said.

CHAPTER 22

The phone rang shortly after four, and a moment later, the judge's intercom buzzed.

"There's someone named Derek Moxley at the desk to see you," said Carol. "Should I say you're too busy?"

"Better that I go out," said Tom. He gathered several yellow pages into a pile and went through the middle room and into the outer office.

"Derek Moxley, you said?" he asked Carol.

"Big muckety-muck," piped Elliott.

Tom scowled. "Any idea what he wants?"

"Didn't say," said Carol.

Tom paused, waiting for Elliott to say something else. But Elliott slouched in his chair and said not another word. Got him trained, thought Tom.

At the security desk, Moxley ignored Tom except for the briefest glance. He was in the middle of telling a story to the court officer, who seemed not only entertained but thrilled that someone with Moxley's courthouse stature would pay attention to her. Tom backed away. He grinned indulgently—Moxley's story actually was an elaborate joke delivered with the timing and polish of an after-dinner speaker—but inwardly he churned. He had reached a critical point in writing the *Berne* decision, and he hoped this interruption bore him good news.

"Ah, Mr. Carroway," Moxley said, then turned to the officer and bowed with a flourish. "A pleasure, ma'am."

The officer giggled.

Tom followed Moxley through the tiny foyer and into the circular corridor. Above the bare radiators, large windows looked out into the empty space over the rotunda. Dark snow swirled out of the flat gray sky.

"I conveyed your offer, just as any good lawyer would," said Moxley. "But I stopped short of a recommendation because the fact is, Tom, I don't know you enough to place a client's case in your trust."

"It's already in my trust," said Tom.

"True. But you are also asking for the client's money. Because ultimately, Tom, no matter how we carry this expense on our books, the client pays."

"I can do this," said Tom.

"I know you can write the decision," said Moxley. "But will the judge sign it?"

"He listens to me."

"You told me. But my firm is not one of his favorites."

"He'll sign it," said Tom.

"Which brings me to my next point," said Moxley. "No one has seen the judge today. Is all well with him?"

"He's fine," said Tom. "He wasn't sent a trial, so he's been working in chambers."

Moxley turned toward the window. The snow swirled heavier now, and Tom felt himself swirling, too, as if the circular corridor was an amusement park ride that started to spin before he belted himself into his seat. This deal with Moxley was his last chance to save himself, and it was about to fly off. He gripped the windowsill, trying to bring the ride to a halt. Could he say something? Should he say something? Could he somehow divine the element of Moxley's doubt and explain it away? He started to speak, but stopped. Speaking now only would reveal weakness and need, and Moxley would distrust the weak and the needy.

"Seven and a half," said Moxley. "Tomorrow. No renegotiating. I'm just the messenger, and a reluctant one, so don't press your luck."

Tom gripped the windowsill harder to prevent himself from fainting dead away with relief.

At four thirty, Foxx was in the locker room, changing out of uniform and into civilian clothes. At the far end of the row of lockers, several officers talked as they changed.

"Was Elliott out today?"

"Nah, I saw him early at the mags."

"Poor guy's taking this overtime thing hard."

"You would, too, if you had a wife like his. She's crazy with credit cards."

"So's my wife."

"You ever declare bankruptcy? Because Elliott did."

There were groans of disbelief all around.

Foxx zipped up his jacket and slipped around the lockers to the door.

"Any word on the union's lawsuit?"

"We got a guy in the Motion Office. He'll get the word out soon as the decision's filed."

Foxx climbed the stairs to the rotunda, headed out through the main door, and made a quick left for the south side of the colonnade, away from the huge, lantern-shaped chandelier that hung from a thick iron chain. The snow had stopped, leaving just enough of a coating on the frigid pavement to brighten Foley Square.

Down below the courthouse steps, foot traffic swelled into rush hour. Foxx leaned his shoulder against a column and remembered that he had smoked only two of the six cigarettes he allotted for the day. He lit up, lifted a foot onto the base of the column, and took a long drag as he watched the pug circle to the back side of the fountain.

They came out at five fifteen, after the tide of departing workers had ebbed. They were all together, Tom and Carol side by side with Elliott a step behind, his head pitched forward as if butting into their conversation. Tom carried a briefcase; Carol, her purse; Elliott, a duffle bag.

Foxx started down the steps as the trio crossed Centre Street. Tom lived on the West Side, Carol went up the East Side to Grand Central, and Elliott lived in Queens, which meant that only Carol would split off at the first subway entrance. But as Foxx reached the bottom of the steps, Carol stayed tight against Tom while Elliott steered them both across Foley Square and past the Federal Building. Foxx hurried, then settled in about thirty yards behind them. The pug crossed in between and followed on their right flank. If he noticed Foxx, he did not give any sign.

Foxx never had tailed anyone. He figured he needed to give

his quarries some space and keep them in sight, easy tasks on a crowded sidewalk. It also helped that, by deductive reasoning, he figured their destination now must be Tom's apartment. The pug followed much closer, apparently not caring if Tom spotted him and just as apparently not intending to make contact. After three long blocks, they descended into a subway station at the corner of West Broadway. Foxx crossed the street toward a different set of stairs. He boarded the same uptown train, one car behind, the four of them visible through the connecting doors. Tom, who sat beside Carol while Elliott loomed over them, studiously did not look at the pug. They got off at Seventy-second Street. Tom, Carol, and Elliott formed up as before. The pug followed twenty paces behind, and Foxx another thirty paces behind him.

Tom's apartment was a three block walk on Seventy-fifth Street. Foxx set up across the street where a minivan and a tree gave him cover. Tom, Carol, and Elliott went inside. The pug followed as far as the glass entry door. Then he pulled out a cell phone and stabbed in a number.

Tom actually had spotted Dominic sallying out from behind the fountain as they crossed Foley Square. He resisted a second glance, bracing himself for an attack. But the attack never came, and, when he next looked back, he saw that Dominic had settled in to pace them about twenty yards behind. They locked eyes twice from opposite ends of the subway car, and each time Dominic had mugged a curiously nonthreatening expression. Yet Dominic's presence alone was a threat, and coming up out of the subway station and for the walk to his apartment, Tom knew that Dominic was still on his tail.

Tom opened the door and led the others inside. There was

a small foyer with a mirrored coatrack hanging from the wall and a small table with a pewter dish labeled KEYS. Tom dropped his keys into the dish, then headed quickly into the living room. He looked down at the street, then tightened each of the three window blinds. Carol set her purse on the coffee table and settled lightly on the couch.

The phone rang.

"You going to answer that?" asked Elliott.

Tom picked up the phone slowly. He already knew who was calling.

"Hey, asshole, look out your window," said Dominic.

"Who is it?" Elliott demanded.

Tom cupped the phone.

"Someone tailed us. He's on the street. Wants me to look out."

Tom started toward the window, but Elliott stopped him.

"Who is he?" Elliott asked, parting the blinds.

"Guy I owe money."

"Him?" said Carol.

"What does he want?" asked Elliott.

Tom uncupped the phone. "What do you want?"

"I need to talk to you," said Dominic.

Tom cupped the phone again and told Elliott.

"Tell him you're busy," said Elliott.

"I'm busy," Tom said into the phone.

"You get your ass down here or I'm coming up."

Again, Tom cupped the phone and told Elliott.

"Who is he?" asked Elliott.

Tom started to answer, but Carol cut in.

"He's a client who's mad at Tom about a dumb deal that went bad."

"He won't go away," said Tom.

Elliott took one more look out the window, then let go of the blind.

"We both go down," he said. "You go out and talk. I'll stay in sight. And you," he turned to Carol. "You stay here."

Carol nodded. For the moment, she was glad anyone was here. Even Elliott.

Tom and Elliott took the stairs to the lobby. Tom went outside, while Elliott stood just inside the door and watched through the glass.

"Did you settle your guests in?" said Dominic. He took a step toward Tom, and Tom stepped back to stay out of range.

"Yeah," said Tom, his eye on Dominic's right hand. "What do you want?"

"I wanted to tell you I collected from all those other sorry mutts today," said Dominic. "All except one."

"Me?"

"Besides you. You can read about him in the newspaper tomorrow. But the boss's giving you extra time."

"You already told me," said Tom. "But thanks."

"Don't thank me. He bought your sorry-ass story about paying him off by selling a decision."

"He understands my situation?"

"Nah. He just likes the idea of corruption in the courts. But he needs to know where things stand."

Quickly, Tom explained how one deal fell through but that he found a second deal that would pay off his debt in full.

"So why the entourage tonight?" asked Dominic.

"That's part of the first deal. That guy inside, he's here to make sure I get it done. And the secretary . . ." Tom did not want to refer to Carol by name . . . "She's caught up in this mess."

"Too bad for that," said Dominic. "So you're writing two decisions?"

"Nobody knows about the second, except for you. One is done, the second is close."

"And how do I know this second guy isn't going to snake you out, too?"

"He's a reputable lawyer with lots of money at stake," said Tom.

"A reputable lawyer. What's that like, the winner of an acid fight?"

Tom laughed nervously, worried that Moxley might not be as reputable as he needed him to be.

"You remember," said Dominic, "tomorrow at eleven is the end of the yo-yo."

"I know," said Tom.

Dominic turned to walk away, then pivoted on his toes and hit Tom in the gut with a left jab. Tom wobbled, but stayed on his feet, sucking air and listening to Dominic laugh as he walked away. He took one more deep breath and stumbled back into the lobby.

"Did he punch you?" asked Elliott.

Tom nodded. "Let's wait here a few minutes. I don't want Carol to know."

The bar was six blocks uptown on Broadway. Through the windows, Foxx checked out a crowd that was thick enough to give good cover. The door opened, and a big guy in boots and bike leather came out on a gust of heavy metal music.

Foxx caught the door before it shut and curled toward the opposite corner from where Dominic sat, his cap off, his elbows on the bar, his fists pressed against his jaw. The bartender set a shot glass and a beer mug in front of him. Dominic tilted his head downward, gazing at the drinks. A line of people pushed past, obstructing Foxx's view. When they cleared, the shot glass and beer mug were empty. Dominic slid off the stool, leaving his cap on the bar, and swam against the current of people toward the back. Foxx followed.

The men's room was at the far end of a long, dimly lit corridor. A cold draft carrying the strong odor of disinfectant blew out of the ladies' room door. Two guys came out of the men's room. Dominic pushed between them, not giving up any space, not even turning his shoulders. Foxx waited thirty seconds after the door to the men's room closed. He wanted Dominic alone and engaged.

Dominic leaned into a urinal, his hips thrust forward, his head thrown back, his eyes hooded. He pissed dreamily, swaying back and forth. His bare head was not quite shaved, but cut close enough to expose several dents in his scalp, like divots in a fairway.

Foxx quickly noted the three empty stalls and the two empty urinals. He eased the door shut, sealing out the bar noise, and twisted the lock. Dominic's stream thundered. He stopped swaying, rocked his head back and forth on his wide, bulging neck, shook himself off.

Foxx chopped his forearm against the back of Dominic's neck, slamming his forehead into the flush pipes. Dominic tried to twist free, but Foxx jammed his pistol into the flesh under his jawbone.

"What's up with you and Tom Carroway?"

"Don't know no Tom Carroway."

Foxx screwed the pistol deeper into Dominic's neck.

"You want to think that over?"

"Why you interested in Carroway?"

"I have my reasons," said Foxx. "Put your hands behind your back."

Dominic did, slowly. Foxx, using one hand, cuffed him, then frisked him. He found a wallet, looked through it, and shoved it back into a pocket.

"This a stickup?"

"No."

"Then whaddaya want?"

"I want to know about Carroway."

"That's none of your goddam business."

Foxx yanked the cuffs upward.

"Hey. Shit. You're breaking my goddam shoulders."

"Not yet I'm not."

Foxx yanked the cuffs higher.

"Oww. Shit. Stop that."

"I will when you tell me."

"Okay. Okay. I'll tell you."

Foxx let go of the cuffs. Dominic leaned against the wall, his face taking all the weight until Foxx straightened him up.

"My boss is in the private loan business," said Dominic. "Carroway's supposed to pay up. I'm supposed to collect."

"How much?"

"Eight grand. He paid me one this morning. Told me he'd have another four by ten o'clock. Asked me if the boss would wait a couple of days on the other three. The boss went for it."

"Hasn't been a couple of days since this morning."

"Yeah, well, he didn't come up with the four."

"Why not?"

"He showed me a briefcase full of papers. Said it was a court decision. He works for a judge, but said someone was paying him to write the decision."

"He say who?" said Foxx.

"No."

"So if your boss is giving him a couple of days, why did you tail him from the courthouse?"

"I don't like getting jerked around, and I think he's jerkin' me and the boss around. I wanted him to know I'm onto him."

"And?"

"He says one deal fell through, but now he got a different deal with someone else."

"Did he say who?"

"No."

Foxx stood there, thinking about who the first guy and the second guy might be.

"Hey," said Dominic. "That's everything I know."

Foxx dragged the pistol around Dominic's neck and down his back to the center of his spine.

"Move to your left, slowly," he said.

Dominic shuffled sideways, his face to the wall until Foxx could reach the doorknob.

"Stop right there," said Foxx.

"What about the cuffs?" asked Dominic.

But Foxx did not answer. He unlocked the door and slipped outside. Dominic had not laid eyes on him, and Foxx knew he would not follow. His dick was still dangling from his fly.

CHAPTER 23

They had Mexican delivery at Elliott's insistence, and after dinner they each repaired to separate corners: Elliott to the living room, Carol to the bedroom, and Tom to the dining area. Elliott settled into an easy chair and took off his shoes. Carol closed the door and sat on the edge of the bed. Tom opened his laptop and pulled the papers out of his briefcase.

Elliott turned on the television and immediately ran the volume down to zero. Then he channel-surfed till he found a Clint Eastwood Dirty Harry movie. He knew the dialog by heart.

"This okay?" he called to Tom.

"Just as long as the sound is off."

Elliott settled in to watch. The night reminded him of the nights he spent home while Denise went out with her friends. He would put the kids to bed, then sit in a chair and watch television with the sound turned down, his belt loosened and one hand tucked into the waistband of his boxers. They really hadn't been able to afford her going out once a week, not on his salary and with her refusing to work. But she felt she deserved one night out a week for all the time she spent home with the kids, and if he wouldn't take her out she would go out herself. When she eventually tipped her way back into the apartment, the odds were even money they would fight or fuck.

Now the kids were grown and gone, one in Boston, the other in Philly. They rarely visited, rarely called. Denise still went out with her friends, and now when she came home they neither fought nor fucked.

Elliott went into the bathroom and sat down on the toilet lid and called home. He thought she would be out and that he would leave a message on their machine, but she answered and sounded bored.

"I won't be home tonight," he said. "I'm working."

"I thought you said overtime was over," said Denise. "That's all you've been harping about."

"I'm kinda like moonlighting tonight."

"You got another job? The laziest man in the world?"

"This is a big job, and when it's done, overtime will be back."

"Oh yeah," said Denise. "Tell me about it. You always think some big payoff's coming."

"This time it's different," said Elliott.

"Right. Just like all the other times."

Elliott cut the call without saying good-bye and went back into the living room and switched from Dirty Harry to undersea footage about sharks. He watched the sharks until his cell phone rang.

"Yeah, Bobby," he answered. "Hold on."

He hauled himself out of the chair and hurried into the bathroom.

"How's it going there?" asked Bobby.

"Quiet. Carroway's working on his laptop, Carol's in the bedroom keeping to herself."

"Good. Carroway say how the decision's coming?"

"Not to me. And I stopped asking. He won't give me a straight answer." Elliott paused a moment. "Bobby, I want to ask you. You got me involved in this, and I'm happy to help you. I really am. But you never told me exactly what's in it for me."

"Jerry, I involved you because we go back a long way and you're one of the few officers I can trust completely. You are getting overtime back."

"But what if this decision gets reversed? Where am I then?"

"What do you want, Jerry?"

"I want out of the courthouse. I want a job with you at the union."

"We'll need to talk about that some time."

"Tomorrow."

"Not tomorrow. But next week, okay?"

"Yeah," said Elliott. "Next week."

"I'll call you in the morning with final instructions."

They rang off, and Elliott returned to the TV. He ran back through the channels to the Dirty Harry movie again. Harry loomed on an overpass as a bus full of hostage school children curved into sight and the maniac on board fell into a panic. Elliott liked this scene; it was one of his favorites in all the movies he ever had seen. But he couldn't concentrate. His head was a jumble of voices. Not just Bobby's, but Denise's, too, squeaking like a rusty axle in his head.

Carol quietly cracked the door and pressed her eye to the slit. Elliott still sat in front of the TV with his head bent to his chest.

He had twice gone into the bathroom and spoken on the phone, brief conversations that came to her in gruff mumblings separated by short lengths of silence. The last had been two hours ago. She had been uncomfortable with him in chambers, but now had to admit that her worries were misplaced. He had kept his distance from her.

She eased the door shut. It was after ten, close to her usual bedtime. She stripped down to her panties and rummaged through Tom's dresser drawers, finding an oversized Pace Law tee shirt and a pair of boxers. She lay on Tom's bed.

She had experience to draw on, not like when she was young and naïve. She had made mistakes, seen other people make mistakes, too, and one thing she had learned was that most mistakes were errors of omission: the words you didn't say, the hot iron you didn't strike, the bull you didn't take by the horns.

There had been a time, she remembered, when she first suspected that He was having an affair with his secretary. Looking back, she remembered one particular Friday night in winter when she was four months pregnant and they sat, as they often did, eating dinner on snack tables facing the TV. She almost brought it up, almost demanded, "Who is she?" But she refrained. She thought the time wasn't right, she thought her suspicions could be wrong, she thought that she would come across as paranoid, as if the pregnancy drained the good sense from her head. She assumed there would be another time, a better time with more evidence and less paranoia. There never was, and, thinking back, she wondered whether the outcome would have been different if she had voiced her suspicions that night. Not that she wanted a different outcome. Not now.

*   *   *

A big guy with the look of a college jock turned stockbroker banged into the men's room. He took three long strides to the urinal, then did a double-take at the little man backed up to the sink. The little man's dick was out of his pants and his hands were locked behind him.

"Hey, little man," said the big guy, "what's the problem?"

"No problem," said Dominic.

The big guy looked over Dominic's shoulder. He could see handcuffs in the paint-stained mirror.

"Who the hell did that to you?" The big guy spun Dominic around and then started laughing. "These are fuckin' toys."

"Are you shittin' me?"

"Hold still."

Something snapped, and Dominic could move again. He lifted his wrists in front of his eyes and he could see that the handcuffs were toys. He opened the jaws and let them drop to the floor. He felt like an asshole.

"You should find little friends who play nice," the big guy said as he bellied up to a urinal.

Dominic packed his dick into his pants. Back in the day, when he was the Gramercy Glider, he developed a technique for fighting taller men that he called the jump punch. He used the jump punch now. Landed it right on the big guy's jaw. Dropped him on the wet rubber mat below the urinals. Dusted his hands as he walked out.

By ten-thirty, Tom was just a few paragraphs away from finishing the *Berne* decision. Had he been an impartial law clerk, applying the law to the facts of the case, he would have denied the Berne family's application for permission to serve a late notice of claim. Tragic as this case was, the law was not in their favor. But spinning this decision in the opposite direction had been easier than recasting the union decision, and the result, in terms of legal reasoning, was less of a stretch.

Carol came out of the bedroom. She tilted her head against her hand to signal that Elliott was asleep, then padded across the living room. Tom clicked the mouse, replacing the *Berne* case with the union's as Carol ran her hand along his shoulder. She had changed into an old Pace Law tee shirt and a pair of boxers, a combination that looked sexy on her. She knelt beside him, her hand caressing his neck. One breast, loose under the *P*, bumped his elbow. Her thighs pressed together, sparking a particular memory from New Year's Eve at the judge's apartment and immediately making him hard in his pants.

"How's it going?" she whispered.

"Almost done."

"Can we talk? Soon?"

"Sure. About?"

"Something."

"I'm at a sensitive part. Ten minutes?"

Carol stood up. She trailed her hand back across the same shoulder and went into the bedroom, not quite closing the door behind her.

Tom finished the *Berne* decision within those ten minutes, then took another five to proofread and make corrections. Twice in those five minutes, Carol's shadow crossed the band of light leaking out through the slit in the door. Then the mattress creaked and the light dimmed but did not completely darken.

He was done. Both decisions in the can. He linked them into a single file and saved them to his flash drive. It was then, with his brimming sense of accomplishment, that his thoughts turned completely to Carol. He thought of her lying on his bed, his boxers riding up her thighs, her breasts firm beneath his tee shirt. He got up and went into the bedroom.

Carol was not lying seductively on the bed. She sat on the edge, her bare feet pigeon-toed on the floor.

"Hey, doll," Tom said, and settled beside her. He nuzzled her cheek and pinched the tee shirt, but she stopped him before he struck flesh.

"We need to talk," she said.

Tom nuzzled her cheek again, rubbed a finger inside the curl of her hand. When she did not respond, he pulled away.

"What do you want to talk about?" he asked, trying to keep a sigh from creeping into his voice.

"Have you noticed anything different about me today?" she asked.

"It's been a strange day. Stranger than we expected, even though we knew it would be strange."

"There's something else."

"Something besides all this?"

Carol nodded. "Something I never wanted you to know."

About seven years earlier, before Tom came on board, the judge asked Carol to accompany him to his fortieth high school reunion. Not as his secretary, not as a casual date, but as his girlfriend. His classmates remembered him as this skinny, whip-smart nerd, and he wanted to show them he turned out all right.

The plan seemed innocent enough, and, after all, he and she were more than just boss and secretary. He was her mentor, benefactor, academic advisor. She was his student, so to speak, but more importantly, she was someone who listened to him because of who he was, not because of the robe he wore.

The reunion was fun, the reactions Alvin Canter and his young girlfriend elicited were a mix of admiration, amazement, and surprise. The judge drove her home in his Buick. It was way past midnight, cold and clear. They sat in her driveway with the car running and the heat pumping. The windows in Carol's house were dark except for the flickering night light in Nick's bedroom.

He thanked her. She clutched her purse, leaned over and kissed his cheek, started to back out of the door when he closed his hand over her wrist.

He had a confession, he told her.

She settled down, and even though he released her wrist, even though the reunion had been fun, she felt the night take a sinister turn. The confession was simple: he had feelings for her that he should not have but could not deny. He refused to admit that he was in love, though they both understood that was what he meant. He was embarrassed, he hastened to add. He always had prided himself on his control, his balance. And now he felt he was out of control, out of balance. He pleaded with her, not for her love, which he morosely assumed she would not give, but for her understanding.

Carol, when she finally got to bed, slept hardly at all. Her boss, the most important man in her life, had fallen for her. Now what was she going to do?

Monday morning came, and the judge walked in. Carol tried to read him in the few seconds it took him to round her desk and head into his office. She had spent a sleepless Sunday night as well and still had reached no conclusion on what to do. But she consciously had dressed differently today, selecting a skirt that showed off the curve of her butt and heels that sculpted her legs.

She heard the rattle of the coat hangers as he hung up his coat, the squeak of his chair as he settled down, the whisk of paper as he opened the *Law Journal*. She waited for him to call; she wanted him to call. But calling for her now was not part of the chambers ritual. She got up, fixed his coffee, brought it in to him.

"Ah, Carol, thank you," he said. Over his glasses, his eyes looked soft and kind.

Normally, she stood right in front of him when she passed him his coffee. That day, she stood at an angle, implying a desire to go around to the other side. She handed him the mug, shifted her weight to cock her hips. Normally, he took a sip to assess both the strength and the temperature. That day, he lowered the mug to his blotter and looked her square in the eye.

"Carol," he said, "I want to apologize . . ."

She didn't let him finish. If she had, he might have tossed off his midnight confession as a product of booze or nostalgia or bravado. In the length of that phrase, Carol weighed fear and attraction and survival. She walked around to the other side of the desk, turned his chair, and sat on his lap.

The affair lasted three months. There were Friday night dinners and buffets at the judge's luncheon club. Otherwise, they confined themselves to chambers. Even the law clerk, Tom's predecessor, did not know. They waited for him to leave at the end of the day, then Carol would shut off the lights in each of the three rooms as she drifted back to where the judge waited in his chair. His desk became their pallet, the glow of his laptop their guttering candlelight.

By late winter, with the sun heading back north, they needed to wait longer for the darkness that had become, in the judge's words, the sine qua non of their trysts. At home, Rose dropped comments, asked pointed questions. Carol ignored the comments, turned the questions back on her mother. But each comment and question had landed like jabs to the jaw of her subconscious. She began to play out scenarios, to ask herself questions laced with the word *future*.

She wavered, of course. There was this and there was that. There was the possibility, even the probability, that he would fire her if their relationship ended. What pushed her over was simple, even trite. At dinner one Friday night in early March, she noticed he moved his lips as he read the menu. Afterwards, they went back to his apartment—her first and only time there until New Year's Eve—and rather than go to bed with him, she filibustered until he fell asleep. The next Monday, she broke it off.

Tom pushed himself up, swung his legs off the bed, and stared at the floor.

"Why did you tell me this?"

"Because I needed to tell you. Because you needed to know."

"I didn't need to know this. It was years ago, and now he's dead. You didn't need to tell me."

"It's more complicated than that," said Carol. "Someone hooked up a webcam to the laptop and took pictures. Bobby has them." She stretched her legs beneath the comforter, working one foot under Tom's thigh. "I wanted you to know because we're going to get through this, and I don't want there to be any secrets between us. So what about you, Tom? Is there anything you need to tell me?"

"Like what?"

"Like anything. An ex-wife. A girlfriend I don't know about. A genetic trait."

Tom moved off her foot.

"No, Carol. There's nothing you need to know."

On the street, Foxx waited. For a time, he thought Dominic might come back. But time passed, and now Foxx's reason for waiting was more personal.

His phone buzzed against his chest. He pulled it from his pocket, tilted it into the wash of the streetlight. Bev's number pulsed on the readout. The phone buzzed three more times, then went still. A few moments later, the screen showed he had one new voice mail. He dropped the phone into his pocket.

At about ten thirty, the blinds opened in Tom's apartment. Foxx ducked behind the van, then slowly peeked out. Tom stood at the window, looking down at an angle toward Broadway. After a moment, Carol joined him. She rubbed her cheek against his shoulder, but Tom spun out from under her and disappeared.

PART FOUR

January Third

CHAPTER 24

The sound spiraled into Tom's ear. It reverberated there, unexamined, until his thoughts coalesced around it. *A voice.* And then, *a loud voice.* And then, *a loud but muffled voice.*

Tom pushed himself up on an elbow. The bedroom was dark except for the green glow of the alarm clock on the night stand. Tom squinted, the light rays resolving enough in the narrow aperture between his eyelids for him to make out that the first number was a six.

The voice boomed again. *Yes,* three times in rapid succession, then a *gotcha, Bobby.* The voice belonged to Elliott.

Completely awake now, Tom heard a cell phone snap shut and then the creak and rustle of Elliott pushing off the chair. There was a pause, and then Elliott cleared his throat and opened the bedroom door.

"Tom," he whispered. He was a silhouette against the vague light from the living room. "We got to move. Bobby wants the decision filed as soon as the Motion Office opens. I'll shower first, then you two."

He receded and closed the door.

Tom pushed himself up until his back rested against the spindles of the headboard. His eyes could make out Carol lying stiffly on her side with her face close to the wall. Two pillows lay like a barrier between them. He listened carefully; her breathing was slow and even.

"Carol," he whispered.

Her breathing caught, then returned to its long, slow draughts. She was pretending to sleep.

Through the wall, water thundered in the bathtub, then turned pebbly as Elliott switched the flow to the showerhead.

Tom got out of bed, picked his glasses from the nightstand, and went into the living room. He parted the blinds and looked down. Seventy-fifth Street was just as dark and quiet as last night. He had stood here right after Carol told him her story. She came to him, nestled against him, whispered, "I hope you don't think badly of me," then retreated when he did not respond. In truth, Tom did not know what to think. He was still now, as he had been then, of several minds. The judge had a catchphrase to describe working in chambers: *It's like living in each other's pockets.* Tom wondered now whether a more accurate image was that he and Carol were loose change in the judge's pocket.

The shower stopped and the curtain hooks rattled. Tom backed away from the window and peeked into the bedroom. Carol lay as stiffly as before.

"You sleep," said Tom. "I'll shower next."

Foxx found a seat in the last car of the subway train. Court officers were taught not to travel to and from the job in uniform. The institutional dark blue pants were innocuous, but the uniform shirt with its collar studs, shield, and bars might draw officers into situations best left to other law enforcement agencies. So Foxx wore his usual winter garb of uniform pants, pullover sweater, and medium-weight jacket. A sharp observer—of which there were none in the half-filled car—would have noticed two departures from Foxx's early morning norm. First, instead of his plain black oxfords with thick rubber soles, he wore black leather sneakers. Second, the jacket bulged slightly below his left armpit from the pistol and shoulder holster.

Foxx quickly noted the other passengers in the car before closing his eyes and settling into the rhythm of the train as it crossed the Bronx on the elevated tracks. He folded his arms and slouched against the rail. He had no real plan yet other than to get to the courthouse.

His chest buzzed, and he worked his cell phone out of his pocket in time to see Bev's call go into voice mail. Even he knew ducking her like this was getting old. Still, he waited a full minute before retrieving the message.

"Foxx," said Bev. "I'm getting tired of playing phone tag with you, but this is what I have. Anton Vuksanaj was a court officer for thirteen years. He was fired after repeated incidents of drunkenness and leaving his assigned post. He went missing for a while, then was hired by Bobby Werkman as the union's director of security. We have no jurisdiction over him as a union employee. Call me."

Foxx shut the phone and noted the time as the train descended from the elevated tracks and entered the tunnel. He closed his eyes again and plugged himself into the different but no less rhythmic underground beat. East Harlem became the Upper East Side. The Upper East Side became Midtown. He felt an influx of passengers at Grand Central and then the train hit the hard curve going downtown. Three stops later, he was calculating his ETA at 60 Centre when the train stopped, the lights dimmed, and the blowers cut off.

Dominic waited outside the courthouse door with a group of people holding red and white jury summonses. The day was cold and clear, the wind coming straight out of the west and buffeting the colonnade. Dominic wore no gloves. His peacoat hung open with only a thin black tee shirt underneath. The bruises on his forehead and cheek were still raw. As a boxer, he had been cut through the entire circumference of his head, and he always wore his bruises like emblems of courage and resilience. Not today. Whenever someone stared at his face, he started punching his right fist into the palm of his left hand. Instead of consoling himself with thoughts of valor, he dreamed of revenge.

Eventually, a court officer unlocked the revolving door. Some of the people grumbled about waiting in the cold, and the court officer said something about reduced hours of operation. Like Dominic fuckin' cared. He followed the crowd into the lobby. The court officer directed everyone to use all three lines, where three other officers worked the magnetometers. Dominic stopped, his eyes focused on the empty desk beside the information booth. He replayed the voice from three days ago in his head: *This is a courthouse, not a coffee house.* And from last night: *Hasn't been a couple of days since this morning.*

Dominic had an ear for voices the way some people had an eye for faces. These voices matched.

He waited his turn on the mag line, punching his right fist into his left palm. The officer working the machine was a slim redhead, and though Dominic doubted she would be any good in a fight, she certainly added to the scenery. He emptied his pockets into a small plastic tray, waited for the officer to beckon him through the mag, then lifted his arms as she wanded him.

"Thank you, sir," she said, avoiding eye contact.

Dominic took his sweet time scooping out his tray and returning his change, keys, and money clip to their proper pockets.

"You know a guy who works here named Tom Carroway?" he asked.

"It's a big building," said the officer. "Like six hundred people work here."

"I think he works for a judge."

"Do you know which judge?"

Dominic shook his head.

"There's an information kiosk in the rotunda. Touch the box for Justices and then Chambers Information."

"Thanks," said Dominic. He pointed over his shoulder with his thumb. "You know the officer who sits up at that desk?"

"Lots of officers sit there."

"I mean a weasely guy with silver hair."

"That sounds like Foxx," said the officer.

Foxx, thought Dominic. What a perfect name. He lifted his watch from the tray, but shoved it into his hip pocket rather than strap it onto his wrist. He didn't want to break it when he encountered Officer Foxx.

Dominic strolled down to the information kiosk. He followed the officer's instructions and quickly found that Carroway worked for a judge named Alvin Canter. He liked touching his fingers to the bright electric boxes and seeing the screen change. He felt like a wizard.

He rode the elevator to the fifth floor and checked out the territory. The elevator opened onto a circular corridor that was connected by a single hallway to an outer corridor. A court officer sat at a desk in that hallway, stopping anyone who tried to get by.

Dominic milled around and watched. There were a few lawyers at this hour, but mostly messengers and coffee deliveries. The officer turned away the lawyers and piled the messengers' envelopes on the desk. The only people he let through carried coffee.

Dominic rode back down to the rotunda, waited near the kiosk, then got back onto the elevator with a small man carrying a large plastic bag. The man pressed the 5 button.

"Coffee for the judge?" said Dominic.

The man smiled.

No one else got on the elevator. Dominic pressed 4, and when the door opened he pushed the man off. The man protested, but Dominic flicked his hand and a crisp ten dollar bill opened like a switchblade.

"Get me onto the fifth floor and this is yours."

CHAPTER 25

Tom went back to work at the judge's desk. He already had printed the two decisions from his flash drive, looming over the printer while Carol measured grinds for the morning coffee and Elliott buttoned his uniform shirt over his gut. Now, with the aroma of coffee thick in the air, Tom emptied his briefcase and assembled the two motion folders. The union decision already was signed, but the *Berne* decision still needed a signature. Tom settled into the judge's chair, leaned forward with his spine straight and his elbows out, his right hand holding the pen in what his grammar school nuns called "penmanship posture." Carol could have dashed off a perfect *AC* in a second. But after last night, Tom definitely did not want to involve her directly in his deal with Moxley.

He practiced on a legal pad, and after a dozen flourishes, felt ready for the real thing. He set the signature page at an angle, inhaled deeply, and exhaled slowly. He lowered his head, slackened his jaw, tried as an impersonator would to assume the physical being of the judge. His hand jerked across the page. He relaxed, dropped the pen. The *AC* looked just like any

AC the judge would have written. Tom tore the top sheet off the legal pad, ripped it into long strips, and flushed it all down the toilet in the judge's lavatory.

In the middle room, Tom went back through the pile of motion folders Carol had been working on when Elliott interrupted yesterday. He removed each of the decisions from the rubber bands, added the union and *Berne* cases, and tapped the edges into a uniform sheaf.

"It's ready," he announced.

"What's your filing procedure?" asked Elliott.

"Carol photocopies the decisions in the library, then she assembles the folders and loads the cart."

Elliott mulled what Tom just told him. Carol sipped from her coffee mug, ignoring them both.

"You do the copying," Elliott told Tom. "I'll stay here with her."

The library was empty. As the copier ground out the copies, Tom peered down onto Foley Square and wondered how different his plight might be if he hadn't tried to avoid Dominic on New Year's Eve. Not much, he concluded. Not much.

His cell phone buzzed. Monty's name flashed on the screen.

"What's up?" asked Tom.

"Just checking in," said Monty. "Haven't heard from you in a couple of days. Everything all right?"

"Everything's good," Tom replied.

"You being straight with me? No backslides?"

"Not one."

"Good to hear, but we still need to meet. I have an appointment on Prince Street today. Let's meet for lunch."

"Today's no good."

"Tomorrow?"

"Yes," said Tom. "I think tomorrow will be a fine day for lunch."

Tom returned to chambers at eight thirty, half an hour before the Motion Office opened. He told Carol he would reassemble all the motion folders and file the chambers' copies in the file cabinet. Carol only shrugged.

Things had to happen in the proper order today, so Tom moved slowly to fill the available time. Filing the union decision would get Bobby off his back and Elliott out of his hair. He would need to prove to Moxley that the *Berne* decision was filed before he could get paid, and he would need that to happen before he and Carol became visibly concerned about the judge's absence. At least he hadn't seen Dominic waiting near the fountain. Maybe his boss had called him off for a while.

Elliott came into the middle room just as Tom slipped the last of the photocopied decisions into the filing cabinet. He held out his cell phone.

"Bobby," he said. "He wants to talk to you."

Tom took the phone.

"I want you to read me my decision," said Bobby.

"The whole thing?"

"Every goddam word."

Tom took the decision copy out of the file cabinet and went to the judge's desk. He read in a sharp whisper so his voice would not carry into the corridor. Bobby listened quietly, grunting several times during the section that involved OCA's contractual argument. Tom's mouth ran dry toward the end, and as he reached the end a tickle crept into his throat.

"I like the way you handled the contractual argument," said Bobby.

"That's why I needed that extra time," said Tom. "The judge back in his apartment?"

"He returned early this morning."

"How does he look?"

"Like he died yesterday. At least to the untrained eye."

"What about the trained one?" asked Tom.

"That's a problem."

"But you said you had all your uncle's skills at your disposal."

"And I do," said Bobby. "Just as long as no one inquires, we're all right."

"What about your political connections?"

"I can't quash an inquiry before anyone knows he's dead."

"But then you can, right?" asked Tom. He hated the pleading, whining tone he could hear in his voice.

"I already told you," said Bobby, "we can dress up a body on the outside but can't change what's happening on the inside. We can't change the fact that the last time he ate was probably breakfast on New Year's Eve. We can't change whatever forensic trail you left behind in your idiotic scheme to move the judge out of the courthouse. The best we can hope for is that no one gets suspicious enough to start poking around. So you need to trust me and don't do or say anything stupid. Get the decision filed ASAP and don't worry about the judge till later. Okay?"

"Okay. Fine. Yeah. I'll do it," said Tom.

"Of course you'll do it," said Bobby. "You have no choice."

Foxx prided himself on never wearing a watch because, as he told anyone who would listen, he never needed to be in any specific place at any specific time. Time for him was neither an element nor a dimension, but simply a curiosity. Until today. Today time definitely was an element, and here he was, stuck in a dark, overcrowded, and rapidly chilling subway car. And, because he had no service underground, he could not even read the time off his cell phone.

A synthesized voice scratched over the loudspeaker.

"We are delayed because of train traffic ahead of us. We apologize for the inconvenience."

Train traffic my ass, thought Foxx. A dark car meant the power had been shut off to the third rail, and power only shut off when something happened. He turned to look out the window behind him. Across the tunnel, a train rumbled uptown on the local track. He fiddled with his cell phone again. Sometimes service wavered underground, and moving the phone even a few feet could make a difference. But he could not find a hint of a signal.

"Does anyone have the time?" he asked softly.

Someone close tapped Foxx's wrist. A young woman illuminated the dial of her watch. It showed eight forty-five.

At 8:58, Carol wheeled the cart out of chambers and, escorted by Elliott, headed toward the elevator. All along the corridor, the *Law Journals* were gone from the mail slots, which meant that more staff were back from the long holiday. As she steered the cart around the first angle, a door farther down the corridor opened and a secretary stepped out with an armful of motion files.

"Hi, Carol," she said cheerfully. "Are you heading to the Motion Office, too?"

Oh no, Carol thought. *Anyone but her. She'll pump me about New Year's Eve, about whether Judge Canter decided the union case.*

But then a voice call from within chambers, and the secretary went back inside.

"Narrow escape," whispered Elliott as they hurried past the chambers door.

Carol sighed. They agreed on that, at least.

They made the elevators without meeting anyone else, rode down to the rotunda, and went into the Motion Office. There a clerk expertly made runic markings on the front page of the decisions, hit them with a file stamp, and then entered them into the court computer system. Carol sensed a subtle but definite wave of excitement as news of Judge Canter's decision rippled out from its electronic entry point. All around the office, workers leaned close to peer at their computer screens. Some fought back grins, other picked up their phones. In a corner, a court officer pumped his fist as he leaned over a woman's shoulder to read the screen.

Elliott followed Carol as she rolled the empty cart out of the office. They crossed the rotunda, took the elevator up to the fifth floor, and rolled the cart to chambers. Inside, Tom paced in front of the conference table.

"Done?" he asked, as Elliott held the door and Carol pushed the cart inside.

Elliott clapped his hands, then rubbed them together.

"Yep. Overtime has been officially reinstated." He looked at the ceiling. "Thank you, Judge Canter."

"Are you done here?" Tom asked Elliott.

"Should be soon," said Elliott. His cell phone rang, and he fumbled it out of his pocket. "Yeah . . . right . . . done . . . be right there." He closed the phone. "That's it. I am done. It's been real. Carol . . ."

She waved away whatever he planned to say. He got into his

parka, shouldered his duffle bag, gave Carol one more long look before going to the door.

"Sorry," he muttered and left.

"What was that all about?" asked Tom.

"Nothing. He's a jerk, that's all," Carol replied.

Tom waited for more, and when Carol said nothing else he pushed the cart into the middle room, then padded to the file cabinet and quietly rolled a drawer open enough to pluck out the copy of the *Berne* decision. He folded the decision once lengthwise and stuck it in his back pocket. He turned. Carol stood in the doorway. She had her coat under her arm.

"Going somewhere?"

"Home. I have a son who's sick and a mother who can't function alone."

"But we need to finish this."

"You can do it yourself, Tom. You don't need me."

"But I do," he said. And he did, in his mind. But his words fell flat.

Carol smiled dimly. "I'm leaving anyway, but first I have some questions for you, and I need answers."

"I'm happy to answer any questions you have. There's just something I need to do first."

He stepped forward, angling for the space between Carol and the doorjamb. But she slid sideways to block him.

"Carol," he said. "I need five minutes."

"And I need answers."

"Carol . . ."

"No. Not in five minutes. Now." She leaned her left shoulder against the jamb and braced her right hand against the other.

"Hey, Jerry left without giving us back our cell phones."

"Don't try to change the subject, Tom."

"Okay," he said with a sigh. "Are these more questions about what Foxx told you?"

"No, they're my own. But they started with him coming here yesterday morning looking for the judge." Carol took a breath, searching for the precise words. "How did Bobby Werkman find out the judge was dead?"

"I told you. A court officer must have seen us taking him out that night and reported it to Bobby. They all knew the judge had the case. They would have told Bobby if they saw anything strange involving the judge. Hey, maybe it was Jerry. He's tied in with Bobby."

"That's your story?"

"Carol, I really need to go." Tom tried to push his way through, but she stiffened.

"That's your story?" she asked.

"That's not my story. It's the truth. And I don't see why this is so important."

"It's important because I want to trust you, Tom. I really do. But ever since Foxx came by yesterday morning asking for the judge, I've been replaying the last few days over and over in my mind. And things just don't add up. I don't like that, Tom. I don't like it when I think I don't know the whole story. That's why I told you about me and the judge. I knew it was a stupid thing to do. But I wanted to clear the air. I wanted there to be nothing between us, and I hoped you would come clean with me."

"I have come clean with you, Carol. Honest."

"Honest?" She smirked. "Well, here's what I think, Tom. I think you went to Bobby Werkman and told him the judge was dead. Why? I don't know."

"Look," said Tom. "I can answer all your questions. I just can't answer them now."

"Then when?"

"When I get back. Five minutes. Ten at most."

Carol smiled faintly. It was not a happy smile, more like a reaction to a bet with herself that she would have preferred to lose but actually had won. She stepped back, letting Tom brush past her. He circled her desk, stopped with his hand on the doorknob.

"Ten minutes," he said.

He opened the door, and then suddenly he flew backwards.

CHAPTER 26

Time passed slowly. The subway car grew colder. The announcements grew more garbled and scratchy and then stopped.

Foxx tapped the shoulder of the young woman, who lifted her arm and touched the button to light the dial of her watch. One minute to nine. Court was opening now. The lines for the mags would be filling up, the doors to the back offices would be swinging open, the clerks in the big courtrooms would be gearing up for the nine thirty calendar calls. Judges would be shouldering onto the judges' elevator and riding up to chambers.

Foxx had felt the movement of time ever since the train went dark, slow at first but with a muted internal throb as if poised to accelerate. It had now. He needed to get to the courthouse fast. Several trains had passed going uptown, but nothing on the adjacent downtown express track. His best option was to exit the train and run down the express track to the Fourteenth Street station. The rear door of the last car would be locked, so he waded toward the front of the car. The lighting was dim, the people shadowy. Some felt him coming and shifted out of his way, others blocked him till he asked to pass. He was polite, softening the edges of his words, betraying none of his anxiety. He reached the front end of the car, sidling past a huge woman with her arm hooked around the vertical pole. A man, just as huge, leaned back against the door that connected to the next car.

"Excuse me," said Foxx.

The man did not respond.

"Excuse me," said Foxx.

Again, no response. Foxx squinted, moved his head to change the angle of the light on the man's face. His eyes were closed.

"Excuse me," said Foxx. "I need to get through."

The man's eyes opened.

"Illegal to pass between cars," he said.

Foxx reared back a bit, allowing himself a better look. The man was broad, a head taller, too. He spoke like a conductor or a brakeman, but he wasn't wearing a transit uniform.

"I know, but I need to get through."

The man shifted his weight, which Foxx took to mean that he would let him pass. Foxx started to move, but the man grabbed him by the front of his jacket, lifted him off the floor, and shoved him back against the pole. The woman screamed. Several people moved out of the way.

"Illegal to pass between cars," the man said. He grabbed Foxx's jacket again and this time pinned him against the pole.

Shit, thought Foxx. Thousands of goddam trains, ten thousand goddam cars, and I got to be on the one with a crazy citizen-conductor.

He freed one of his hands and worked it into his jacket. He fingered his wallet, then his pistol.

"I'm a peace officer," he said.

"Yeah? Prove it."

"Let me down."

The man lowered Foxx to the floor but kept a grip on his jacket. Foxx quickly weighed the stupidity of pulling his pistol in a crowded subway car against the reaction of this huge knucklehead to a court officer's shield. Then a third idea struck. In pinning him to the pole, the man had moved away from the door, leaving enough room for him to fit behind.

"I just need to get my shield," said Foxx.

The man let go of his jacket. In one swift motion, Foxx pulled out his hand, grabbed the man's wrist, and twisted it behind his back. The man yelped in surprise until Foxx shoved his wrist high up his spine. Then he screamed in pain.

Foxx doubled him over, pushed him down, then yanked open the doors. Outside, he straddled the two narrow ledges and shook the chains that hung between the cars. The chains were meant to prevent people from riding between cars, but to Foxx they only stopped people who wouldn't dare and could not stop those who did. He shook one of the chains, saw how it was hooked, then just crouched under the upper chain and stepped over the middle one. Luckily, the third rail was on the other side of the train. He sat himself on the ledge, then pushed off and landed on the rail bed.

A lattice of upright girders and horizontal struts separated the local track from the express track. He ducked under a strut and planted himself in the middle of the express track. The rails curved downtown for about a train length before disappearing. From somewhere beyond came the glow of the Fourteenth Street station.

The tunnel began to rumble as he picked his way along the ties. He assumed it was another uptown train. But then the downtown rails began to vibrate, and he turned to see the twin headlamps of a downtown express flickering behind him.

"Shit," he said.

He ran forward half a car length, then ducked through the lattice and pulled himself up onto the ledge between two cars of the local just as the express shot past.

Tom slumped against Carol's desk. His face was red, his mouth open with a thin cord of bile stretching and then breaking off. Dominic swaggered into the room and kicked the door shut behind him. Carol immediately sized up the squat body and bowed legs under the peacoat and jeans, the thick skull under the soft dockworkers' cap, the outsized hands poking out from the sleeves like hands in a Thomas Hart Benton painting. This was the guy who punched Tom on New Year's Eve, the guy Tom met in the liquor store that night, the guy who followed them to Tom's apartment.

Dominic lifted Tom by the collar and dangled his face an inch from his own.

"You got it?"

Tom groaned, slurped back red saliva that bubbled in the corner of his mouth.

"Do you got it, asshole?"

"What are you doing?" asked Carol.

Dominic looked at her as if noticing her for the first time.

"I'm interrogating this mutt. What's it look like I'm doing?"

"You're hurting him."

"That's the cost of doing business. My business. His cost." Dominic turned back to Tom. "You got it?"

Tom mumbled.

"I said do you got it." Dominic shook Tom, snapping his head back and forth.

"Stop it," said Carol. She reached over her desk.

"You leave that phone right there."

Carol dropped the phone back on its cradle. "But you're hurting him."

"I start hurting him, you'll know." Dominic measured Tom, then flicked a jab to his jaw. "Like that. I just started."

"Po-ut."

"What'd you say?" said Dominic. He pulled Tom closer, keeping him upright. Tom's legs wobbled and blood dripped from his mouth onto Dominic's shoulder.

"Po-ut," said Tom.

"He said 'pocket,'" said Carol. "It's in his pocket. Just take it and go."

"What's in your pocket? Show me."

Tom painfully reached a hand behind his back and pulled out the copy of the *Berne* decision. Dominic snatched it away and gave it a quick glance.

"Another one of these, huh?" He tossed the decision to the floor, then punched Tom square in the gut. Tom crumpled onto Carol's desk, then melted to the floor.

"Stop it," said Carol.

"This mutt's been jerking me around for three days, lady. I ain't stopping."

"He owes you money, right?" Carol opened her pocketbook. "What is it? A couple of hundred dollars?"

Dominic laughed.

"He told me about you hiring him for your condo deal," Carol said. "He tried to stop you from buying, but you insisted and then you were foreclosed on and now you blame him and want the money you paid him."

"He may be a lawyer, lady, but he ain't ever been mine." Dominic lifted Tom and slapped his cheeks. "He don't owe me nothing except my cut of the eight gees he owes my boss. He's been telling me fairy tales for three days. He tells me yesterday he was sellin' a decision for five gees and he'd pay it over to me by ten a.m. Then he tells me that deal fell through and he was writing another one for seven gees. So now he hands me this. Like I'm supposed to believe him. Like my boss is supposed to believe him. So the time's come to pay. Somehow. Some way."

A sly smile crossed his face. Carol tried to scream, but he was on her instantly, clamping a hand over her mouth, twisting himself behind her, pulling her back against him. She squirmed, but he was too strong. One hand stifled her breath while the other fished for a bandanna inside his peacoat. She swooned. He pinned her against the desk and forced the bandanna into her mouth and tied it behind her head.

He lifted Tom off the floor and flung him into the middle room. Tom stumbled forward, drunkenly trying to catch himself. He crashed into the schefflera, knocking the plant over.

Dominic grabbed a hunk of Carol's blouse and dragged her after Tom. She dug in her heels, locked her hands on the credenza behind her desk, and for a moment held fast until Dominic's strength uprooted her. In the middle room, Dominic kicked at Tom. Tom rolled onto his stomach and crawled through the doorway until he collapsed in the inner office.

Dominic swung Carol onto his hip. She managed to hook her fingers on the doorjamb and held long enough to stop Dominic's momentum. But he just laughed and broke her grip and kicked the door shut behind him.

"Now we're gonna have some fun," he said.

Within minutes after the clerk filed Judge Canter's decision, word that Bobby Werkman had defeated OCA's ban on overtime pay flashed through the courthouse. It was still early. The traditional nine thirty start to court proceedings was almost a half hour away. Except for the dozen officers working the magnetometers and a few security posts, the vast majority of the sixty-five officers assigned to 60 Centre Street were reading newspapers, drinking coffee, or buttoning their uniform shirts in the locker room. Now they began to drift.

Bobby Werkman could feel them. He could feel their footsteps reverberating in the venerable old courthouse. He could feel them flowing, like the blood in his veins, down the elevators and stairways, through the rotunda, up the promenade to the lobby, and out the front door. He could feel the joy in their hearts, the relief in the corners of their minds where they hid their darkest thoughts. He could feel them because he was connected to them. They were his brethren, and he had slain the giant for them. Now it was time to hold up the severed head and receive their adulation in return.

"How many?" he said. He stood at the north end of the portico, around a corner, where the perspective of the columns formed a solid visual shield.

Vuksanaj peeked around a column.

"Forty, maybe forty-five on the steps," he said when he came back. "Lots of clerks, too. More clerks than officers. Still coming out the door."

"I don't give a damn about the clerks," said Bobby. "I want uniforms. I want every goddam officer we can find on the front steps."

Foxx worked his way forward car by car. The train was dimly lit and solidly crowded, but no one tried to stop him and, finally—he estimated seventeen minutes—he reached the front end of the head car. He banged on the door to the engineer's compartment. The engineer turned, ran his eyes across Foxx's face, then shrugged. Another one, the gesture seemed to say.

Foxx banged again and slapped his shield against the window. The engineer focused on the shield and opened the door.

"I gotta get out of here," said Foxx.

The engineer snorted. "You and everyone else."

Foxx cupped his eyes to the front window. Up ahead, the single dark tunnel curved to the rear end of a train lit by emergency lamps.

"When did that wall start?"

A solid masonry wall now ran tight along the left side of the local track.

"'Bout a car length back," said the engineer.

"That's the disabled one there?" asked Foxx.

"Yup."

"It's in the station?"

"Almost, but not quite."

"How long till the power's back?"

"Could be a minute, could be an hour."

Foxx jiggled the front door, but a dead bolt held it shut.

"Man, you must really need out of here," said the engineer.

He turned a key and opened the door. Foxx picked his way through the chains and balanced on the ledge.

"Don't run me over," he said.

Then he swung down onto the rail bed. He jogged at first, calibrating his stride to land on the ties. Then he turned up the speed.

CHAPTER 27

The engineer had been exactly right in his assessment. The disabled train had stopped just short of the station with half of the last car off the platform. Foxx used the triple chain hanging across the rear door to pull himself up onto the ledge. The car was empty, its doors closed. Toward the far end, light from the station flooded in through the windows.

Foxx shuffled along the ledge to the corner of the car. He could hear the dull hum of voices and, through the narrow gap between the metal skin of the car and the sooty wall of the tunnel, he could see a thick guardrail painted bright yellow and beyond that the platform jammed with people.

He jumped down and crouched on the rail bed. There was space between the tunnel wall and the undercarriage, but the body of the car bowed out, leaving only a four- to six-inch gap at the platform, which meant he would need to crawl the entire length of the car before he could use the space near the coupling to climb out.

He pulled himself back onto the ledge and looked down the side of the car. A rain gutter ran along the line where the wall curved into the roof. He reached up and gripped the gutter with four fingers. The gutter offered good support, but there was no ledge to stand on. Four feet of smooth silver metal separated him from the rear doors and a two-inch doorstep. Beyond that, there was another ten feet of smooth silver metal before the middle doors and another doorstep. The tunnel ended and the platform began another two feet beyond.

Foxx retracted his arm, flexed his fingers, then balled his hands into solid fists. The rail bed or the gutter. Scylla or Charybdis. The rail bed offered the quicker route, but so did running down the express track and he well understood how that idea might have ended.

He leaned back around the corner of the car and reached his left hand as far as he could along the side. His four fingers snagged the gutter. He flexed them, tested their hold. He let his left foot swing free. Then he snaked his right hand up along his chest to the gutter. He snagged that, too, and tested his hold.

Here goes, he said to himself.

He dropped his right foot. Immediately, his fingers screamed with pain. He tucked his chin to his chest, pushed his hands along the gutter. Left, then right. Left, then right. The cold metal scratched against his face as he scraped along. He was just about to lose his grip when his left foot caught the first doorstep, allowing him just enough leverage to take the pressure off his fingers. Huffing, he stood on the doorstep and leaned back against the tunnel wall to rest.

Ten feet, he thought. Another ten feet till he reached the next set of doors and he could stand again and rest. From there it was just another few feet before he could jump to the guardrail and flip onto the platform.

He balled his fists, flexed his fingers, rubbed his palms on the front of his jacket. The hum from the platform rose in pitch, then resolved into words. *Some guy. Hanging on the last car. Get someone. Conductor.*

Foxx told himself not to listen to the voices. He took a deep breath, pushed himself off the wall, and reached as far as he could to insert his fingers in the gutter. He got halfway before his fingers locked and his arm muscles screamed. He swung his left leg and pointed his toe, but his foot kicked only at air. He dropped down, letting his arms go limp to rest the muscles, relying only on his fingers, locked like those of a dead man into the gutter. A dead man, he thought. That's what he could be if he didn't move.

Get someone. Open the doors to the last car. Help him.

Foxx tensed his muscles, pulled himself up, slid his left hand another six, eight, nine inches toward his goal. He started to move his right hand, and then his arm muscles gave out. He dangled, panting, praying his fingers would hold. He kicked out his left leg, but his foot still swung short.

He tried to pull himself back up. A chin-up, he told himself. One damn chin-up. But his arms would not move. He closed his eyes, pressed his cheek against the cold skin of the car, decided to breathe the strength back into his body. One breath, two breaths. Long and deep. The same technique he used for meditating. Maybe he could levitate himself and float to the platform.

A buzz sounded in his ear. The skin of the car vibrated against his cheek. He opened his eyes. Lights blazed inside the car. The power was back on. Which meant the doors could open. But the doors didn't open. Which meant the train could move. And if the train moved, the platform would literally cut him off at the ankles. He tried to pull himself up, but his arms quickly gave. He took a breath, tried again. No luck.

The air brakes hissed. He tightened his grip on the gutter, pulled with his arms. He felt himself rise a bit, then a bit more. The hissing stopped. He pulled harder. The train lurched forward. This was it. Either he'd clear it or he wouldn't.

The tunnel wall peeled back. The brightness of the station enveloped him. The guardrail slipped past, the platform grazed the soles of his sneakers.

The train stopped. He let go of the gutter, fell to the platform, nestled onto the hard tiles like a mattress.

Bobby had made some phone calls to the criminal court and the lower courts and dragooned a few dozen officers to join the gathering. Even with Vuksanaj's estimate now comfortably over one hundred officers, the steps were nowhere near full; it would take at least a thousand people to fill them. But photographers from the tabloids were on their way, and Bobby knew that photos framed just right would depict a solid wall of blue.

Elliott finished setting up the portable podium on the sidewalk and trudged up between the two brass rails that ran down the center of the steps.

"All ready," he said.

Bobby and Vuksanaj exchanged a glance.

"I want you to relieve the officer at the Worth Street post," Bobby told Elliott.

"Aw, Bobby, I wanted to listen."

"You've heard it all before. When I'm done, meet me back at union headquarters."

"Really?" Elliott said.

"That's what I said." Bobby shook Vuksanaj's hand. "Good luck."

Then he walked out from behind the columns and paused between the brass rails. No one noticed him at first because the podium focused everyone's attention downward. But eventually someone in the back row spotted him, and word of Bobby spread through the crowd. The applause started slowly. A few staccato claps to his left, and then a few more to his right. Then it started to roll, quickening and filling in before finally erupting.

Bobby began his descent. He spread his arms wide and slapped palms with officers on both sides of the rail. A chant rose: "Bob-by, Bob-by." By the time he reached bottom, the chant had changed to a more rhythmic, "Bob-by Werk-man." Clap clap, clap-clap-clap. "Bob-by Werk-man." Clap clap, clap-clap-clap. He stood in front of the podium, pumping his arm in time with the chant.

He went behind the podium and tapped the mike of the portable amplifier. Loud thuds pulsed out of the speaker. He dropped the mike, lifted his arms, and tamped down with his hands. But the applause continued, so Bobby walked along the front row of officers and slapped each one a high five. Whoever invented the high-five was a genius, he thought. It was a great gesture, combining the joy of victory with the spirit of camaraderie. He hoped a news photographer caught him at the height of a high-five. That would be the picture he wanted to see in the newspapers.

Bobby went back behind the podium and scanned the crowd again. This time, he spotted Vuksanaj at the top between two columns. That silver spike-job looked dumb in most contexts, but not when he needed to pick him out of a crowd.

Bobby lifted the mike, and the applause finally died.

"I am happy to see you all here," he said.

His amplified voice rolled up the steps, bounced off the façade, and then, a quarter-second later, echoed off the federal building across Foley Square. The acoustics gave the impression of Bobby speaking in stereo.

"I want to know," he said. "Does anyone have anything to say?"

On cue, Vuksanaj shouted, "Thank you, Bobby!"

Competing shouts rose, mostly unintelligible. Vuksanaj shouted again, and the crowd picked it up. "Thank you, Bobby. Thank you, Bobby."

Bobby raised his arms. As the crowd noise died into silence, Vuksanaj signaled a thumbs-up and melted into the columns.

"I appreciate your sentiments," Bobby said. "But I ask you not to thank me. Yes, I brought the case against OCA. But I didn't sue for myself. I sued for you. That's my job as union president, and it is a job I take very seriously.

"The person who truly deserves your thanks is not here. We wouldn't expect him to be. He is the kind of man who comes to the courthouse every day, does his job, and goes home. That person is Justice Alvin Canter.

"*Justice* Canter. Think about that for a moment. We call them judges as shorthand, but the men and women who sit in New York State Supreme Court are justices, not judges. A judge might merely choose sides between two opposing parties. A justice does what is right.

"Think, too, about how many justices recused themselves because they did not want to be caught between OCA and the court officers. Not Justice Canter. He read the facts, he applied the law, and he did justice.

"I'm sure Justice Canter is back in chambers now, working on his other cases. I'm sure he would be surprised to learn that his decision led to this impromptu gathering. So when you see the Justice Canter, whether it's today or tomorrow or . . ."

Tom woke up in bed. It was a hard bed with a single scratchy sheet beneath him and no pillows or covers. He had a terrible headache, an unbelievable headache, the migraine of all migraines. Two distinct lines of pain started at his chin, ran up his cheekbones, curved at his temples, and knotted themselves at the top of his skull.

"No," came a voice. "Stop. Please."

The voice sounded like Carol speaking under water.

Tom forced open his eyes and saw blurry brown fabric. Not a sheet, but a carpet. The carpet in Judge Canter's office. He tried to lift his head, but that knot at the top of his skull exploded and his head fell sideways.

"No," Carol gurgled again. "Please."

Tom tried to focus. Above him, a blurry Carol knelt on the couch with her face shoved into the corner. Dominic stood behind her, one foot on the floor, the other knee on the couch, his crotch pressing into her.

"Tom," said Carol. "Help."

Dominic lifted her head by the hair, leaned his mouth to her ear.

"You're boyfriend's out of it."

Dominic untied the bandanna, stuffed a wad of cloth into her mouth, and knotted the bandanna tight against the back of her head.

"Enough outta you," he said.

Carol gagged.

Tom pushed himself up on his elbows. The room swayed as he crawled. Another wave of pain started at the top of his head and rolled back to his chin. He lowered his head to the carpet, rubbed his forehead against the stiff nap.

Carol gagged again. She was doubled over in the corner of the couch. Dominic worked one hand in between her legs while the other tugged at his belt buckle. Tom shoved himself forward until he reached the couch. He rose up on his knees, laced his hands together, and clubbed Dominic in the kidney. Dominic turned around and pushed Tom over. Tom got up again and tried to gather himself for another blow, but Dominic lifted his foot off the floor and kicked back like a donkey. His heel caught Tom square in the chest and knocked all the air from his lungs. The last thing Tom heard was Dominic say, "It's just you and me, babe."

Above ground, Foxx rode a bus for three blocks before he jumped out and ran. He ran like a bastard now down the east side of Centre Street. Below Canal, traffic thickened both in the street and on the sidewalk. He weaved, he feinted, he stopped short and cut sideways. A traffic signal changed as he crossed a side street, and he spun to avoid the fender of a car. He reached the Criminal Courts Building. Another block, and 60 Centre would be in sight.

People who met Foxx thought him to be of indeterminate age. His silver hair said fifties, but his unlined skin and clear blue eyes said thirties. But right now, running hard, anyone could determine his age; he was too damn old for this.

Reaching the intersection at Worth, Foxx spotted a crowd on the courthouse steps. An organized crowd was an occasion in any kind of weather, and especially in the cold of early

January. As he crossed into the north end of Foley Square he could see that court officers made up most of the crowd. He could see that a man stood at a podium at the bottom of the steps. He could hear now, through the pounding of the blood in his ears and his feet on the pavement, a voice echoing across the square.

". . . and when you see Justice Canter in the courthouse, whether it's later today, or tomorrow, or next week, you don't need to thank him. Justice Canter simply did his job. He did the right thing."

Applause erupted as Foxx skirted the courthouse steps and opened the brass door of the street level entrance. The security post, manned only during the morning hours, was deserted. The door to the judges' elevator was open, the car empty. Foxx got on, pressed the button for five, felt the gears engage and the car rise.

Judge Canter's chambers was unlocked. Carol's computer was on, and a chair lay on its back between Tom's desk and the conference table. Foxx lifted the chair. As he pushed it back into place, he saw that a plant was knocked over in the middle room and the door to the judge's office was closed. He padded to the door, listened long enough to hear that no noises came from inside, then yanked it open. A body lay facedown in front of one of the couches. Foxx checked for a pulse, then went to Carol's desk and called the captain's office.

"It's Foxx. I'm in Judge Canter's chambers. You need to get here."

He went back inside and crouched beside the body. A hand twitched, then an arm moved, then the head lifted off the carpet to show a face so bloody and swollen it was unrecognizable.

CHAPTER 28

"What the hell is going on?" the captain called from the doorway. He was in full winter uniform, right up to the dark blue vest and, on his head, the peaked cap with his shield. "Who is that?"

Rather than answer, Foxx stood up to give the captain a clear view.

"That's not the judge," said the captain. "Where's the judge?"

Foxx shrugged.

The captain unclipped a radio from his shoulder and started barking commands. Foxx got down on one knee.

"Where did they go?" he asked.

The eyes loosened.

"You?" The voice cracked. "You were on my list."

"Me?" said Foxx. "You couldn't even handle Carroway."

"Carroway's a pussy . . . He din' do this."

"Who did?"

But Dominic closed his eyes and sank into himself.

"Foxx." The captain was off the radio. "What was that all about?"

Before Foxx could answer, two officers carrying medical bags rushed in. Foxx stood up and drew the captain aside.

"His name's Dominic McGlinchy. Works for a loan shark. Been tailing Carroway for a couple of days."

"Carroway did this? The man looks like he's been tenderized."

"Wasn't Carroway."

"Then who?"

"He didn't say."

"Well, if you knew that this man was tailing Carroway, but that Carroway didn't do this, then who else?"

Foxx said nothing. Two more court officers came in. The two with the medical bags stopped working on Dominic and the two new ones lifted him onto the couch. Dominic immediately slouched sideways, so one of the officers righted him while the other rearranged the cushions for support.

"Didn't there used to be an Oriental rug here?" said the captain.

No one answered.

The captain crouched in front of Dominic.

"Sir, do you know who did this to you?"

Dominic's head rolled against the cushion. His mouth opened, but nothing came out.

"Sir, do you know who did this to you?"

Dominic's eyes opened halfway. He leaned forward, lost the support of the cushions, and toppled to his left. One of the officers pulled him upright.

"He's somnolent," the captain said. "I can't question a man if he's somnolent."

An officer took a capsule from a medical bag and broke it

under Dominic's nose. Dominic's head snapped backwards. His eyes blinked.

"Sir," said the Captain, "do you know . . ."

"Alls I know is my head hurts," said Dominic.

"Now we're getting somewhere," the captain said.

Foxx slipped out of chambers and phoned Bev as he pelted down a set of stairs toward the rear entrance of the courthouse.

"Finally," she said. "Where are you?"

"Sixty."

"We heard Judge Canter ruled against OCA and Bobby Werkman held a rally on the courthouse steps. True?"

"All of it," said Foxx. "But there's more you need to know."

Foxx talked the entire long block to Broadway.

"Unbelievable," Bev interjected several times before asking, "Where are you now?"

"Outside union headquarters."

"Keep Werkman there. We're on our way."

Foxx took the stairs to the second floor, where a large decal of a court officer's shield adorned a frosted glass door. Beside the door, riveted to the plaster wall, was a gold plate embossed with ROBERT WERKMAN, PRESIDENT. The doorknob turned, the latch clicked, and the door creaked open from its own weight.

Foxx heard Bobby's voice from deep inside. The voice was loud and full of itself. Foxx pushed the door slowly through the rest of its arc to expose a secretary's desk with no secretary behind it.

"What the hell you doing here, Foxx?"

Around the door, Jerry Elliott stood at the window looking

down on Worth Street. His parka was open, showing his uniform shirt beneath.

"Came to see Bobby," said Foxx.

"Oh yeah? Why do you want to see Bobby? You want to reap the spoils of victory?"

"That's pretty good turn of phrase, Jerry. You used your few hours of comp time well."

"Not as well as I'll use my overtime," said Elliott. "Bobby's on the phone with *The New York Times*. This is a big deal."

"It is," said Foxx. "A judge ruling in favor of a union that didn't have a chance in hell to win its case is a big deal."

Bobby's voice boomed inside his office. "The right judge made the right decision. You can quote me on that."

"The right judge," said Foxx, shaking his head. He stepped toward Bobby's door, but Elliott blocked him.

"You can't go in there," he said.

"I'm going in there, Jerry. My question to you is, what are you doing here?"

"I'm helping Bobby."

"Like you helped Bobby last night by escorting Tom and Carol to Tom's apartment."

Elliott stuttered.

"I followed you, Jerry."

"Tom needed protection," said Elliott. "Some guy's been hassling him about money."

"I know all about him. I just scraped him off the floor of Canter's chambers."

"When?"

"Fifteen minutes ago," said Foxx. "Do you know where Carol and Tom are?"

Elliott said nothing, and Foxx knifed past him.

"It's a victory for the common man and the common woman," Bobby was saying. "Especially in an environment where public employees are demonized by the same private sector that ruined the economy. You can quote me on that, too."

He sat sideways behind his desk, swiveling his chair back and forth. He smiled when he first spotted Foxx, assuming he had appeared to deliver more accolades. Then he caught Foxx's grim expression and covered the phone with his hand.

"Can I help you?"

"I'm looking for some people," said Foxx.

"Are you a member of my union?"

"I'm a member of the union."

Bobby raised one eyebrow at the distinction.

"Have a seat outside. I'm on with *The New York Times*."

Bobby swiveled toward the window again, apologizing to the reporter for the interruption and listening to the next question. Foxx walked around the desk and stood behind Bobby.

"No," Bobby said. "The ruling is not a license for my membership to pad retirement benefits. It never has been and it never will be. Not as long as I'm union president."

Foxx pressed the GOOD-BYE button on the telephone.

"Hello? Hello?" Bobby spun his chair. "Who the hell are you?"

"Foxx."

"And you're a member of my union. I'm going to look into you."

"No need. I'll tell you anything you want to know and a few things you won't. But right now I'm looking for Carol Scilingo and Tom Carroway."

"Who are they?"

"Judge Canter's staff."

"Don't know them."

"That's funny, since I saw all of you together yesterday in a restaurant in Chinatown."

"Who the hell are you?" asked Bobby.

"I told you already. My name is Foxx."

"You get your ass out of my office."

"Not until you tell me where they are."

"I don't know. How the hell would I know?"

"But you already told me you don't know them, and I know that's a lie."

"Meeting in a restaurant ain't a crime."

"Who's talking about a crime? Unless you met to discuss a judge who was on ice in a funeral home while he supposedly was working on a decision in his chambers."

"He decided it on New Year's Eve," said Bobby. "You can see for yourself."

Foxx smirked. "So what was there to discuss?"

"Hey, Jerry," Bobby called out. "Come in here and toss this guy."

"He's not going to toss me," said Foxx. "The only person leaving this office is you, but only after you tell me where Carol and Tom are."

"I don't know where they are," said Bobby. "Jerry!"

"Jerry's not coming," said Foxx. He could see out Bobby's office to the entry door, which closed as Elliott departed. "Where are Carol and Tom, and where's Vuksanaj?"

"I don't know."

Foxx flung Bobby's chair. The ball-bearing wheels rolled freely on the plastic mat behind Bobby's desk until the chair crashed into the window. Foxx grabbed a hank of Bobby's hair.

"You gonna tell me?" he asked.

He rubbed Bobby's face against the window, leaving a greasy smear on the glass.

"Jerry," Bobby tried to yell.

"I told you, he's not coming," said Foxx. "Where are they?"

"I don't know."

Foxx slammed Bobby's forehead into the window.

"He didn't tell me," said Bobby. "He doesn't tell me anything. He has stuff locked away that I can't even get to."

"Can you reach him?"

"No."

Again Foxx slammed Bobby's head. A line of blood opened above his eyebrow. The glass was strong, and Foxx knew he would not be able to break it with Bobby's head. But Bobby didn't know that.

Carol had been certain she would die:

She was choking on the wad of cloth in her mouth, blubbering into the back cushion of the couch, her neck twisting painfully each time Dominic thrust against her from behind. He pulled up her skirt and scratched at her skin, trying to snag her panties. His belt was unbuckled, but his pants were still closed. She could feel the rough edges of his jeans rubbing the backs of her thighs.

Tom, she thought. If only Tom could save her.

Dominic's fingers hooked the waistband of her panties. He yanked down, slid his fingers sideways, and yanked again.

Or Foxx, she thought. He came to chambers yesterday. Maybe now, with the decision filed . . .

Dominic slid his fingers the other way and pulled. He thrust his crotch harder against her. His belt buckle jingled.

Then, suddenly, his fingers let go of her panties, the thrusting stopped. She heard grunts, slaps, the woody knock of bone on bone. She pushed herself up, loosened the knot of the bandanna, spit the wet wad from her mouth. She rolled over.

Dominic was a bloody mess on the floor, and Vuksanaj was helping Tom to his feet. Vuksanaj noticed her moving, came over to help her up, and, in a way that was clumsy and yet somehow sweet, fixed her clothes. Then he went into the lavatory and moistened a few paper towels.

"We can't stay here," he said as they wiped their faces.

"Why not?" asked Carol. She looked at Tom, but he seemed too woozy to speak.

"We need to meet Bobby at the judge's apartment. He needs your help to finish this thing."

"But I need to get home," she said. "My son has been sick."

"I'm sorry," said Vuksanaj. "Please, this will not take long."

Carol had not heard Vuksanaj speak so much at one time. Despite his forbiddingly odd appearance, he sounded polite, with just a hint of Eastern Europe in his inflections. Plus, he had saved her from Dominic. She looked again at Tom, saw something in his still-addled expression that suggested Vuksanaj's words had registered, and agreed for both of them.

"What about him?" she added with a glance at Dominic.

"What do you care?" Vuksanaj answered.

And so, after Vuksanaj had wet a few more paper towels, and Carol and Tom had wiped and dried every trace of blood, sweat, and tears from their faces, they departed chambers.

Vuksanaj led them on a circuitous route of back stairs and catwalk corridors down and past the emptier reaches of the courthouse. They encountered no one on the way. Not a clerk, not a court officer, not even some wayward member of the public trying to find a restroom. Carol thought it strange that the courthouse would be so deserted now, two days removed from New Year's. But when they landed at the Worth Street entrance and she heard the loud voice booming amid shouts and cheers, she knew that something was happening on the front steps.

Elliott was at the security desk. He nodded to Vuksanaj, but did not meet Carol's eye. Outside, Carol recognized the amplified voice as Bobby's.

"I thought he would be at the apartment already," she said.

"He'll catch up," Vuksanaj assured her.

And so, despite a twinge of misgiving, a suspicion of something not quite right, but still not thinking clearly in the wake of Dominic's attack, Carol followed Vuksanaj across Worth Street.

They skirted Columbus Park and walked half a block up Mulberry Street, where Vuksanaj opened the back door of a green 4x4. Tom climbed in and Carol followed. Vuksanaj got into the driver's seat, started the engine, and drove slowly through Chinatown. They headed north on the FDR Drive until just past the Manhattan Bridge, where Vuksanaj announced he needed to get something from the trunk. He pulled off the highway onto the shoulder of an exit ramp and got out. Cold air filled the truck when he opened the rear deck. Carol heard metal clanking, but when she looked over her shoulder she saw the entire trunk covered by a dusty red canvas.

Vuksanaj slammed the rear deck. When he got back in, he held a pistol and a handful of white plastic strips.

Foxx slammed Bobby back into his chair.

"I don't know, I don't know," Bobby said. A curtain of blood poured from a gash that creased his forehead from eyebrow to eyebrow.

Foxx unlocked the window and lifted the sash. He hauled Bobby out of the chair, pushed his face out into the cold air, then bent him over the sill. He was not going to push Bobby out the window. But he had not intended to break the window glass, either, and right now the glass was cracked and bloody.

"You got one more chance," he said into Bobby's ear.

"I can't tell you what I don't know."

Foxx grabbed Bobby under the arms and started to lift. Bobby flailed at the air, tried to kick himself backwards.

"Foxx! Stop!"

There was a rushing sound, and before Foxx could turn, four big men in dark suits and wraparound sunglasses peeled him off Bobby. Foxx wrestled until he caught sight of the woman standing in the doorway.

"Bring him to me," she said.

She meant Foxx, and two of the men dragged him into the outer office.

Foxx had not seen Bev since she had given him the cell phone and turned him into her eyes and ears at 60 Centre Street. He noticed she had developed laugh lines around her mouth, and that the lines added character to an already attractive face. But these thoughts were incongruous, and vanished as soon as she spoke.

"What the hell are you doing? You knew I was coming here."

"Judge Canter's staff is missing. I think they're in danger."

"That's not my immediate concern."

"It's mine," said Foxx.

"I'll see what I can get out of him. But this is my entire squad. Not much I can do even if I find out."

"Try."

"Sure. But you should call the cops."

Bev went into Bobby's office. Bobby was seated behind his desk. Two of Bev's men flanked him, a hand on each of Bobby's shoulders while Bobby pressed a handkerchief to his bleeding brow. The other two stood on each side of the desk, their arms folded. Bev paced, took off her gloves, slapped them against the palm of her hand.

Fuck it, thought Foxx. This'll take too long.

He rushed out of the office and down the stairs. Elliott stood at the bottom.

"Who was that lady?" he asked.

"Inspector General."

"She's questioning Bobby?"

"Yeah, but not the right questions."

"She gonna want to talk to me?"

"Soon as Bobby gives you up."

"You got any juice with her?"

"Some," said Foxx.

"I might know where he took them," said Elliott.

CHAPTER 29

Carol had only an inkling of where they were. They were somewhere north of White Plains. Not far north, maybe only three or four miles as a crow flies. But in Westchester, a small city could change quickly into back country with only a narrow buffer of suburbia in between.

The road switched back on itself as it climbed a steep hill. Trees with boughs still caked with old snow pressed close on both sides. The 4x4 spit gravel as it hugged the curves. Vuksanaj clung to the wheel, eyes squinting through a windshield streaked with dried salt.

Another sharp curve threw Carol against the door. She wished the door would fly open and she could tumble out. She saw herself rolling across the gravel and ice and shrunken snowdrifts, then springing up to run swiftly into the brown woods. Because if that happened, if she somehow miraculously had that chance, no one would catch her.

It was not going to happen. Tom sat across from her, directly behind Vuksanaj. A white plastic strip bound her left wrist to his right. Two other strips lashed their other wrists to the door handles. She wasn't going anywhere, and neither was Tom. And yet they were going somewhere.

They passed a small reservoir, then burrowed back into the trees. The road followed the spine of a ridge, slipping off at some curves then pulling itself back up on others.

Carol glanced at Tom. He was slumped with his head bobbing, his eyes closed, and his mouth open. Only the plastic strips prevented him from sloshing around as the 4x4 took the turns.

They crested the ridge. The trees fell back from the road, opening up on a bright but overcast sky. The engine whined as the truck accelerated, and then Vuksanaj hit the brakes. The truck skidded, then slammed to a stop broadside in the middle of the road. The engine stalled. Vuksanaj, cursing under his breath, turned the ignition key. The engine sputtered, then rumbled, then evened out. Vuksanaj worked a broken U-turn and headed back slowly in the direction they had come, fifty yards, a hundred yards, until he forced the truck onto a turn-off. The road was dirt, rutted and frozen. Twenty yards in was a chain-link gate.

Vuksanaj got out of the truck, walked to the gate, and rattled it.

"Tom," Carol whispered. "Tom, wake up."

Tom's eyes loosened.

"He's out of the truck. Look."

Vuksanaj kicked at the gate, then walked to the rear of the truck and opened the hatch. Cold air blew in. He sorted through tools that made heavy metal clunks, then headed back to the gate brandishing a bolt cutter. He clamped the jaws on the padlock and jammed the handles together. The padlock snapped and fell to the ground. Vuksanaj kicked it away and swung the gate open.

"Tom," Carol said again.

Vuksanaj threw the bolt cutter into the back of the truck, then got in and drove through the gate. He stopped when the truck was clear, got out again, and swung the gate closed. A dented sign beside the gate read QUARRY CLUB in peeling paint. The name meant something to Carol, but she could not place it exactly.

The road curved up between two rocky outcrops, where it turned completely to gravel and started to descend to the quarry. The pit was a perfect figure eight, with rugged stone walls that pinched in around a large circle of ice and then curved again into a more distant circle. In the distance, the walls were eighty or ninety feet high. Treetops stood beyond the wall, and fuzzy clumps of dried underbrush hung over the rim. The stone faces were weathered, with bare saplings and more dried brush clinging to the ledges. On the near side, a semicircle of sand met the gray glass surface of the frozen lake.

Vuksanaj rolled to a stop in a parking lot outlined by railroad ties. There were several buildings, each in a different stage of decay, with broken windows, cracked siding, and peeled roof tiles.

Vuksanaj leaned through the opening in the two front seats.

"Hold up your hands," he said.

Tom did not move, but did not resist when Carol raised her left hand and lifted his right along with it. A switchblade snapped open in Vuksanaj's hand. He slipped it between their wrists, blade up, and severed the plastic strap with a flick of his wrist.

"Don't move," he said.

He got out of the truck, opened Tom's door, and cut the strap lashing him to the armrest. The force of the movement tumbled Tom out of the truck. Vuksanaj caught him by the collar and pulled him the rest of the way out. Tom's legs were rubbery. Vuksanaj dragged Tom around the back and slammed him against the rear fender. Then he opened Carol's door and cut her loose from the armrest.

Carol got out of the truck herself. Vuksanaj pocketed the switchblade and pulled out his pistol.

"Walk," he said, then screwed the muzzle under Tom's chin. "That means you, too."

He pushed Carol to get her started, then picked Tom off the truck and flung him in her direction. The sand felt crusty underfoot. Carol tried to listen past their crunching feet and Tom's huffing breaths, and what she heard was not mere quiet but a total absence of sound. No birds, no wind, no traffic. They were far away from anyone and anything.

They crossed the sand to a break in the trees, where a tilted sign read NATURE TRAILS. A wood-chip trail rose steeply, curving behind the back edge of a sudden upland that had become the quarry and then leveling at a fork. Another sign pointed right for TEA BERRY LAKE TRAIL and left for QUARRY HEIGHTS. Vuksanaj looked at the sign, rubbing his chin with the hand that held the pistol. A thick tangle of thorn bushes swirled like western tumbleweed behind the sign. He stepped in and gingerly plucked out a piece of cardboard. Someone had written LOVERS LEAP in red marker. Below the words, a crude arrow pointed left.

Vuksanaj grabbed Tom by the arm and yanked him down the trail. Carol stayed rooted to the ground at the point of the fork.

"Hey, you," said Vuksanaj. "C'mon."

But Carol could not move as her vague memories of the Quarry Club resolved into brutal clarity.

Vuksanaj grabbed her arm and flung her so hard she began running until her foot caught a root and she sprawled face first onto the trail.

Foxx drove the Crown Vic, fighting his way toward the Hudson and then getting on the West Side Highway and then weaving through traffic. Elliott looked sick. He slumped in the passenger seat, his skin completely white. He had said only two words since getting into the car. *North,* he had said. And then, once Foxx had turned in that direction, *Westchester.* Foxx didn't question him on any more details. He knew that, wherever they were going, he needed to haul ass, and so he wanted to concentrate on getting through all the obstacles in the city. That's when he would turn the screws on Elliott.

But Foxx didn't need to question Elliott. As soon as they crossed the Henry Hudson Bridge and into the Bronx, both traffic and Elliott opened up.

"I set up the podium for Bobby's speech this morning. He and Vuksanaj were waiting at the top of the steps. Bobby told me to relieve the officer at the Worth Street entrance post, then he told Vuksanaj good luck and shook his hand. I didn't think anything of it till Vuksanaj came down later with Carol and Tom."

The trail alternated steep winding climbs with straight level runs. During the climbs, the trees were small, the brush thick, and shelves of rock broke through the earth. But on the runs, the terrain fell away gently. The trees were tall, the underbrush sparse, the forest floor carpeted with last summer's dead leaves. Snow filled the hollows. The cold air and the walking revived Tom.

"I'm sorry," Tom said. He spoke in a huffing whisper. They were climbing a steep stretch side by side. Vuksanaj was a few yards behind them, and the scuffing of their feet on the rocks masked Tom's words.

"Forget it," Carol whispered back.

"You need to know."

"You need to shut up. We need to get away from him."

"How?"

"We run. Can you run?"

"Guess so."

"We both run at the same time. Different directions."

"What about the gun?" whispered Tom.

"He's not going to use it. He has something else planned."

"What?" asked Tom.

But they reached the top of the climb, and Vuksanaj caught up enough to hear.

"Stop," he said, and moved past them to look ahead.

They were at a high point on a ridge. The path curved out of sight, following the shape of the quarry. Farther ahead, the quarry walls were visible.

"Move," Vuksanaj said, and prodded each of them with the muzzle of the pistol.

They stumbled across the top of the ridge, each step bringing them closer to those quarry walls. Tom was still huffing as he had on the climb, and Carol felt rubbery in the legs herself. Part of it was the climb, but it could not all be the climb, not in the shape she was in. She was scared. She was scared not only for herself or for Nick and Rose. Those were the obvious fears.

She also was scared because she still had it in her power to resist, rather than go along politely and quietly. She needed to act, and right now that scared her.

She watched the terrain change. There was no more talking now; Vuksanaj was too close. There was just watching and breathing the strength back into her legs and waiting for the right combination of footing and tree cover. And there was hoping she had convinced Tom to follow her lead.

They walked another ten yards, twenty yards. To their right, the side away from the quarry, the underbrush ended. The trees grew tall and thick. Leaves and snow covered the ground. Carol checked the trail ahead. It was clear and firm. No ice, no roots. Ten yards farther ahead, a tree grew tight along the trail. Beyond it, more trees formed the best combination of cover and running room she would find. That was the place to make their break.

Elliott leaned forward in the Crown Vic, his hands on the dashboard and his eyes peering through the windshield.

"Turn left here," he said.

Foxx swung onto a narrow road that climbed steeply through a forest in tight turns.

"This is the road," said Elliott. "I remember it now. There'll be a reservoir on the left."

And two hundred yards later, the trees thinned to reveal a circular body of water.

"There's an old quarry filled with water," said Elliott. "Used to be a swimming club, but now it's abandoned. These four kids, like late teens, go there one night. They climb the quarry, hold hands, and jump off. Three of them die, the two girls and one of the guys, and for a long time everyone thinks it's a double suicide pact. But then it turns out the kid who survived planned the whole thing because he was involved with both girls and wanted to get rid of them. He was prosecuted for three counts of inducing suicide and a bunch of other charges. I worked the trial. We took the jury to view the scene because the D.A.'s theory was that the kid knew exactly where to jump so he would survive but the others wouldn't. It's been known as Lovers Leap ever since.

"I was part captain back then. Bobby was in my crew. So was a scrawny officer who spent half the time drunk. Never could remember his name, and yesterday was the first time I seen him in years. Didn't recognize him at first with the silver hair and all."

The ten yards passed slowly for Carol.

At seven yards, her heart began to thump wildly. At five yards, she touched Tom's arm. He did not react, and at three yards she squeezed. Maybe he would understand the signal, maybe he wouldn't. She couldn't gamble there would be another opportunity to talk, couldn't gamble there would be another break point up ahead. At one yard, she let go of Tom's arm.

At zero, she ran. The ground fell away from the trail, and after a few choppy strides she was sprinting. She curved left around one tree, right around the next. She kept running that way, making random turns around trees in case Vuksanaj shot. Her breath huffed, her eyes teared. Gunshots never came.

She was twenty yards away and then she was thirty and she began to wonder whether it could be this easy, whether she could simply keep running and running all the way through the woods and back to her life. She could not hear anything beyond the blood in her ears and the padding of her feet on the dead leaves. What luck she had kept her sneakers on and her coat off. She felt alive, her legs strong, her feet light and quick. She wanted to know if Vuksanaj was chasing her, but she could not risk the slightest glance. She needed to concentrate on the ground ahead of her, to avoid the patches of snow, to turn randomly at each tree.

Now she was fifty yards away from the trail, then sixty yards. The ground leveled. A small creek cut in front of her, and she leaped it easily, not even breaking stride. Another twenty yards fell behind her. The ground began to rise, the footing loosened. She balled her hands into fists, pumped her arms, lifted her knees. She ran on the balls of her feet, concentrating on digging in each step before pushing forward to the next.

The trees stood thicker at the top of the rise. She would have enough cover there to turn and look for Vuksanaj. Look for Tom, too. She wondered if he had run in a different direction. Because if he did, Vuksanaj could not chase them both. And if he couldn't chase them both, there was a chance he wouldn't catch either of them.

She couldn't wait. She began to turn before she reached the top of the rise. She never saw the stone.

She stumbled forward, banged her opposite knee, gripped her ankle and rolled onto her back. The gray-brown world spun over her. The pain was intense. A bad sprain, maybe a break. She twisted onto her side, pulled up her knee, rubbed her ankle with both hands.

She looked up to the top of the rise and saw two large dogs loping through the trees. They had golden fur, but the shape of German shepherds. Perhaps their owner was trailing behind them and he would see her and come down to help her and the very presence of the dogs and their owner would scare off Vuksanaj.

She looked down the rise. Someone was climbing up among the trees. A shoulder, an arm, sometimes a leg. Blue against the copper-brown of the dead leaves.

She looked back up the rise, hoping to see the dogs running toward her. But they were gone, if they ever existed. She heard car doors slam from far, far away. But it might have been her imagination, just like the dogs.

She pushed herself back, crab-walked on her palms and the heel of her good foot. Behind a tree was a hollow where the roots spread away from the trunk. She nestled into it with her bad leg stretched out. The pain brought tears to her eyes. No way she could outrun Vuksanaj now. No way she could run at all.

Quietly, she scraped leaves together, covering her feet, her legs up to her knees and then up to her waist, the opposite of a snow angel. She stopped and listened. A stiff wind rustled the trees, shaking down some of the leaves still clinging to the crown of an oak. The breeze died. She could hear the crunch of feet walking deliberately on the dry leaves.

She gathered more leaves together, covering her stomach. She replayed the images of Vuksanaj climbing the rise. The shoulder, the arm, the leg; blue against the copper-brown leaves. She didn't remember seeing his face, and if she hadn't seen his face, then he couldn't have seen her.

She gathered two more armfuls of leaves, then stopped. The crunching approached, but it was impossible to tell exactly where or how close. She sank deeper into the hollow, made herself small, closed her eyes. The crunching stopped.

She took a deep breath and held it. A leaf tumbled across

her face, tickling her nose to the point where she needed to stifle a sneeze. Then something cold and hard touched her cheek. She turned her face toward it and stared into the muzzle of a pistol.

"Bang bang," said Vuksanaj.

CHAPTER 30

They passed the entrance before realizing it—Foxx because he never had seen the place before, Elliott because it looked different. His one visit to the Quarry Club had been during the summer. The club was two years out of business by then, but its chain-link gate still shined in the sun, the driveway was still smooth, and the hemlocks were still shapely. Now, several years later in the dead of winter, the rusted gate sagged on its hinges, the driveway was rutted, and the hemlocks had been stripped by deer.

Foxx reversed the Crown Vic and turned in toward the gate. Elliott jumped out.

"Padlock's been cut," he said, kicking it away. He unlatched the gate and pushed it open enough for Foxx to drive the Crown Vic through.

They ascended for a long stretch, with nothing visible but the rock walls and the gray sky. The drive crested the hill, and the quarry jumped into sight: the figure-eight lake, the sheer stone walls, the dilapidated buildings, the hardpan parking lot with railroad ties scattered like dark matchsticks. There was one vehicle in the parking lot—a green truck.

Foxx pulled alongside the truck and cut the engine. It was an old truck, as beat-up as the surroundings. The windshield was streaked where the wipers swept, and Foxx felt heat when he touched the hood.

"How do I get there?" he asked.

"It's a hike," said Elliott. "Follow me."

"No. You stay here in case he comes back."

"But he's crazy," said Elliott.

"So am I."

Elliott took Foxx as far as the beach and pointed out where the nature trails began.

"The trails will fork," he said. "Take the left one. It'll climb up behind the quarry. Keep going until you can't go any higher."

Carol kept her knee bent and her bad ankle up and hopped on her good foot as Vuksanaj dragged her down the rise. The pain was terrible, and she could barely lift her head enough to see in front of her. She wondered if Tom got away. She hoped that Tom got away. She prayed that he was out at the highway now flagging down a car for help.

They reached the bottom of the rise, then started up the gentle incline toward the trail. Vuksanaj pulled harder. Carol could not hop fast enough.

"Stop," she said.

"You stupid to run, you stupid to hurt," said Vuksanaj.

Eventually, they made it back to the trail, and Carol's heart sank. Tom lay in the dirt with plastic straps binding his wrists and ankles. Vuksanaj dropped Carol beside him, then used his switchblade to slice the straps.

"Get up," he said.

Tom got to his feet. He shook each foot and rubbed his wrists. He kept his head down, avoiding Carol.

"Pick her up," said Vuksanaj. The switchblade was gone and the pistol was back in his hand.

Tom did not move until Vuksanaj jammed the pistol into his back. He bent over Carol and worked his hand under her arm and across her stomach. She did not groan, but he could feel her fighting against the pain as he lifted her up.

"I think I broke it," she said tightly.

They headed down the trail, Carol limping as she leaned heavily against Tom, Vuksanaj prodding them in the back whenever their slow pace moved even slower.

"I tried," Carol said. "Could have made it if . . . I wanted you to run, too."

"I did," said Tom, "but he tackled me right away."

The trail curved, and the brush thinned, and soon they were walking along the edge of the cliff. Down below, the lake was a flat gray.

Tom stopped at the point where the trail was closest to the edge. The drop down to the lake looked like seventy or eighty feet. He was bad at estimating distances; all he knew was that heights made him dizzy.

"Move it," said Vuksanaj.

Tom readjusted Carol on his hip and started walking again.

"You were right," he said to her.

"When was I right?" She did not think she had been right about anything in a very long time.

"In chambers, when you asked me all those questions. Before Dominic came in."

"Tom, I don't think . . ."

"No, I need to tell you. I had a gambling problem. Years. Always thinking I would win my way out of it. Never happened. Eventually, I got help. Stopped gambling, but still had the debt. So I went to a loan shark. Been paying him monthly for over a year. That's why I needed to keep my job. I needed to keep my job to keep paying. That's all I wanted, really, and it was good enough for me until New Year's morning when Dominic's boss called in the entire loan. I needed money fast. So I went to the courthouse and nosed around chambers and came up with the idea of rewriting the union decision and selling it to Bobby. He agreed, even gave me a thousand bucks down payment. But the next day, when Elliott brought us to the funeral home, that was Bobby telling me he wasn't going to pay. My payment for writing the decision was to stay out of jail. I already had the decision written, but I didn't tell him. I made up a problem to buy myself more time so I could make another deal on another case. So, yeah, you were right about everything, and I'm sorry."

The trail rose away from the cliffs through an area of bare saplings and frozen scrub. Vuksanaj told them to stop and wait. He climbed ahead of them and dropped out of sight.

"You can run," said Carol. "You can, you know. Drop me here and run."

"No," he said. "I've been enough of a shit."

"But . . ."

"It was a gamble right from the start. Getting to midnight, then calling Bobby."

"But you didn't plan that. They called in the loan."

"What I planned didn't matter," said Tom. "Fact is, I liked it. The action, the adrenaline rush. Something made me keep pushing the chips out onto the table. You, I think. But I couldn't tell you. Because if I told you, I knew you would hate me."

"Tom, that's ridiculous. If you had told me . . ."

"I didn't need to. You figured it out by yourself."

"Oh, Tom, that was my frustration speaking."

"Didn't mean it wasn't any less true." Tom looked up at the spot where Vuksanaj disappeared over the trail. He knew he could run, that he could sit Carol on the trail and truly live the rest of his life as a total shit. He would not take the chance. He had doubled down enough over the last three days. His gambling was over.

"You know," he said. He could hear twigs breaking in the distance, Vuksanaj picking his way back. "You know the happiest I've been in a long time was eating dinner at your house."

"Really?" said Carol.

"Really," said Tom.

"Come." Vuksanaj stood at the top of the trail, waving the pistol.

Tom tightened his grip on Carol and felt her melt against him.

"Even with Foxx there?" she asked.

"Even with Foxx there."

They climbed slowly. Vuksanaj stepped aside to let them pass, then pushed them forward.

"I'm sorry, too," said Carol. "For being a bitch. Being self-centered when I should have understood that whatever you were doing must have been for a good reason."

"A reason, but not a good one," said Tom.

"I could have helped you. There was that money the judge gave me."

"You don't know how many times I almost asked you for it."

"Why didn't you?"

"It wasn't enough. It wouldn't have changed what I needed to do."

"I would have given it to you," said Carol.

The trail steepened and turned rocky.

"That's why I didn't ask," said Tom. "No, that's not true. I didn't ask because I didn't want you to know."

"It wouldn't have mattered."

"It might have then."

"Well," said Carol. "It shouldn't have."

She accidentally set down her bad foot. The sudden jolt of pain forced her to the ground.

"Move," said Vuksanaj.

"She can't," said Tom.

"Carry her," said Vuksanaj.

Foxx had no idea how far he had walked or where he was in relation to the lake or the cliffs. Whatever young Nick Scilingo might have thought about their day trapping squirrels in the backyard, Foxx had no outdoor skills beyond tilting a milk crate on a stick with a peanut butter pinecone underneath. He could tail an obtuse person on the streets of Manhattan, but didn't know how to track people through woods except to look at the frozen ground and hope to see something obvious. Right now, he saw nothing but frozen mud embedded with pebbles and sticks.

He stopped to listen. The air was cold, which meant it was

dense, which meant it conducted sound well. But right now he heard nothing but random clicks and snaps and the wind rustling the curled copper leaves of oak trees high over his head. He started walking again, padding silently so he could probe with his ears as well as his eyes. He had a sense of having walked in a large semicircle, which meant the parking lot and Elliott were somewhere over his left shoulder, with the quarry lake somewhere in between.

After more walking, the terrain opened up to his right. The ground fell away from the path for a couple hundred yards before rising again to a thick stand of trees. The ground was carpeted by leaves and dotted with dollops of snow. There were trees on the slopes, but they were well spaced, giving him a clear view of a large expanse.

Then he saw something. Just beyond a large oak that grew directly beside the trail, he saw signs of a scuffle. There were scrapes in the frozen ground; pebbles and twigs had been dislodged. And off the path, in a jagged line, the dead leaves had been disturbed by something that had been dragged.

He struck out down the slope, following the line and scanning ahead through the trees. After a hundred yards, the jagged line stopped at a narrow stream.

Foxx jumped the stream and climbed halfway up the other slope. The line did not pick up again. The carpet of leaves was undisturbed. That clock in his head started ticking again, and he ran back to the trail.

Tom picked up Carol and held her under her arms and behind her knees. She hugged him tightly, her face buried against his neck. The last several yards of the climb were steep. The footing was tough, and he needed to pick his way up shelves of exposed rock that broke beneath his shoes. Carol's lips trembled against his skin. At first he thought she was kissing him. Then he thought she was muttering, "Oh, Tom. Oh, Tom."

He pulled them up to the top. It was a smaller clearing than the last one, but much higher—in fact, the highest point around. There was no vegetation, no trees, not even dirt. Just a tiny moonscape of exposed rock, cracked and fissured. A crude sign, made of weathered plywood and lettered with fading spray paint, was wedged into the deepest fissure. LOVERS LEAP, it read.

And that was when Tom realized Carol was not muttering his name. She was muttering, "Oh God. Oh God."

"Over here," Vuksanaj said, pointing to the edge of the cliff.

Tom stood his ground and hugged Carol tighter. He could feel her quake in his arms. He could feel a cold tear hurry out of her eye and run down his neck. He could feel her lips quivering against his chest. He could hear, very clearly now, her repeated, "Oh my God. Oh my God."

"Get over there," said Vuksanaj.

He waved the pistol. Still, Tom stood his ground. Not out of courage, not even out of obstinance. He simply was paralyzed, his legs quickly turning to jelly.

"Goddam you," said Vuksanaj. With two quick strides, he crossed the rock. For a slight man, he was surprisingly strong. He grabbed Tom by the arm and flung him. Tom stumbled toward the edge, managing to fall to one knee and somehow keep his grip on Carol. Her hair tickled his nose. Beyond, the gray lake spread out a hundred feet down.

"Get up," said Vuksanaj. He hooked the muzzle of the pistol under Tom's collar and lifted.

Tom stood up, somehow, with Carol still in his arms. His

legs shook. A cloud powdered with bright pinpoints darkened his vision and then faded. He felt a sudden ooze of warmth in his crotch. He had pissed himself.

"Put her down." Vuksanaj spoke directly into his ear.

"No," said Tom.

Vuksanaj twisted the muzzle into the back of Tom's skull.

"Put her down."

Tom dropped the arm beneath Carol's knees, but held tight with the other arm. She swung down slowly, Tom holding her as she balanced herself on her good foot.

"Take her hand," said Vuksanaj.

"What?" said Tom.

Carol's *oh my Gods,* louder now, changed into real prayer.

"Oh my God, I am heartily sorry . . ."

"Take her hand," said Vuksanaj. "Like lovers."

Lovers, thought Tom. His mind slowed down, that single word stretching and deepening. *Lovers.*

Still, Tom did not move. It was all too absurd, too crazy ending like this. There had to be a way out. There was always a way out. He had written hundreds of decisions, and many of them could have come out either way. Because there was always another option, another answer, another way out. He just needed to find it.

"Take her hand," said Vuksanaj.

"No," said Tom.

Vuksanaj stepped close behind him and pressed the muzzle of the pistol behind his ear.

"Take her hand," he said. "Like lovers. This is Lovers Leap. Get it?"

Tom got it, but he also got more than the sick joke. Vuksanaj had no intention of shooting them. The plan obviously hinged on him and Carol committing suicide, or something that looked like suicide. There was no room for a bullet in the brain.

He looked down at his feet. His toes were two feet away from the edge. The rock itself was broken, not smooth, like the rock on the last part of the trail. He wondered what type of rock it was: granite, limestone, shale. He didn't know one type of rock from another. A rock was a rock was a rock.

". . . and I confess all my sins . . ."

Vuksanaj pulled the pistol away from Tom's head.

"You jump," he said.

"I'm not going to jump," said Tom.

"You jump or I shoot."

"You're not going to shoot."

"You jump," said Vuksanaj. He butted Tom from behind, not hard enough to knock him over but enough to push him right to the edge. Tom wobbled, dizzy from looking straight down. There was a slight curve to the cliff wall. There were shallow ledges where weeds and saplings grew. All the way down, a shelf of ice clung to the rocks.

". . . but most of all . . ." said Carol.

"Jump," said Vuksanaj.

Tom set himself as best he could to ward off another push. But no push came.

"Jump," said Vuksanaj.

"No."

". . . but most of all . . ." Carol repeated.

"Jump or I shoot," said Vuksanaj.

". . . because they offend you, oh Lord."

"You're not going to . . ."

The pistol exploded. The bullet hit the rock behind Tom and Carol and ricocheted between them.

The shot startled Tom into losing his balance. He pitched forward over the cliff. He seemed to float for a moment, wildly spinning his arms, before gravity took hold and pulled him, screaming, into the quarry.

Carol stood on the edge, balanced on her good foot, her prayers silenced by the horror of Tom's fall. She turned and looked at Vuksanaj.

"Please," she said, and lifted her arms. "Please."

And then the ledge broke away beneath her.

CHAPTER 31

Elliott was sitting in the Crown Vic, idling the engine to run
the heater, when he heard a crack followed by two echoes.
Across the quarry, on the far side of the lake, something fell
from a ledge. That something was a figure, small and dark and
featureless at a distance. The figure tried to flap its arms and
then arrowed down, slamming into the rock face, turning over
in the air, and then plummeting out of sight.

Elliott pressed his hands to his temples, unable to look. But
he did look again and saw debris raining down. He groaned as
if he had been kicked in the gut.

Foxx was climbing a steep part of the trail when he heard the
shot. It came from high above and relatively close. Instinctively,
he dove into the brush. He was just below a small clearing.
Beyond, the trail disappeared into the sky. That must have been
the top, as Elliott told him, the place where you couldn't go any
higher. Lovers Leap.

He listened, but heard no other sound. The trail now seemed
too exposed, so he worked his way up on the other side of the

brush, scrambling from one rocky ledge to the next. As he drew even with the clearing, movement caught his eye. Vuksanaj came over the top, then began to sidestep down the steepest part of the trail. He was alone, and his hands were empty.

Foxx watched Vuksanaj start down the next incline. Vuksanaj whistled tunelessly. Foxx pushed through the brush and into the clearing and began to follow.

The trail descended from the brush and rocks of the upper cliffs and into the trees. It seemed darker here than it had only a few minutes before, more like dusk than midday. Foxx pushed his pistol snug into his shoulder holster and quickly calculated how fast he needed to run, how much distance he needed to close. He ran gently at first, his feet perfectly silent on the trail.

Then he sprinted full out.

Vuksanaj sensed him coming. He turned around and squared himself to meet Foxx with a punch. Foxx ducked under and drove his shoulder into Vuksanaj, body-slamming him against a tree. Vuksanaj melted down the trunk, but got his legs under him. He pushed off, swinging a wild roundhouse. Foxx caught the punch, turned Vuksanaj around, and twisted his arm up against his spine. Vuksanaj buckled in pain.

There was a gun somewhere, Foxx remembered. He frisked Vuksanaj with his free hand, but only could reach his right side. He didn't notice Vuksanaj work his left hand free and reach back over his shoulder. Foxx felt a hand on the back of his neck, the fingers probing his spine. What the hell is he doing, he wondered. And then, suddenly, he couldn't form a coherent thought. He couldn't remember who Vuksanaj was or why they were fighting or what they were doing out in this forest. His arm went numb. His vision darkened.

Vuksanaj spun out of Foxx's grasp and slammed a left into

Foxx's jaw. Foxx reeled backwards. His heel caught a root, upending him. Vuksanaj pounced, pinning him to the ground. He pulled Foxx's pistol from his shoulder holster and tossed it away.

Foxx's mind slowly came back to him. Whatever Vuksanaj had done to him—he knew it had something to do with nerve pressure—was wearing off quickly. He knew that Vuksanaj had disarmed him, was straddling his stomach and reaching for his own gun. Vuksanaj was compact and muscular. But he was still relatively small and relatively light, and Foxx knew his only chance was to knock him off balance. Fast. Once Vuksanaj drew his gun, it was over. Foxx's right arm was pinned to his side, his left lay numb on the ground. But he still had his legs and he still had his gut. He arched his back and dug in his heels, lifting his stomach in a wrestler's bridge. The move surprised Vuksanaj before he could grab his pistol from his shoulder holster. He toppled sideways off Foxx.

Both men scrambled to their feet. They circled each other, measuring, feinting, probing. Now that Foxx was upright, he realized he still was lightheaded. His arm felt like a slab of chopped meat.

Vuksanaj lunged, then backed up. He lunged again, then smiled as he dug for his shoulder holster.

Foxx had only one chance. A roundhouse kick to Vuksanaj's chest. Crack a few ribs, knock the wind out of the bastard.

He spun. His foot crashed weakly into Vuksanaj's side. Vuksanaj caught it, forcing Foxx to hop on his other foot to keep his balance. Vuksanaj smiled. He raised Foxx's leg higher and higher until Foxx thought he would snap like a wishbone. Then Vuksanaj shoved.

Foxx flipped backwards. He hit the ground hard but managed to tuck himself into a ball and roll onto his feet. Vuksanaj had his pistol out. Foxx charged. He lowered his head and drove his shoulder into Vuksanaj's chest.

The twin blows of Foxx to his chest and the tree to his back squeezed every molecule of air from Vuksanaj's lungs. His pistol flew from his hand. He sank to the ground.

Foxx staggered momentarily, then lifted Vuksanaj by the collar and turned him around. Pinning him face-first against the side of the tree, Foxx unhooked the handcuffs from his belt and cuffed Vuksanaj to the trunk. Vuksanaj twisted his head and stared icily at Foxx.

"Gone," he said. "Jumped."

Foxx pulled back Vuksanaj's head and smashed it into the tree. Blood spurted from Vuksanaj's nose. Foxx picked up both pistols, holstered his own, and stuck Vuksanaj's in his waistband. Then he headed back up the trail.

CHAPTER 32

There were branches, lots of branches, woody and prickly, and as Carol slid down the face of the cliff she had tried to grab whatever she could. Thirty feet down the cliff face curved out into a series of ledges. Carol had hit the first ledge hard, literally bounced into the air, and spun over the side. The next one caught her for good.

She lay as she had landed, facedown, her left arm bent beneath her belly, her tongue tasting the dirt. She tried to move, but couldn't. It wasn't just her ankle. Her left arm hurt like it was on fire. Both hands were raw from grabbing at branches during her fall.

Carol lifted her head. She wasn't crying. Crying was something she did only when she was frustrated. This was different. The pain in her arm was unbearable. Gasping, she used her good arm to roll herself onto her side. Her hand was bent completely backwards at the wrist. Blood oozed from a gash. Two white splinters of bone stuck out of her flesh.

Her stomach heaved. Darkness clouded over her eyes.

She felt herself falling, not off the ledge, but right through the ground, toward the center of the earth. She shook her head. The falling stopped, but the clouds did not clear. In fact, they only intensified, and Carol realized the clouds were not in her eyes. A snow squall was blowing across the quarry.

"Help," she cried. "Help me."

But her voice came out as barely a whimper. Her words swirled in the air, tumbled down, landed uselessly on the frozen lake.

Carol pushed herself onto her knees. She was freezing without her coat and with the snow peppering her face. She hugged her bad arm to her chest. For a few seconds, the pain drained away. She could smell her own blood, almost taste it as if she had bit the inside of her mouth. Then the pain crashed back over her. She swooned.

She thought about how much she missed Nick. She thought about how her mother couldn't survive without her. She wondered why all this had happened. Then she heard branches breaking above her, the quick patter of debris followed by the thud of something heavier landing on the ledge. Maybe Vuksanaj had fallen, too. She turned to her left. A dog was splayed over the ledge, two paws dangling. It looked like a German shepherd except it was scrawnier and had lots of yellow in its fur and a long tail that curved over its back.

The dog gathered itself, then crept toward her, its head lowered, its sharp yellow teeth bared. It sniffed the toe of her sneaker. She kicked, and the dog recoiled. The ledge was pure snow now. Her kick had dislodged her, and she slid toward the edge before catching herself.

She dug in her heel and pushed back from the edge. Neither

her arm nor her ankle were hurting now, but she knew the pain hadn't gone away. She was too scared to feel it because the dog wasn't a dog. It was a coyote.

Carol knew about coyotes because they had been much in the news the previous summer after several attacks on small children playing in their yards at dusk. Their populations were growing and becoming more aggressive, the experts had said. Loud noises should scare them. Waving your arms should scare them. But the more they came into contact with humans, the less the loud noises and waving arms scared them away. They reverted to their basic nature of opportunistic hunters with a keen sense of smell. If she could smell her own blood, a coyote could, too. And on the instinct scale, the smell of blood outweighed the bang of a single gunshot.

The coyote crept toward the spot where Carol had landed and sniffed at the dark stain where the snow and dirt and Carol's blood mixed together. Then it looked up, locked its yellow eyes on Carol, and pulled its mouth back into a grin.

Carol tried to press herself into the cliff wall. The coyote lunged. Carol kicked and caught the coyote square in the snout. The coyote spun away, yelping. Then came that same sound of branches breaking overhead. Something else landed on the ledge, this time to Carol's right. Another coyote shook itself off.

The two coyotes crept toward her, one from each side. They seemed to grin at each other, and then took turns lunging and backing off.

"Get away," Carol screamed. "Get away."

But the coyotes ignored her screams. One snapped at her foot. The other tore a hunk out of her sleeve. Carol pushed away from the wall. If her choices were being mauled to death or falling, she would choose falling. She began to slide, but then one coyote clamped its jaws on her sneaker. The other loomed over her head.

She screamed.

Foxx fought his way up the steepest part of the trail. The snow had come sudden and thick, quickly covering the cold ground. He scrambled up the last several yards on all fours, finally pulling himself up onto an empty shelf of rock.

He brushed himself off. This was the highest point around the quarry. Lovers Leap. There was no sign of Tom or Carol. Foxx moved slowly toward the ledge, careful of his footing. There were paw prints in the snow. Large ones, like a big dog's. Or dogs. There were enough prints for at least two. They went right to the edge and did not turn back.

"Get away!" screamed a voice from down below.

Foxx never had heard such fear or panic or pain in a voice. He stepped forward, but felt the ledge crumble beneath him and jumped back. Bits of rock crackled as they bounced down the cliff face.

Foxx knelt and then stretched himself out to peer over the ledge. The cliff was steep, but not as sheer as he expected. Several bare saplings grew out of cracks in the face. Some twenty or thirty feet down, at the limit of visibility in the thick snow, there seemed to be a ledge. And on the ledge, blurry figures wrestled.

"Nooooo!" screamed Carol.

"Carol!" Foxx yelled.

"Foxx? That you?"

"Yeah. What's happening?"

"Coyotes," Carol yelled, and then let out a terrible scream.

Foxx twisted himself and swung his legs over the ledge. He

focused on the saplings. He could start off with a controlled slide, catch one, then let go and catch another. Or so he hoped. With the snow, he had no true idea how far down Carol could be. But he had to jump and the jump would hurt. He had no choice.

Carol screamed again.

Foxx moved Vuksanaj's pistol from his waistband to his jacket, took a deep breath, and pushed off.

Hearing Foxx's voice heartened Carol, but not for long. She tried to curl into a ball, but the coyotes would not let her. One snapped at her neck and tore away a chunk of her collar. The other locked his jaws onto her sneaker. Carol pulled her toes back just as the teeth ripped through. The coyote shook its head. A hunk of rubber and leather fell from its mouth.

Carol barely could defend herself. One arm and one leg were useless, so she squirmed and screamed, anything to keep the yellow teeth from reaching her skin.

The coyotes lunged in unison, and finally Carol tucked herself into a ball and hugged her arm to her chest. One coyote nipped at her shoulder, raking its teeth across her flesh. She felt her blood ooze across her skin. This was it. She woke up this morning on Manhattan's Upper West Side, and by noon coyotes were mauling her. How absurd.

Foxx controlled his fall at first. He grabbed one sapling, swung himself past it, then grabbed another. But the drop was steeper than he expected, and gravity took over. Wood snapped and cracked as he plunged through the whirling snow. He groped for branches, but they burned through his hands.

His foot struck something solid, but rather than break his

fall the impact tipped him forward. He was tumbling now, headfirst. He saw a ledge rushing up at him. He tucked his head just in time.

He crash-landed right beside them.

For a split second, they didn't react, and in that split second Foxx took in the entire scene. Tatters of cloth lay on the bloody snow. Carol was curled into a tight, lifeless ball while two coyotes dug at her with their paws and snouts.

Is she dead? wondered Foxx. The thought sank from his brain to the hollow of his gut.

The split second passed. The coyotes turned toward Foxx to defend their prize. Foxx got up on one elbow, kicked himself back. The scrawnier of the two coyotes peeled away from Carol. A bloody scrap of cloth dropped from its mouth.

The coyote slinked toward Foxx, its head low, its yellow teeth bared in a grin. A guttural growl rumbled deep in its throat. Foxx, still kicking himself back, reached into his jacket.

The coyote lunged. Foxx snapped his leg, catching the coyote squarely under the jaw. He felt the sinews and jawbone through the toe of his boot, heard the teeth clap shut.

The coyote spun away, yelping. Foxx sat himself straight up and took out Vuksanaj's pistol. The coyote turned back toward him, gathering itself, tensing its muscles. Foxx aimed at the triangle of skull right between its eyes. He squeezed the trigger once and then twice.

Nothing happened.

Foxx squeezed twice again. The pistol clicked like a broken toy. The coyote lowered its head, ready to pounce.

Foxx had no time to draw his own pistol from his holster. The pistol in his hand was jammed, and it would be quicker to clear the jam. He slammed the bottom of the magazine with the heel of his hand. He racked the round with the slide. He squeezed the trigger. Nothing.

The coyote leaped.

Foxx threw the pistol, but it glanced off the coyote's flank. Foxx caught the coyote, the impact knocking him backwards. They rolled in a heap. Foxx locked his hands around the coyote's neck. The coyote raked its claws and thrashed its head. Bare teeth grazed Foxx's chin.

Foxx flipped the coyote over and tossed it away. He tried to stand, but the coyote quickly leaped at him. For a moment, they seemed to embrace. The coyote's paws clawed at Foxx's shoulders. Foxx clamped his hands on the coyote's head. Face to face, the coyote's breath stank so much of blood and decay that Foxx gagged. The coyote snapped its jaws. Foxx gave the head a strong twist. Something inside its neck cracked. Its eyes bugged, and then its whole body went limp.

Foxx dropped the dead coyote to the ground. Ten feet away, the other coyote stepped over Carol. Foxx reached into his jacket. His pistol wasn't going to jam. He was going to finish this one off quick. But before he could get the pistol out of his holster, the coyote leaped.

The coyote sank its teeth into Foxx's right wrist. Foxx whaled with his other fist, pummeling the skull, the eyes, the snout. But the coyote hung on tenaciously and each blow from Foxx's fist drove the sharp teeth deeper into his flesh. The pain was searing. Foxx collapsed, and the coyote began dragging him toward Carol.

Flat on his stomach, Foxx reached across his body for his pistol. He managed to hook a finger inside the trigger guard. The pistol popped out of the holster and landed in the snow. The coyote pulled hard. The pistol slid out of reach.

The coyote pulled again. Foxx slid on the slick rock. It wasn't pulling him toward Carol now; it was pulling him toward the edge. The pain was so intense he worried he might black out. If he did, he was done. He flipped himself over, twisting his arm in the coyote's teeth. Fighting the pain, he flailed at the pistol with his other hand, but could not reach.

The coyote was right at the edge, its hind legs barely hanging on. Foxx managed to work his fingers into a crack in the rock and pull himself back from the edge. He pulled a second time, rested for a moment, then pulled again. One more pull and he could reach his pistol. But then his fingers lost their grip, and he slid, and even the crack was beyond his reach. The coyote was back at the edge again, twisting its body as if to whip Foxx past.

Then something slid against Foxx's shoulder. His pistol. He looked back, saw that Carol was no longer curled into a ball but lay flat out. Her eyes focused momentarily on his, and she smiled faintly.

Foxx grabbed the pistol. As his feet slid over the edge, he sat up and pressed the muzzle under the coyote's jaw. The animal's eyes tightened as if it realized how quickly its advantage had changed.

Foxx squeezed the trigger. The bullet ripped through the coyote's throat and brain and blew off the top of its skull. The rest of it tumbled off the cliff.

Foxx dragged himself to Carol. She was warm, but barely breathing. He stripped off his jacket and covered her shoulders and stretched himself out alongside her. His eyes closed, and when he opened them again, the snow squall had vanished. Down below, Tom lay crumpled on the ice, the blood that had spilled from his head bleeding through the layer of new snow. One coyote lay beside him.

Foxx touched Carol's cheek, and she half-opened her eyes.

"You're not a coyote," she said.

"It's Foxx."

"You're not a fox, either."

"Officer Foxx."

"Officer Foxx," Carol said dreamily. "How could I forget?"

CHAPTER 33

Foxx stood just inside the doors wearing his dress blue uniform and white cotton gloves. The mags had been pushed to the side, clearing the long, sloping promenade. Rows of folding chairs filled the rotunda, and Foxx could see that most of the chairs were taken. Still, people kept coming in through the revolving door, bringing with them slabs of humid air from the outside. Foxx clapped his hands twice. The gloves muffled the sound into solid thuds.

When all the guests were seated and the front doors closed, Foxx joined the honor guard beside the podium at the back of the rotunda. Carol and Nick sat in the first row. Nick looked like any other kid at a function like this, fidgety and bored, uncomfortable in a jacket and tie. Carol looked good. She always looked good, and the stress of the last few months added character to her face. Foxx liked character in a woman's face. Plus, she had her legs crossed.

Nick locked on Foxx's eyes, and Foxx knew the boy caught him staring. Foxx arched his eyebrows, and Nick bit back a laugh.

* * *

After their rescue from the face of the cliff, Foxx and Carol had been admitted to the Westchester County Medical Center. Foxx stayed only one night as a patient, then posted himself outside Carol's room for the entire week before her discharge. He let no one in except for Nick, Rose, and a lawyer friend from City Island he had summoned by phone. Carol's interview with the lawyer lasted more than an hour. Afterwards, Foxx drifted in.

Carol's condition had improved. Most of the superficial scratches and cuts were healed. But her arm was still in traction and her ankle in a hard cast. Foxx's arm was on the mend, though he could still feel the coyote's teeth whenever he thought about being dragged toward the edge. His solution: Don't think about it.

Carol opened her eyes as Foxx settled onto the stool beside the bed.

"What did you tell him?" she asked.

"What I believe to be true."

"But I didn't tell you the judge was dead until I met you in Chinatown."

Foxx said nothing.

"The truth is that I went along with Tom's plan," said Carol. "I was scared, sure, but I wanted it to work. I needed it to work."

Foxx lifted Nick's third-grade school portrait off the night-stand and handed it to her.

"You can pick whatever truth you want to tell. There is no one left to contradict you. But make sure you pick the right one."

Carol stared at the portrait for a long moment, then handed it back to Foxx and closed her eyes.

In the end, the grand jury did not indict Carol. It indicted

Bobby Werkman and Anton Vuksanaj for manslaughter, attempted murder, kidnapping, and a host of other charges. It indicted Jerry Elliott as an accessory to all crimes except for the manslaughter and attempted murder. Only Vuksanaj was stupid enough to go to trial. He was convicted on all counts and sentenced to consecutive terms that added up to essentially a life sentence. Bobby Werkman's plea deal had him serving ten years, assuming good behavior. Jerry Elliott, through the intercession of the IG's Office, would serve a maximum of three years. He planned to spend that time filing for a divorce.

Dominic McGlinchy was murdered in Rikers Island while awaiting his trial on attempted rape.

A rabbi spoke first. He had only a passing acquaintance with Judge Canter, rarely seeing him in his congregation except during the High Holy Days. But he spoke with the confident knowledge of an old friend, describing Canter's passion for the law, the pleasure he took in the disputational aspects of the adversary system, the emotional energy he poured into his decisions.

Jacob Canter, the judge's older brother, spoke about growing up in a small two-bedroom apartment. Their mother had doted on Al, he said, had dreamed of Al becoming a doctor. He remembered her taking Al to the park as a toddler and drilling him on the multiplication tables because she believed that the multiplication tables, like good manners, were the key to a man's success in the world. But Al turned out to have an affinity for words, and their mother did not fret when he became a lawyer—until he announced he was becoming a judge.

"Why?" Jacob quoted her as saying. "Who wants those headaches?"

To which Al replied, "Respect, Mom. You get respect as a judge."

The administrative judge picked up on this theme of respect. She said the young Al Canter had misled his darling mother. One did not become honorable simply by being called "the Honorable." One did not obtain respect by believing he deserved it. One needed to earn honor and respect, and Al Canter had earned both. Everyone who walked out of his courtroom believed they had received a fair shake, whether they won, lost, or had a settlement rammed down their throats.

The portrait of Judge Canter that usually hung outside the Supreme Court library stood on a table beside the podium. The gray heads of the judges sitting in the first two rows nodded as the A.J. extolled another of Canter's virtues. Foxx, rocking on the balls of his feet, stole another glance at Carol's legs.

The ceremony and the eloquent words could not paper over the scandal that played out in the tabloids during the winter and spring of that year. Judge Canter became the "Phantom Judge" and Tom Carroway became a "mad genius addicted to living on the edge." The legal problems the scandal left in its wake were not confined to *Werkman v OCA* and *Berne v City of New York*. Every decision the chambers of the Honorable Alvin Canter issued in the days surrounding New Year's had been declared null and void until examined by a panel of judges, senior court clerks, and computer techs. The IG conducted an internal investigation and issued an eyes-only report to the chief judge as well as a public version that proposed procedures for preventing any future scandals. The report characterized Foxx only as "a diligent and alert court officer."

* * *

The memorial service ended. Foxx and the other members of the honor guard flanked Judge Canter's portrait as the crowd slowly moved toward a reception held in a nearby courtroom.

Later, Foxx stood at the top of the courthouse steps and smoked his fourth and last cigarette of the day. The sun was still high, and the heat of the day radiated off the stone. Nick ran out past him, and then Carol slipped her hand under his arm.

"That was quick," said Foxx. He dropped his cigarette and stubbed it out. "How did it feel, now that you actually came back?"

Carol had not been inside 60 Centre Street since leaving with Tom and Vuksanaj on the morning of January third.

"Like I don't belong," she said. "Too many judges."

"In the broader sense," said Foxx.

Carol smiled faintly, taking his meaning. Nick tugged on her sleeve.

"Can I go watch?" He pointed down at the square, where a group of teens performed extreme skateboard tricks on the edge of the fountain.

"Okay, just be careful crossing the street," said Carol.

"I will, Mom." Nick turned to Foxx and offered a fist bump. "See you later."

"You got it," said Foxx.

Carol watched Nick run down the steps, then took something out of her blouse.

"I brought this with me as a symbol. Someone needed to be here for him." She handed Foxx a photograph that showed herself and Tom, several years younger from the look of them, standing in chambers.

Foxx had been thinking of Tom during the service, too,

specifically about the brief conversation they had had about instant family on New Year's Day. In some ways, Tom was a better man than he was.

He handed back the photo, stole a head-to-toe glance at Carol as she worked it beneath her blouse. She still wore a flesh-colored support on her ankle; she had two red gashes on her wrist where the skin was healing itself around the plastic surgeon's stitches.

"I'd better collect Nick," she said. She lifted her head, and they kissed. "What time can I expect you?"

"The usual," said Foxx. There was no usual.

Foxx watched her go. She did not look back once as she descended to the fountain and shepherded Nick toward the subway entrance.

Instant family.

Foxx lit another cigarette. He was one over his daily quota, but he needed to think about whether it was time to add water.